Discovery

A Novel by Gordon W. Fredrickson

BEAVER'S POND
PRESS

This is a work of fiction. Names, characters, places, and incidents are either the products of the author's imagination or are used in a fictitious manner, and any resemblance to actual persons, living or dead, businesses, events, or locales is purely coincidental.

Edited by Kellie M. Hultgren

Front cover artwork: Acrylic on canvas by Judy Malz, 2023.

Back cover image credits:
- Front view of a toy, 1930 Ford, Model A, five-window coupe: Photo by Nancy A. Fredrickson, 2023.
- Ducktail hairstyle on wig: Photo by Nancy A. Fredrickson, 2023.
- Sporty: Photo by Gordon W. Fredrickson, circa 1955.
- Concrete stave silo (14′ x 50′), at the Gordon H. and Helen Fredrickson farm, Scott County, Minnesota: Photo by Nancy A. Fredrickson, circa 1988.
- Butler steel granary on the Gordon H. and Helen Fredrickson farm: Photo by Nancy A. Fredrickson, circa 1975.
- Front and back views of a peddler with horse and camper: Photo by Rita Schoenecker, circa 1955.
- Barn with driveway to haymow: Fredrickson family photo, circa 1955.

ISBN 13: 978-1-64343-611-1
Library of Congress Catalog Number: 2023919135
Printed in the United States of America
First Printing: 2023
27 26 25 24 23   5 4 3 2 1

Book design and typesetting by Dan Pitts.

Typefaces used in the interior are P22 Stanyan and Minion

BEAVER'S POND
PRESS

Beaver's Pond Press
939 Seventh Street West
Saint Paul, MN 55102
(952) 829-8818
www.BeaversPondPress.com

Contact Gordon W. Fredrickson at www.gordonfredrickson.com for more information about the author.

This is a work of fiction.
None of the events in this novel happened.
None of the characters existed.

CONTENTS

Map of the

Neighborhood

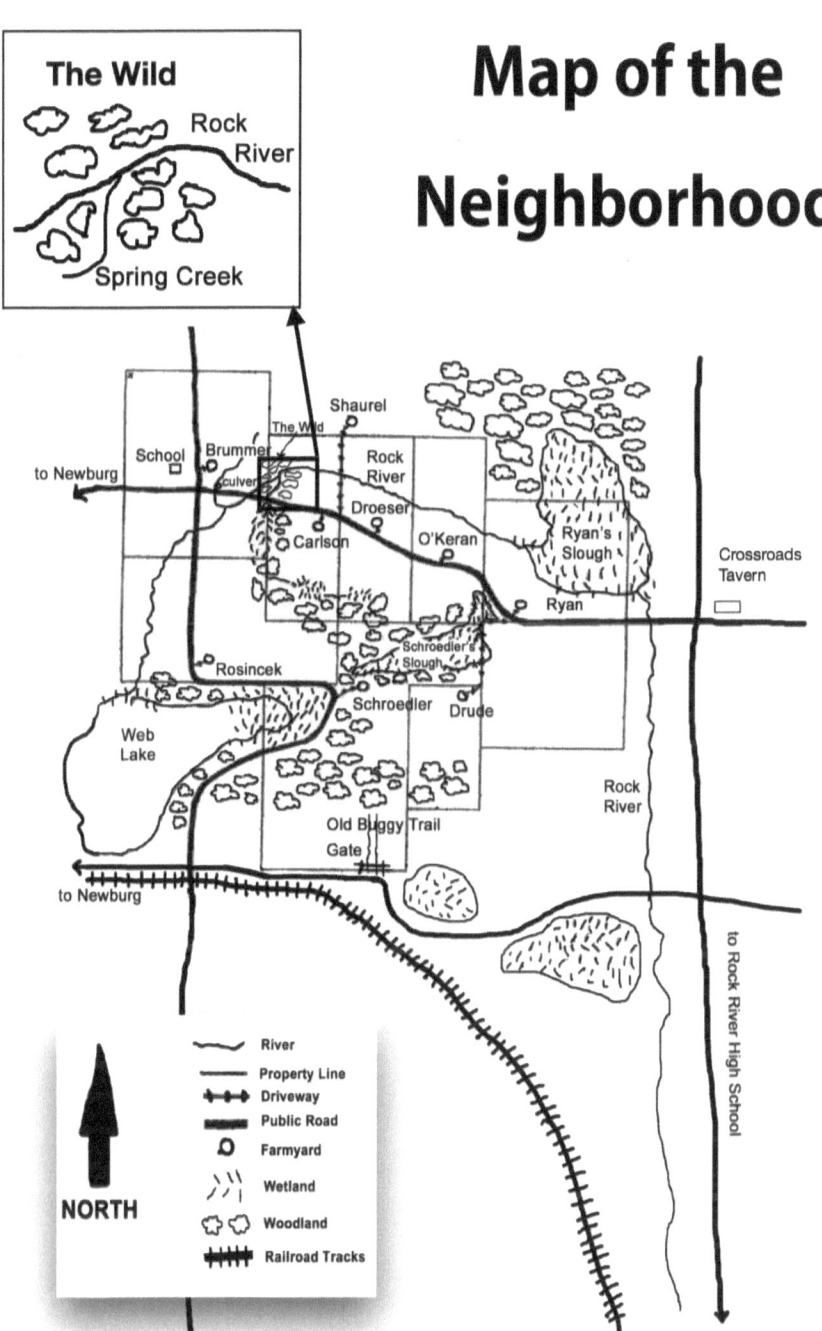

The Wild

Rock River

Spring Creek

CHAPTER 1

A RIDE

Glancing back to see the black Model A Ford approaching on the gravel road behind her, she wanted to run. Instead, she stopped and, like a wounded animal, turned to face her predator as the car pulled alongside her body.

The driver reached over to the handle of the passenger-side door, pushed it open, and demanded, "Get in the car!"

"I don't want to!" she barked, taking a few steps down the narrow dirt road.

He inched the car forward.

She shivered as the open door brushed her arm.

His command was louder this time. "Just get in!"

She stopped, turned to face him, and asked with as much defiance as she dared, "And if I don't?!"

"I'll tell everyone about *you*, Mary Schroedler. *Everyone.*"

Hesitating, as if dipping her toe into ice water before a plunge, she stepped on the running board and rotated her petite body onto the cushioned seat. Immediately, the car jerked forward, pinning her briefly against the back of the seat even as she slammed the door shut. The vehicle sped off toward its destination.

CHAPTER 2

LOCKER ROOM

Twenty-five ninth-grade girls funneling through the double-door entry of the girls' locker room created the standard chaos before sixth-hour physical education class at Rock River High School. Most of the girls hated gym class for a number of reasons—undressing in front of each other, getting all sweaty doing calisthenics, getting wet hair while showering, and then having to go back to a classroom. But today was Friday, which lent enthusiasm to everything, even gym class.

Maggie Carlson pushed through the crowd to get close to her locker and rotated the combination lock to pop the door open. Like most of the other girls, she kept to herself as she tended to the business of stripping off her skirt and top to step into the white one-piece gym suit, which had been stored on a hanger in the long, narrow locker. She placed her regular clothes in the locker before plopping down on the bench to pull on her gym socks and tennis shoes.

Satisfied, she straightened the little collar around her neck and looked down at the rest of her gym suit, which extended about halfway to her knees. She felt ridiculous! When she was in the eighth grade, her last year in the one-room country schoolhouse, no one had to change into a stupid uniform just to get a little exercise! Maggie appreciated that some girls looked good in the uniform, though, especially if they had tan legs that filled out the loose-fitting garment. But her own legs were slim and muscular, with pale white skin that reflected the sunlight when she had gym class outside, announcing to the world that *Maggie Carlson does not belong.* She was glad they seldom had gym outside.

She gathered up her plain, reddish-brown hair, pulled it into a ponytail, and snapped a wide rubber band around it.

"I was wondering what you were going to do with that mop of rust," Janet Morrett commented, as if she were joking. Janet had smooth, light-brown hair tied back into a ponytail, and the gym suit fit her perfectly. "You should cut it short. If it were really red-red, instead of whatever color it is, it would be really pretty, though."

Maggie didn't reply. No use taking the bait.

"Your brother Jimmy has nice hair. He keeps it long and combed back—very cute. I'd give him my phone number, but I know your family doesn't have a phone."

Maggie stayed silent, thinking, *Could Janet be any snottier?*

"Say, where's your farm-girl friend?" Janet continued. "Mary Schroedler, right? I saw her leave school after she talked to you before class. Where did she go?"

"What do you care?"

"Truthfully, I don't," Janet said. "But I always like to see whose legs are whiter when the two of you are beside each other in gym class."

"You're a funny girl, Janet. You should be on stage. The first stage out of town."

"That's *not* a new joke."

"Well, neither is your white-legs crap. I have white legs. I had them yesterday, and I'll still have them tomorrow," Maggie said evenly.

"You could try to get a tan." Now Janet pretended to be helpful.

"Look around, Janet." Maggie tried to be calm but firm. "No one here aspires to be like you, especially me!"

A loud, gritty voice rang through the locker room, announcing, "If you're dressed, get out to the gym and run laps! If you're not dressed, you're late!" Aware that her students called her "Genghis" behind her back, Mrs. Kahn enjoyed using her harsh voice to cement her tough reputation. The sturdy, agile, thirtysomething gym teacher added, "We'll skip calisthenics but do extra laps today before we count off for volleyball teams."

Trading *cal*, as the girls called calisthenics, for extra laps brought cheers from some and groans from others, but Maggie was just glad to exit the locker room. Running laps was better than speaking with Janet.

Once in the gym, Maggie easily kept pace with the leaders of the group and allowed her mind to wander. She had missed Mary all week. Today had been Mary's first day back after staying home for several days to recover from severe bruises and scratches incurred when she fell from the hayloft onto the barn floor. Maybe she wasn't feeling well, but then why walk home? And why not check out with the office to avoid getting in trouble? Jeez, she'd been held back last year because she missed so much school after her mother died. Wasn't she concerned about getting held back again?

All Mary had told her was "I turned sixteen last month. I don't have to be here anyway." Maggie couldn't bear the thought of her only friend quitting school. Even though Mary had always been a grade ahead of her in school—until this year, anyway—they had been best friends ever since Maggie started first grade. Although Maggie felt bad that Mary had to repeat grade nine, she was secretly delighted to have most of their classes together this year.

Maggie spotted the dark-haired Anne Busch running alongside her. Everyone envied Anne's good looks and mature figure. She had rolled up the fabric on her uniform's legs, a practice which might elicit an accusation of "Young hussy!" or even detention from Genghis.

"I heard Morrett's comments, Maggie," Anne said, keeping her sentences short to facilitate breathing while running. "You told her off good. She's a pain. Thinks she's hot stuff. Sure, I wouldn't mind trading places with her sometimes. She lives in a new house by the lake. All she does during the summer is swim. While you're working on the farm and I'm working in my parents' restaurant, she goes to some fancy summer camp somewhere. For a month or more! But don't let her bug you."

Maggie felt the warmth of Anne's words but was unsure how to respond. Finally, she nodded and said, "Thanks," wondering why Anne was so nice to everyone and Janet was so mean.

"And I think your hair is unique *and* pretty," Anne added. "I agree with her about one thing, though."

Maggie turned slightly to look at her, expecting some kind of negative comment, but caught the grin on Anne's face.

"You do have a cute brother. But don't tell him I said so."

"Your secret is safe with me." Maggie returned the grin.

As Genghis ran backward ahead of them, calling out the names of those who fell behind, Maggie felt grateful that farmwork made gym pretty easy for her—and unnecessary too. *Lucky me*, she thought sarcastically. *I'm a farm kid.* But no matter how much she envied the townies, Margaret Emma Carlson had to settle for being a plain farm girl, even though she was tired of doing her chores and tired of farm life. A song had come to her mind as she lapped the gym: "How 'Ya Gonna Keep 'Em Down on the Farm? (After They've Seen Paree)." Rock River High School was no Paris, but glimpsing the way others lived made her hesitate to embrace the identity she had owned from birth.

In the hallway after class, Maggie ran into Jimmy's classmate Robert Plathe, who always talked nonstop, as if he feared losing his audience. It seemed to her that he recently had been finding reasons to meet her in the hall. Liking the attention, she made a mental note to ask her brother about him.

CHAPTER 3

THE ROPE

The small high school gym smelled of fresh perspiration as boys in yellow-white tees and red gym shorts ran laps after calisthenics during last-hour gym class. As usual, Jimmy Carlson was out in front of his tenth-grade classmates. He took no pride in finishing first because it wasn't a real competition. No one had challenged him for the lead, and there was no prize other than the privilege, awarded to the first six finishers, of being volunteered by Coach Sutter to drag the tumbling mats from their storage space against the wall to a position under a thick rope that hung from a beam about thirty feet above.

The boys easily pulled the mat into place as the coach blew his whistle and hollered, "Sit on the mat in four even columns facing the rope. You're going to get your chance to try climbing the rope today."

As the boys scrambled to sit in four columns, Robert Plathe, a short, thin boy with hair combed back into a ducktail, commented to Jimmy, "Hey, you can do this! Climbing the rope is right up your alley. Maggie told me that you practice climbing rope every day in the hayloft."

"I do," Jimmy replied. "But this rope is twice as thick. Don't know if I can grip it." He held up his right fist to remind Robert that he could not bend his index finger.

"Oh yeah," Robert joked, "when you make a fist, it looks like you just fished out a booger and don't know where to put it."

The two boys burst out laughing.

"Now, pipe down and listen up! Plathe! Carlson! Especially you, Plathe! Pay attention, and maybe you can drag yourself out of that D you're getting in this class!"

Jimmy gave a sideways nod to Robert, signaling the time for horseplay was over. Medium height, with hard muscles in his limbs and torso, Jimmy was the only other boy in the class who combed his long hair back into a ducktail, a style and length frowned upon by the school administration. However, the difference between him and his friend was stark—the mop of hair on Robert's head seemed to unbalance his thin body, making him look almost comical, while the mop on Jimmy's head fit his mature torso, revealing that he was one of the few fifteen-year-olds who could grow dark sideburns. Both boys turned their eyes to Coach Sutter, who stood by the rope.

"Each of you will get your turn to climb the rope. I don't expect many, if any, of you to succeed, because it takes a great deal of strength, balance, and practice. Do the best you can and try it every day we have gym class, and maybe by spring some of you will be able to climb it." He paused authoritatively before he continued. "I'll demonstrate the correct form."

Jimmy watched closely. Although Sutter was difficult to like, he was knowledgeable and appeared as a model of fitness in his red shorts and white T-shirt.

Sutter explained, "The correct way to start is to sit with your legs extended on either side of the rope. Then pull yourself up by reaching hand over hand until you get to the top. Most of you will want to use your legs because your arm strength is insufficient to lift your whole body and your abdominal muscles are not developed enough to hold your legs out straight. Well, go ahead and use the legs when you need to, but give the correct form a try."

Jimmy watched as Sutter climbed the rope by lifting himself hand over hand until he reached the top. Wow! Impressed by the demonstration, he gave the coach his full attention.

Sutter returned to the floor and checked his red gradebook for a name. "Anderson, you're first."

"Guess what," Carter wisecracked. "Anderson is first. The curse of the alphabet."

Jimmy smiled but said nothing. He watched intently. If anyone could do this, Jerry Anderson could. He was an athlete, skilled at football, basketball, and track. Despite his popularity, he was friendly with the nonentities, the students outside of the social and sports circles.

"Come on, Jerry. You can do it!" came cheers from the onlookers. Anderson sat on the mat, straddling the rope with his legs, and pulled himself up, first with his right hand, then with his left, and once more with his right. His cheeks puffed out, and his face showed strain. His legs eased downward to the floor. He took a leap, grabbed the rope as high as he could, and used his feet to anchor himself as he reached up again with both hands. Accompanied by cheers of "Go, Jerry! Go, Jerry!" he came within about ten feet of the top. But the effort had taken its toll on his strength, and he lowered himself to the mat, letting go with his feet about six feet from the floor and landing with a loud *thump!*

As if purposely defying Carter's wisecrack, Coach Sutter called off the remaining names at random as he walked among the students seated on the mat. Students cheered on classmate after classmate, but each of them failed to make it even halfway up the rope. Sutter marked their attempts in his gradebook. After Robert tried and failed, only Jimmy remained.

As Robert walked back to his place, Sutter mocked, "Maybe if you cut that hair, you'd be a little lighter. I could cut it for you."

Some of the boys snickered and jeered, and Jimmy heard one suggest, "Let's cut his hair!"

Robert stayed on his feet, waiting until the noise subsided before saying, "I usually charge fans for a lock of my hair." Then he slowly sat down on the mat.

Jimmy laughed loudly. That was Robert. He'd say anything to anyone.

Some of the boys laughed cautiously, but Sutter said nothing as he strode over to where Robert sat. Then, grabbing a bunch of Jimmy's hair above his ears, Sutter lifted hard, nearly pulling him off the mat, as he mocked, "See if this long hair will help you climb, Carlson. You're next."

Eyes watering from Sutter's surprise stunt, Jimmy quickly stood to take his turn amid laughs and jeers from his classmates, many of whom took pleasure in his pain. He swallowed hard to manage his anger as he moved toward the rope with his usual exaggerated swagger—an overcompensation for his natural shyness rather than a cocky strut.

Without a word, he sat on the mat with a leg on each side of the rope. Motivated by anger and pride, he inhaled deeply, reached up with his left hand, and pulled. Without any pause, he reached up with his right hand and gripped the rope hard to pull himself up until his left hand found the next grip high on the rope. He continued hand over hand toward the top and heard jeers turn to cheers.

At the top, he reached up with one hand to touch the beam and then backed off, switched hands, and touched the beam with his other hand. The entire class cheered as he descended hand under hand, still keeping his legs on either side of the rope.

At the bottom, Jimmy forced himself to stand up despite aching abdominals and wobbly legs. Holding the rope, he looked at Sutter and demanded, "Now give me an A for the quarter! I did what no one else could do."

His classmates began to chant, "Give him an A! Give him an A!" His courage and anger grew as the chanting grew louder, leading him to assert, "And I did it without using this finger, *Mr. Sutter.*" He held up his right hand with the index finger extended. "Remember, I can't bend it! This gives me four-fifths the grip others have with their right hand, but I did it anyway. Long hair and all! I deserve an A!"

The chanting grew, but Sutter did not move. He blew his whistle and waited for the chanting to stop before he said evenly, "You have to be out for extracurricular sports to get an A in gym, Carlson. You know that."

Jimmy yelled, "And that rule is just a bogus recruitment tactic, and everyone knows it!" The words echoed against the dull yellow walls of the gym, making them louder and more disrespectful than Jimmy had intended.

Sutter's red face showed anger, but his voice was steady and calm. "That's an hour of detention for you, Carlson. And the whole class has just earned the privilege of running laps for the rest of the period."

The boys groaned as they rose to begin lapping the gym, but before Jimmy could leave, Sutter demanded, "Wait up, Carlson."

Jimmy expected more scolding or maybe even more hair-pulling, but as both student and teacher cooled down, Coach Sutter offered him a deal. "Look, son—normally, there is no detention held on Fridays, but you can serve yours today, if you want, and get out early. Just show up at the locker room at quarter after three to help Jerry Snider put away uniforms for the season. He's a ninth grader, but he knows where everything goes, so you guys will finish long before four and you can get out early."

Jimmy stood there in surprised silence. He hated it when anyone but his parents called him "son," and he was reluctant to trust Sutter's deal. And yet, glad to have the chance to get out early from detention, he suppressed his many gripes about Sutter—though he did wonder if the coach handed out detention just to recruit students to put away uniforms.

"I'll be there," Jimmy heard himself say, and he moved to run laps with the others.

"Wait up a second," Sutter called to him. When Jimmy returned, Sutter asked, "What happened to your finger? Why can't you bend it?"

Reluctantly, Jimmy said, "I was teaching my little brother how to split wood. I was eleven. He was six. I held the wedge while he swung the sledgehammer."

Sutter nodded, and Jimmy left to run laps, muttering, "As if he really gives a rip." Catching up to Robert, he asked, "I'm doing my detention today. Could you get my green notebook and my literature and geometry books out of my locker and give them to Maggie before she gets on the bus home?"

"Glad to," his friend replied.

CHAPTER 4

THE FIGHT

Jimmy let the locker-room door close on its own behind him as he hurried toward the exit at the end of the three-story red-brick high school. His sister would be getting off the school bus at home around now. He could run the five miles to his folks' farm in about thirty-five minutes and arrive home in time to do his pre-supper chores before dark.

He tugged on the leather strap attached to a belt loop to retrieve his pocket watch from his jeans, which hung low on his hips. It was a couple of minutes to four—not exactly "long before" four, as Sutter had claimed. Dad was right when he advised, "Trust everyone and you'll soon find yourself among the deceived."

Jimmy stopped at the lavatory to relieve himself before the long trek home. After he washed his hands, he reached into his back pocket for a comb, a habitual motion. He wetted the comb under the faucet and then gripped it in the four working fingers of his right hand. Using familiar strokes, he combed his hair back on each side, following the comb with his left hand to form his signature ducktail in the back. He used water and frequent combing to keep his hair in place, not hair oil or any greasy substance.

He'd never trust Sutter again, that's for sure. Coach Sutter, the guy who bullied every kid with long hair. Coach Sutter, the champion of clean-cut style and the adviser of the Rock River High School Letterman's Club, where most club members wore either a flattop or a crew cut. Having longer hair on top was okay as long as the sides were cut short. Jeez, Sutter had even convinced his country friend Tom Ryan to tell Jimmy and Robert to cut their hair short. It irked Jimmy that Tom chose to abandon old friendships formed in the farm neighborhood to become a lackey for the coach. "You'll just make it harder on yourself if you don't comply!" Tom had threatened.

Sutter also tried to convince his club members to wear khakis or other slacks instead of jeans, but if they did wear jeans, they must not wear them below their waistlines. Doing so would hint at the daring new style of wearing them low on the hips, which identified the wearer as some form of "juvenile delinquent," the current term for a bad boy.

Storming out of the lav, Jimmy exclaimed, "I might even like school if it weren't for all the stupid rules."

Arriving at the exit, he stopped, donned his fur-collared brown leather jacket, and fished a wool cap out of the pocket. He folded out the earflaps and pulled the cap down tightly over his head, making sure his hair was set neatly underneath. Once outside, he took a brief moment to examine the overcast November sky, feel the sharpness of the cold against his cheeks, and smile at how much he loved being alive.

November had produced little snow so far, giving the ground a scattered whiteness, like spilled milk on a landscape of varied browns, yellows, and dull greens. The ground was frozen, but the roads would not be slippery, and the pastures would not have deep snow that would prohibit him from taking a shortcut home. It was a fine day to run!

He ran easily at first, musing that the rule against long hair—like the rule against chewing gum—had just made it a point of pride, no matter how many teachers pulled the boys' long hair. He cleared the school parking lot and pulled a large red handkerchief out of his back pocket, the kind that all farmers carried. Slowing his pace slightly, he folded the hanky diagonally, placed it over his nose and mouth, and tied it behind his head over the back of his wool cap. The mask kept the cold air out of his lungs as he ran, but he didn't like to wear it before he left town. It made him look like some robber fleeing a crime scene. When Robert had first seen him wearing the mask, he'd tagged him with the name *Bandit*.

About a hundred yards beyond the school, he picked up the railroad tracks—an illegal path for pedestrians, but no one had ever bothered him as he ran. The space between the rails was free of snow and ice, but the distance between the wooden ties forced him to adopt an unnatural gait, either stretching or holding back each step to avoid the space between them. Worth the effort, though, because running the railroad tracks cut off about half a mile compared to running the roadway. He smiled at the geometry of the configuration: the tracks were the hypotenuse connecting the roads, which were the two legs of the triangle. He ran the tracks in peace, allowing the day's events to turn over in his mind.

He felt no remorse about his run-in with Sutter, who strutted around like the biggest rooster in the henhouse. One thing was for sure: Sutter had totally forgotten what it was like to be young. He had no clue what it was like to be a teenager in 1955. Maybe Maggie was right when she advised, "Dear big brother, you need to try to get along with people." *Get along,* he thought, *but at what price?* And then he said aloud to the railroad tracks, "Ha! Robert always tells me I need more *diplomacy* if I'm going to be a smart-ass."

But Jimmy didn't feel diplomatic. He poured his anger into running, his feet making hard *thumps* on the railroad ties. Sometimes he paired a footfall with a shout to the sky, demanding justice and understanding. "Sutter pulls my hair"—*thump*—"then he gives me detention when I deserve an A"—*thump*—"then he has me put away his uniforms"—*thump*. His anger helped both time and distance pass quickly.

Jimmy turned off the railroad tracks onto a small dirt road going north. When the ridge along the road became level with the woodland, he veered off the road onto a narrow, brush-lined trail that led to a gate, which, when opened, was wide enough to allow the passage of horses and wagons carrying farmers to town when roads were blocked with winter snow or rendered impassable by deep spring mud. Taking the old buggy trail across Schroedlers' pasture would save him nearly a mile, and he was glad the weather was good.

Rounding a tight curve to the west gave Jimmy a clear view of the gate, revealing a surprise that stopped him in his tracks. Parked next to the fence line was Jack Drude's Model A Ford, a huge black spot corrupting the purity of the snow-dotted hillside. Although his common sense told him to stay away, a louder voice induced him to mischief. He sprinted toward the car and hit the top of its steel front fender hard with the side of his four-fingered fist, releasing some of his bottled-up anger and creating a *thump* to startle anyone inside or outside of the sturdy old vehicle. He fancied he heard chickens squawking but did not stick around to check. Without pause, he ran onward and cleared the five-wire pasture fence by grabbing a post and swinging himself over without adjusting his stride. Then he stopped, turned to check the car, and laughed as Jack crashed out of the driver's door like a rodeo bull charging out of the gate. Three years older than Jimmy, Jack had always been big for his age, and he had bullied everyone in the neighborhood country school. His tall, square body gave him a brutish appearance, and he was always willing to live up to his past reputation of physically beating others.

Jimmy could easily outrun him and was about to continue on when Mary Schroedler emerged from the passenger side of the vehicle. Why was she in the car with Jack? Slim and graceful, she sprinted toward a post on the fence about ten yards from him and, without slowing her stride, cleared it effortlessly, using the same method he had despite the fact she wore a dress under her navy wool jacket. Landing with grace, she turned to face him. Stunned, Jimmy smiled weakly. She nodded to him before racing up the pasture path toward her home. Without questioning his own motives, Jimmy pursued her, ignoring Jack's warning shout, "Mind your own business, Carlson!"

Jimmy's eyes followed Mary as she ran. Although quite petite, she was also strong and mature for sixteen. To Jimmy she was perfection, not just because she was pretty, but also because she was kind and friendly. And up until recently, he'd thought she liked him in a special way. They'd been friends since they started first grade together in the country school and childhood sweethearts since about grade five. He missed seeing her every day, now that she was no longer in his grade. He missed making her smile, and he missed the attention she had given him. He was keenly aware that Mary's bright blond hair and pretty face drew the attention of upperclassmen, especially after they discovered she was as old as many juniors. He knew he was losing her close friendship, and he had done nothing to keep her attention. How do you go from a childhood crush to dating? He felt like a coward.

Minutes later, the two runners completed the half-mile stretch through the pasture, with Mary reaching the fence next to the driveway about twenty yards ahead of Jimmy. Clearing the fence without hesitating, Mary stopped and yelled, "You need to get out of here! Jack is mad as hell."

Jimmy stopped running and pulled the red handkerchief down to talk. "He's always mad as hell. Nothing new there."

"Not funny, Jimmy. He's kill-Jimmy angry. And he got here before us. See his car parked behind the bushes at the end of the driveway?"

He had not seen the car until that moment, but running at the sight of it would look cowardly. "I'm more concerned about you," he honestly offered.

"He won't hurt me. He's mad at me, but I know how to calm him down."

Jimmy felt a pang of jealousy in his heart. For a brief, painful moment, nothing was said. Jimmy recognized Mary's navy-blue dress as one of the many she had sewn for herself. Her fair skin amplified the faint redness placed on her cheeks by the cold air, and her bright-yellow hair was tied into a ponytail that had bobbed up and down as she ran. Suddenly, her voice broke Jimmy's trance.

"Jeez, Jimmy. You've got to get out of here! Jack is probably in his car waiting for you."

"Well, then," he joked, "I'm glad I'm on this side of the fence—"

Then Jack hit him from behind like a locomotive on full steam.

Jimmy went down under Jack's heavy body; with superior size and strength, Jack could easily manipulate him into any position. Jack's legs and knees churned into his sides and stomach, and his fists flailed at his face. Jimmy tried to relax and keep moving to escape the larger boy's control, but the fight continued as it had begun, with Jack pummeling Jimmy as he lay on his back.

Furious, Mary cleared the fence, grabbed a four-foot dead oak branch from the ground, and pushed its sharp, brittle twigs into Jack's back and neck, exclaiming, "You rotten bully. You know that's not necessary. You know it!"

Leaving Jimmy lying flat on the frozen ground, Jack stood up and warned, "I could take that branch away from you. Easily."

"Go home!" she hollered, pushing him toward the fence with the branch. "Your visit with me is over!"

"Or what!"

"I'll get Mac and Shep!" Mary threatened.

"Those old mutts?" Jack snickered. "I know you keep them locked up in the old chicken coop. By the time you release them from the pen, Jimmy will be pulp."

"I'll get my father!" Mary was desperate.

"You hate old Matt! In fact, ain't he the reason you really better see me?" He laughed and added, "But I'll say no more. I'll just go."

By pushing the top wire on the fence down and swinging one leg over, then the other, Jack crossed the fence as if stepping over a dollhouse. He turned to yell to Mary, "I'll be back. I take what I want, or I find a way to have it given to me. You have no choice, you know." Then he strode toward his car, whistling his signature tune, "She'll Be Coming 'Round the Mountain."

CHAPTER 5

SPORT

Jimmy struggled to sit up. Unable to bear the shame of the moment, he did not want to face Mary, but as soon as Jack left, she was by his side. He expected her to have an "I told you so" attitude, but she untied his red handkerchief from around his neck and started wiping blood from his face. Jimmy tried to stand and felt even more ashamed when he had to accept Mary's help. He needed to move before he stiffened up.

"I'd better get home," he said, as he painfully stooped to pick up his cap. "Sorry to cause such a ruckus. Banging on the car was stupid."

"I'm glad you did it," she said without explanation. "Are you okay?" She looked at him, her face close to his.

Jimmy's ego answered for him, "Yes, I'm fine," though he hurt all over.

Mary abruptly hopped the fence and ran up her driveway.

Pain in his lower ribs and thighs prohibited him from hopping the fence in his usual manner, but he crawled between the barbed wires and began trotting home with a determined but uneven stride. Worried that Jack might be waiting for him around the bend, he decided to stay off the road. He would have more fences to cross and pasture hills to climb, making progress slow, but cutting across the edge of Schroedlers' slough and his folks' pasture would save him over a mile.

After less than a minute of running, he heard someone cackle. "Hey, Carlson, look who I found!"

Turning to look toward the bend in the road on his left, Jimmy saw Jack kneeling by his parked car near the edge of the road. Snuggling up to him was Jimmy's own dog, Sporty. He stood nearly to the height of a German shepherd and was mostly white, but he had enough black splotches on his body to give him a camouflaged appearance against the snow-patched ground. Jack aggressively stroked the dog, a reminder that he could charm dogs as well as people. The only exceptions were Matt Schroedler's big dogs, which Mary had urged to attack Jack many times over the years when he bullied his neighbors.

Jimmy called his dog with a firm enthusiasm he knew Sporty couldn't resist: "Here, Sport! Come, boy!"

Sporty bounded toward the voice of his master. Wincing from the pain of his bruises, Jimmy managed to kneel down to greet and pet his dog, whose tail wagged with such passion that his entire body moved with it.

Jimmy said, "You were chained to your doghouse when I left for school this morning, Sport. Did Mom let you loose?"

Jack's deep voice broke into their reunion. "He was in the pasture chasing old Matt's cows with a smaller black-and-white border collie—a female, I think. Looks like he's got a girlfriend, Jimmy. Nature will take its course. You'll never keep him home now. Tie him up, or one of the neighbors will do everyone a favor and shoot your dog just for the good of the neighborhood. Maybe I'll shoot him myself." Jack laughed at his own cruel joke.

Pretending to ignore Jack's comments, Jimmy whispered, "Let's go, Sport."

The two of them charged toward home. They fell into a game they had enjoyed for years, where Sporty would run behind Jimmy and try to trip him with his front legs. Usually, Jimmy would fall down on purpose as a kind of reward for the dog's efforts, and they would roll around on the ground together, enjoying the bond between animal and human. But Jimmy was too sore for the game today.

Jack's warning stuck in his mind like a bad radio jingle: "Maybe I'll shoot him myself." The unwritten neighborhood rule was that if a dog was chasing a neighbor's cattle, anyone shooting the dog would be doing the dog's owner a favor. Of course, you were expected to visit your neighbor to let him know about the dog's activities and give him a chance to secure the dog, but if the dog was doing serious damage, immediate action was warranted. Jimmy knew Sporty had a habit of running around the countryside, and he decided to chain him as soon as he got home.

Then there was the matter of the female dog. No neighborhood dog fit Jack's description of a black-and-white border collie, but Jimmy had seen Sporty with such a dog several times recently. He and Maggie had named her Little Collie. It was not unusual for stray dogs to appear in the farm neighborhood from time to time. People from distant towns or even the city might drop off pets if they didn't want them anymore, hoping the animals would find a home with some nice country people. Sometimes they could be tamed and given a home. But what often happened instead was the dog or cat stayed in the wild, became a nuisance, and was eventually shot by the locals. Abandoning any animal was considered a crime by those who cared about dogs and cats, but abandoning a female dog created a particular problem in farm county, where free-running males would breed with her when she came in heat, creating a pack that would prey on chickens and cattle.

"Yeah, I'll have to chain you when we get home, old boy," Jimmy muttered to the playmate running behind him.

Every movement created painful throbbing in Jimmy's head, and his bruised muscles screamed for him to rest. Suddenly, Sporty's powerful paws took hold of Jimmy's foot, tumbling him onto the hard ground. Jimmy groaned in pain, but Sport thought it was all in the game and surged forward to roll and play with his master, licking Jimmy's face and wagging his whole body. Despite the pain, Jimmy rolled around with his companion, holding the dog's head away from his own face. Laughing, he said, "I can smell you've been eating frozen cow pies again, Sport. Not a tongue I like on my face, if you don't mind. You're just a shit-eatin' dog."

For a sweet moment they lay together on the ground, absorbing each other's love. Abruptly, Jimmy rose and said, "Only a couple hundred yards to go." He checked his watch to discover he would arrive home only fifteen minutes behind schedule. Then he chuckled and said, "No one can get beat up faster than I can."

CHAPTER 6

HOME FROM SCHOOL

Enjoying the after-school freedom offered by the walk home, none of the group of children hurried as they ambled east down the middle of the narrow, snow-dotted dirt road that connected the farm neighborhood to the country school. While throwing loose pebbles from the road's surface at the base of electric poles, Joey Carlson saw the large black car approaching them from behind and announced, "Car coming." All six children moved to the edge of the road and stood in single file as the car passed. Recognizing the driver of the black Cadillac, Joey raised his hand high to wave and smiled as the driver returned the gesture.

"Who was that?" asked Caroline Shaurel, a sixth-grade classmate of Joey's. "Who do you know who drives a nice car like that?"

"That's Moses Ziton," Joey said with a hint of pride. "Doesn't everybody know him? He's the trader who stables his horse and camper at Crossroads Tavern in Berris's barn. When the weather is nice in spring through fall, he drives his Caddy down to park at Berris's place, and then he hitches up his mare to the camper and drives to farms to sell stuff."

"Like what?" demanded Caroline.

"New and used kitchen stuff, cloth, and lots of other things," Joey answered. "Mom likes to buy his fancy buttons for when she makes dresses. He also sharpens knives and tools, and he'll trade his services for cash or farm produce. His horse and camper make him look like he's from the pioneer days. He lives in the camper all week, and he drives his Caddy back to his house in Minneapolis on Friday evening."

"Why doesn't he come up to our farm?" Caroline sounded hurt about being left out, but the kids knew she was faking.

"Your driveway is too long, Caroline," piped up Katherine O'Keran, an eighth grader. "My brother, Billy Joe, used to talk to him all the time when he came up to our place. Ziton told him he doesn't take his rig up long driveways. He drives his mare slowly down the road, hoping farmers see him coming, and if they want him to stop, they will come to the road and tell him to drive up to the house. That way he saves time by not driving up when people aren't home, and he doesn't pester people unless they want to see him."

"He comes to our place in the summer," offered Mary Ryan, a seventh grader, "and I see him park his rig in Drudes' driveway pretty often. But what's he doing down here in November? Isn't it too cold out?"

Joey explained, "He drives all the way out here just to visit his mare, Sarah, on Friday nights during the winter. He says she misses him if he doesn't visit her once every week." He paused before he added, "I used to be afraid of him because Mom and Dad threatened to trade me for some buttons when I misbehaved. They were just teasing me, of course, and after talking to the old man during his visits to the farm, I got to like him."

"Your folks probably weren't kidding," said the eighth-grade twins Mary and Margaret Shaurel at the same time. Margaret added, "Your mom probably couldn't get more than one button for you."

"Or maybe Ziton didn't want to trade his buttons for a heathen like you, Joey Carlson," quipped Mary. "He probably preferred a real Christian."

"He wouldn't care either way," Joey answered. "I think Ziton is Jewish. Here's my driveway, see ya Monday."

Joey was glad to wave goodbye to the five girls, lamenting his bad luck that all the boys he was friends with lived in the other direction from the school. He began running up the fifty-yard driveway toward the farmhouse, but he slowed to a walk when he noticed the family car was absent from its parking spot. The house would be empty. The school bus would drop off Maggie and Jimmy in a few minutes, and then they would each do their pre-supper chores. Carrying feed and water to the chickens and gathering eggs would take him and Maggie about half an hour. Jimmy would throw down silage.

Joey looked forward to the evening because on Fridays their parents let them put off their schoolwork till the next day; after the evening milking was done, Mom would make buttered popcorn and chocolate milk for the family to enjoy as they watched a couple half-hour television shows before going to bed at nine.

As he trekked up the last half of the driveway, Joey wondered about his schoolmates. What did they really think of him? Why did Caroline hang on him like a wet towel, and why did her sisters always find something mean to say? The twins were the worst! No, Mary and Katherine were just as bad. They were smarter than the Shaurel girls, and Katherine was good at thinking up mean things to say. Mary wasn't so bad when she wasn't around Katherine.

But even his best friend, Ronnie Schoen, called him a heathen once in a while. He didn't really mind, but he didn't know why it was so funny to them. Sometimes he felt like they were all against him. Other times, everybody treated him like one of the group. The kids in his Sunday school were just as bad or worse. Even though they were Lutherans, like he was, they still treated him like an outsider. He was glad he didn't see them often enough to call any of them friends. Mom had told him once, "Don't expect much from other people. After all, they're just people." His big brother was more direct, saying, "Most people are just assholes." Joey didn't like to believe that was true. But he just didn't understand people.

He let the hinged storm door slam behind him as he entered the enclosed porch, but he was careful to push the heavy wooden inner door shut until he heard the doorknob latch go *click*. "No use wasting heat," his dad had told him a hundred times. He took off his overshoes on the porch before he opened the kitchen door to enter and then set his Superman lunch box on the kitchen table. As he removed his coat and cap, he saw the white note on the white-spotted red tabletop. Joey was pretty sure he knew what it said. He reached for it and read, in his mother's small, legible handwriting, *Took eggs to town. Should be back by 5. Fresh bread on the cupboard table.*

The last line hinted that supper might be late. The odor of fresh bread made him smile, and he decided to take Mom up on her hint to make himself a snack. The long bread knife lay in its usual spot by the cutting board on the cupboard table in the narrow room adjoining the kitchen. He expertly sliced off a thick piece of the over-raised loaf. The crust was a creamy, dark tan, and the bread had a coarse softness that Joey loved. A jar of homemade elderberry jelly and a white bowl of butter covered with an upside-down bowl were kept on the cupboard table, rather than in the refrigerator, a modern convenience the family had only acquired, secondhand, last spring. Both condiments tasted better at room temperature anyway and were used up too quickly to spoil. With a table knife, he dipped into the bowl of soft butter and generously spread the slippery substance over the bread, filling most of the small holes. Then he dipped a spoon into the jelly, which was a little runny, just as he liked it, and dumped as many spoonfuls as necessary to cover the oversized slice. He smeared the jelly around, watching it soak into the pores. He poured a glass of cold milk from the jar in the refrigerator and sat on a chair at the metal kitchen table to enjoy his feast.

Holding the bread in both hands, he took a big bite and chewed slowly, savoring the flavor of the sweet jelly mixed with the salty butter on the soft texture of the tasty bread. Life didn't get any better than this. He liked his folks and his brother and sister. He liked most things. What he didn't understand was why some people enjoyed being mean.

Kneeling on the chair's seat and resting his elbows on the table, he reached to the far end of the table for the daily newspaper and positioned himself to read *Henry*, his favorite comic strip. Henry was a weird-looking person without hair who usually did funny things. In today's strip, Henry came home from school, cut a slice of bread, and layered the top with jam. Joey laughed at Henry's antics, but the similarity to his own actions escaped him.

The sound of squeaking brakes told Joey the school bus was stopping to let off Maggie and Jimmy. Although eager to see them both, he kept reading the funnies, trying to assume a nonchalant pose for when they walked in. After a few more minutes, Maggie burst into the kitchen.

Unable to restrain himself, Joey blurted, "Where's Jimmy?"

"Detention. His friend Robert told me about it after school. We may as well start the chicken chores as soon as I put on my everyday clothes. Why aren't you changed?" Maggie was using her bossy big-sister voice.

"It's Friday. I'll wear these clothes for chores."

"Mom won't like that. You know she wants you to save your good jeans. What if you rip them on a chicken feeder or something?"

Joey hated that his sister was always right. "Okay, okay, I'll change."

Maggie read the note, muttering to herself, "Jimmy will probably be home before Mom and Dad are. That's just great. I get to play the dutiful farm girl again."

They both changed to what they called their "everyday" chore clothes, which were washed-out bib overalls with large patches of denim on the knees. Joey's overalls were a bit small for him; they had been purchased new for school two years ago but now showed too much wear on the knees and seat to be suitable for class. Maggie had no cause to buy new overalls, so hers were a hand-me-down from Jimmy. Their coats, too, had first been worn to school but now were too shabby or patched.

After donning their rubber four-buckle overshoes, Joey and Maggie strutted out to do their pre-supper chores together. Maggie filled two pails of water from the hose in the milk house, and Joey fetched a pail of chicken mash from the granary. They carried their burdens twenty yards to the chicken coop and went inside to empty the contents into waterers or feeders before picking eggs together. As they gathered eggs from the corners and the nests made of wooden orange crates and carefully placed them in the bottom of the emptied pails, Maggie commented, "I wonder where Emma is. Usually, she squats at my legs and waits for me to pick her up and stroke her."

"I don't see how you can tell them apart. They're all white chickens. They look exactly alike to me," Joey said.

"Only Emma squats down and chirps to me as I pick her up and talk to her. Her comb is really red, too, which means she's really healthy."

"They're all the same," Joey teased.

"Her comb flops a certain way," Maggie insisted. "She was here yesterday."

"Not as many eggs this time," Joey said.

"Yeah, the nests that usually have several had only one or two today."

"Mom won't be happy about that!" Joey exclaimed.

"Let's not say anything unless she asks," Maggie offered. "It'll just worry her."

"Let's tell her. Maybe we could get by with just her picking them in the morning or us doing it after school."

"No," Maggie instructed. "Eggs have to be picked both morning and evening to decrease the opportunity for the eggs to break or for the chickens to dirty them with poop."

Joey still hated that she was always right.

As they emerged from the chicken coop with the eggs, they saw Jimmy and Sporty charging down the hillside into the yard. They waved their acknowledgment to him and trekked to the house.

CHAPTER 7

JIMMY'S PLAN

Jimmy headed straight for the doghouse to find the end of Sporty's chain. Sporty stopped just short of the chain's reach, squatted down on all fours, and placed his head on his front paws, striking a cute pose that would increase his master's sympathy. Sporty may have been disobedient, but he was not stupid. Jimmy proceeded with the necessary ritual to entice his dog to come closer. He kneeled and pleaded, "Come on, boy. I wouldn't do this to you except I want to save your life, even as miserable as the chain might make it. Please, Sport. You know that I'll pick you up and carry you if I must, and you know you'll let me do it even though you wouldn't have to. You could run away or fight, but you won't."

Of course, the words meant nothing to the dog, but he found Jimmy's voice and posture irresistible and soon crawled up to put his muzzle between Jimmy's elbow and side, allowing the chain to be placed around his neck and snapped tightly in place. Jimmy lingered a moment to give Sporty a hug before he stood up and left without looking back. He'd worry about Sporty's future later. Right now, he had to throw down silage before the light faded. The sun waited for no one.

Once in the house, Jimmy stormed through the kitchen, opened the stairwell door, took the stairway two steps at a time up to the second story of the house, and bounded down the hallway to the room he shared with Joey. He stripped to his shorts and grabbed his everyday jeans from a nail in the corner he and Joey used as a closet. By the time he got to the kitchen, Joey and Maggie were seated at the table, reading the funnies.

"What happened to you?" Maggie exclaimed when she saw the blood and swelling on her brother's face.

Jimmy, as he often did, gave a silly answer. "I was talking when I should have been listening." Such an answer discouraged follow-up questions.

"This didn't happen at school, did it?" Maggie exclaimed.

"No, no," Jimmy assured her. "And the other guy is just fine." He forced a laugh. Noticing the odor of fresh bread, he decided he needed a snack, but he was in a race with the sun. He began putting on his barn clothes over his jeans as he said to his brother and sister, "Who wants to be my favorite and make me a jelly-and-butter sandwich? I have to hurry to throw down silage before we lose light."

Maggie retorted, "Zap, you're a jelly-and-butter sandwich—but you knew I'd say that. Don't worry, I'll do it. I don't think you want Joey to make it. Hands of a ten-year-old are seldom clean."

"Yes, they are!" Joey barked. But there was no rancor in the bickering, just predictable sibling exchanges. "Besides," he added, "I'm nearly eleven. And I'm already Jimmy's favorite, anyway. And I'm everybody's favorite cuz I'm the youngest and cutest."

"Your cuteness will wear off in a few years." Maggie chuckled as she rose to start making the sandwich. Then, putting her face close to his, she said, "Oh, I guess it already has."

The two older siblings laughed, and Joey retorted, "You're both jealous."

After buckling his four-buckle overshoes, Jimmy thanked Maggie for the sandwich as she handed it to him.

"Aren't you going to wash your hands after buckling up your barn boots?"

"No time. Besides, I'll wolf this down so fast I'll barely touch the bread."

"Quite a germ theory you have, there."

The sandwich was gone before he was halfway to the barn, allowing him to slip his yellow chore gloves over his cold hands before he opened the door to the small entryway to the haymow.

As he descended the stairs to the lower level, where the cattle were locked in stanchions, he felt the steamy air in his nostrils and smelled the odors, a combination of corn silage, hay, and gas from cows. Not a bad smell, really. He ran down the center aisle to the door to the silo room, where silage for the next day was stored for the morning feeding. He half hoped Dad had thrown it down before they left for town, but he was not surprised to discover he hadn't. He crossed the six-by-eight-foot space and gazed up through the thirty-inch-diameter steel chute to the reinforced-glass skylight some fifty feet above. Spaced less than a foot apart along the chute, twenty steel doors, each with two steel bars used for steps, provided access to the steadily shrinking heap in the silo. Reaching for the second rung on the second door from the bottom, Jimmy began climbing the steel ladder. His dad's advice rang in his ears as he climbed: "Never release your handhold on a rung until you have stepped on the next foothold and it has borne your weight."

Usually, his father waited until Thanksgiving weekend to "open the silo," a phrase that meant tossing off and carrying away all the spoilage on top, after which they began feeding the fodder to the cows every morning. Two factors had contributed to opening the silo early this year. First, a dry fall had cut down the length of time they could pasture the harvested fields, forcing them to feed silage earlier than usual; and second, a good corn crop had let them refill the silo after each layer of chopped corn settled, giving the contents of the silo more tonnage than usual. The latter fact had convinced Dad they would have enough silage until spring pasture provided high-protein feed for the cattle.

Arriving at the first open door—the second from the top—Jimmy grabbed the step on the door above it, which was fastened in place. Using the step as a handle, he hoisted himself through the silo door below it, feet first. The cold, moist air in the silo gave Jimmy a chill when he took off his coat, but he knew that once he started working, he would warm up in minutes. The fifteen-tine silage fork leaned against the concrete stave where he had left it yesterday, and in a moment he had taken it up, set his mind to the task, and begun furiously pitching silage out the square door.

The fury was not without a plan; it was a sensical method taught to him by his father. Yesterday, Jimmy had taken off an eight-inch layer from the silage to the right of the door. As Jimmy threw from his left side, he could minimize the arm movement needed to pitch the heavy forkful across the fourteen-foot-diameter space and down the chute. He would work his way around to the right and pitch off the last of the layer of silage in front of the door. To start another layer, he would begin pitching again a few feet to the right of the door. A pitcher thus worked his way around, always throwing across the layer that he was about to pitch off, so that any spillage landed on an area yet to be handled, not on the smooth surface left after taking a clean layer. Neatness counted.

Like the constant tick of a metronome, Jimmy's rhythm was marked by the crashing of each forkful of silage he threw against the far end of the metal chute. He had prepared himself mentally to work the rapid pace till he completed the task in twenty minutes or less. Sometimes he timed himself to see if he could break his own record, but he skipped it today. He had other things on his mind.

Jack Drude and the dread of Jack Drude and the scourge of Jack Drude had followed him all his life, from his first day at the country school to the present. No one could fix it for him. He had to be his own hero. Life would be so much better without Jack Drude! And the fact that Jack recently seemed to be able to control Mary Schroedler made it all even worse. Why, after Mary and he had been sweethearts for years, had she suddenly started riding around with Jack? Sure, Jack had a car and Jimmy didn't even have a license, but he'd be getting his permit soon, and Dad would let him use the '52 Ford. But today had been a huge blow. Right in front of Mary, Jack had easily beaten him until Mary came to his rescue! How embarrassing! Embarrassing and painful. Would she ever want to be with a loser like him?

Thoughts flooded his mind as he searched for an answer to his predicament. *Jack is big. He has always been bigger than me, and nothing beats size. Jack is strong, stronger than me, and nothing beats strength. Jack is fast, but I'm getting faster, and nothing beats speed. Jack has stamina, but I have stamina too. I work on it every day when I push myself to throw down silage as fast as I can. Nothing beats stamina.*

Jack has all four of the four necessary components, and in two of the four, size and strength, he is clearly superior. Sure, I'm getting stronger, climbing ropes and exercising in the haymow daily, but a hell of a lot of good my speed or strength or stamina did me today, when Jack mowed me down like a locomotive scraping a peanut off the rails.

He was frustrated, not angry, that he always came up with nothing. He stopped pitching and poked his head into the chute. From over forty feet above the top of the pile of fodder, he could not determine the height of the pile, but he had thrown down a whole layer and was back to where he had started on the big circle. He leaned the fork against the wall of concrete staves, donned his coat, and prepared to exit, a simple task that always brought a smile to his face as he remembered the first time he'd tried to climb out the door. He had been about six years old and should have waited for his dad to tell him what to do, but lacking any plan, he'd climbed out headfirst and ended up with his feet above him as his small hands desperately grasped a handle of the door below him. Luckily, Dad had been watching and grabbed his feet and hauled him back in, explaining, "First, you need a plan. Don't just rush into things. When you get older, here is what you'll do." And then he'd demonstrated. "Facing upward, stick your head and arms through the opening and reach the rung on the ladder above the door. Then climb up until you get your legs out of the opening. Then climb down, being careful to grab the sides of the wall of the open door. But never try it without me for quite a while yet. Until you get older, you will crawl out after me and climb down while I have my arms on either side of you for protection. You couldn't fall if you tried."

Now, Jimmy pulled himself through the door as he'd been taught, but when his feet were solidly on the rung below the open door, he stopped and leaned back against the steel chute, resting in a position he had seen his father take many times and reflecting on the pain he still felt from Jack's blows. Suddenly, he uttered to himself in a loud whisper, "A plan. Maybe that is the component I've overlooked! *Nothing beats a plan.* Maybe Jack's not so invincible after all!" Then, disregarding the pain, he hustled down the chute and ran up the barn stairway, taking the wooden steps two at a time.

CHAPTER 8

MARY'S DOGHOUSE

After leaving Jimmy's side, Mary ran directly to the old chicken coop to seek the safe company of Mac and Shep. Cuddling with her two loyal companions on an old sofa, she confessed her guilt at allowing Jimmy to follow her through the pasture. "You guys understand, don't you? Sure, I should've known the risk and not put Jimmy in danger, but you see, I wanted him to follow. Maybe I'd get a chance to explain about Jack. But what would I have said? I couldn't tell him the truth. Better off saying nothing."

Her dogs lay with their heads on her lap, shedding hair and drool on her good school clothes. "Don't worry, guys, I don't care about the clothes. I'm quitting school anyway." Scratching behind their ears, she lamented, "Wish you guys would've been there. You'd have protected Jimmy and me. All the times I've sicced you on Jack and he ran like a whipped dog. But now you have to be penned up. The days of dogs running free are over, my old, sweet puppies.

"Remember when I first got you guys, and we used to play together late in the day, until Mom called supper? We'd play stick, and I'd chase one of you. Then that one would drop it, and the other one would pick it up and run from me. You were always smart, even smart enough to distrust my brothers and my father and Jack. And they stayed away from me when you guys were nearby. You loved Mom, though. Everybody loved Mom."

Images of her mother brought a smile to her face: milking cows by hand as they sang old songs like "May I Sleep in Your Barn Tonight, Mister" and "Oh, Playmate, Come Out and Play with Me," and their favorite, "You Are My Sunshine," which expressed precisely the feelings between them. And baking cookies. "How Mom loved to bake cookies!" she exclaimed in a whisper to Mac and Shep. "And how Jimmy and Maggie loved to eat them when they visited." She paused briefly before sighing. "Oh, Jimmy. You wanted to say something to me today. But what? We've been friends since the first grade, and now we can't seem to really talk anymore. We used to talk and giggle all the time. Most of the other kids in school looked down on me, but you were always a kind listener. And my protector.

"And the next year, when Maggie started school, she and I became best friends. We walked together to their place after school, and then I'd cut south across the pasture to our place because I just hated going home. Sure, I missed you two guys and Mom, but Matt was so mean."

The thought of Matt clouded her demeanor—how her father tried to isolate his family from the rest of the world. In the fifth grade she'd gotten rheumatic fever. She was weak. All she'd wanted to do was sleep and rest. She lost all her desire to run and play. Jimmy and Maggie had brought books to her a couple times each week, and Jimmy had helped her continue to learn fractions. Her mother always welcomed them when they visited, but one time, Matt had barged into the kitchen, ranting, "Don't waste time teaching her much. She's just a girl, and all she needs to do is learn housekeeping and how to have kids. Her ma and I can teach her that." And with that, he had scooted Maggie and Jimmy out the door without giving them time to finish the cookies or the schoolwork.

Mary whispered, "Yes, everybody loved Mom. Except maybe Matt. After that I never called him Father again. And from then on, any tutoring the Carlsons did was when Matt wasn't home."

She hugged her dogs. "Jimmy was so brave. He came over often. Without his help, I would've never been passed on to the sixth grade that year. Dear Jimmy, I felt a bond grow between us then, a bond beyond friendship. I know you felt it too. A bond of love. Sure, we never speak of our feelings, but

I know we want to. I know I want to. I know my being with Jack is breaking your heart. And mine too. But he has threatened to expose me."

Suddenly, Matt's harsh call brought her back to stark reality: "Are you in there, Mary? Milk the cows before supper today. After you make supper, we'll hit the sack early."

Mary shuddered. She buried her face in warm fur and whispered to Mac and Shep, "I don't know how, but I've got to escape this place. Soon." Then she scurried out of the doghouse to milk the cows.

CHAPTER 9

A TRADE

Late Friday afternoon, Jack parked his Model A in his folks' driveway, far enough around a bend so that most drivers passing by wouldn't notice it, but close enough to be seen if you entered the driveway. Ziton was late, but Jack knew he'd be there for the trade. Today, the final two-chicken payment was due to complete last spring's deal: four payments of two chickens each in trade for Ziton's powerful binoculars, which already hung on a leather strap around Jack's neck.

"Take the binoculars now," Ziton had said after only the second payment of chickens. "I trust you, and you'll have a lot of use for them over the summer."

And today, Jack had needed them really bad. B. J. O'Keran had stolen the other three pairs of birds from his parents' flock, but with him away at school, Jack had scrambled to find another source. The chickens had to be White Rocks, the same breed as the O'Kerans' meaty hens, or Ziton, who had never ventured down the long driveway to Drudes' farmyard, might get wise to the fact that Jack's folks didn't raise any chickens.

Jack made it his business to know the neighborhood. Carlsons raised White Rocks, and with his binoculars, Jack had spied them leaving for town in the early afternoon. After he unchained the dog to keep him from barking, he'd easily had time to steal the chickens and a couple dozen eggs before the kids came home from school.

"Don't have chickens and don't have eggs, but I got my sources," he boasted with a chuckle. He stepped out of his car when he saw Ziton's black Caddy approach.

Sliding out of the vehicle, Ziton explained, "I drove by earlier, too early for our meeting, so I drove over to visit Sarah at Crossroads and make sure she had enough hay for the weekend."

"So that's why you came from the east. Doesn't Berris look after her for you?" Jack asked, feigning interest to charm the trader.

"Sure, but Sarah misses me during the offseason. I like to visit her anyway."

Jack didn't hurry to hand over the heavy hens. Ziton liked to shoot the breeze. He didn't like to be dismissed. Every business deal required some small talk, which might lead to another deal. Best to avoid being too direct.

"Will you be making some rounds around Valentine's Day? You did last year, didn't you?"

"Don't know for sure. That's three months away. It depends how warm it is then. If we get a weeklong warm spell coming on, I might come down. New cloth and used jewelry sell good in February. And fancy buttons and lace, too. But I don't like to take Sarah out unless it warms up to the thirties."

"I get it. You care for your mare."

"She's pretty special to me. Besides, most people don't like to trade when it's cold. Don't know why. The housewives like to get the knives sharpened, though, and trade for eggs. I can sell them in town easily. For a good price. Did you bring any eggs?"

Jack's patience had been rewarded. "I did. Two dozen."

"I don't have anything to trade but some jewelry. I suppose you don't want that."

"Naw, I've no use for it." Best to play it coy.

"I can give you cash. Two cents a dozen below the retail egg market in town."

"Okay," Jack said, and he went around to get the eggs. Then he stopped to add, "Maybe I could use the jewelry. How about cash for one dozen and trade the other dozen for the jewelry?"

"No, it's a nice set. A necklace and bracelet. I would need both dozens for the set."

Ziton showed Jack the pieces, explaining in his salesman spiel, "It's just costume jewelry, of course, but the necklace's gold-colored chain and the setting holding the red stone are beautiful, don't you think? And the matching small red stones on the bracelet make the set really special. You'd be getting a deal."

Jack admired the large red stone, picturing it against Mary's soft, white skin. "I think you're right," he agreed, and took the jewelry to his car.

"Got a girlfriend?"

"Maybe this will help get me one." The men shared a light laugh.

Checking that no cars were about to pass by, Jack transferred the chickens and eggs into Ziton's car.

"I'll call and leave word with Berris when I decide to start my rounds."

The two men nodded their goodbyes, and as Ziton's Caddy pulled away, Jack said aloud, "Maybe the jewelry is just the thing to soften her up. And it's paid for by her best friends' chickens."

CHAPTER 10

HOME FROM TOWN

The headlights of Carlsons' blue 1952 Ford weaved slightly before slicing into the darkness of the driveway and then ambling toward the house, mixing with the dim glowing circle projected by the yard light.

Glad to be home, Mom sang a line from a nursery rhyme, as she often did on such moments, "Home again, home again, jiggety-jig." Then she said, "The house is dark. I knew they'd be milking already. We've got good kids, Martin, but we should have been home an hour ago."

"They could've waited. We're not that late," Dad grumbled good-naturedly.

Mary asserted, "We wouldn't even be this late if you didn't always insist on buying a last round. Then John had to buy a round, and then Emil and then Joe and . . ."

"I suppose it's all my fault."

"I didn't say that. I drank my share. Though I passed on some beer to get a couple nickel candy bars for each of the kids."

"It's a good thing beer is only a dime a glass."

"It still adds up. Takes nearly three eggs to pay for a glass with what we get for them. At the store they are nearly sixty cents a dozen, but we don't get near that much."

Money worries aside, Martin and Mary were in a mellow mood. Feeling good about completing the difficult task of removing the fall fencing from around some fields they had pastured and the stinky task of opening the silo and carrying away the spoilage that week, they had decided to make a quick trip to Newburg, the town where they did most of their personal and farm business. After tending to routine tasks—taking in eggs, picking up a couple of sacks of chicken feed, buying a few groceries, and paying bills—they had rewarded themselves with a few beers at a fairly quiet establishment called McShane's Hardware, which, in addition to hardware for farms and households, also sold tap beer, soda pop, ice cream cones, candy, and other treats. The owners were honest, kindhearted people who ran a good business and also owned the mortgage to Mary and Martin Carlson's farm.

Mary and Martin were in their midthirties and always ready to work hard and enjoy life, seeking every occasion to do either or both. Martin was about five foot ten, strong, quick, and physically fit. Mary was about five foot four and unafraid to compare her ability to do farmwork to any man's or her cooking skills to any woman's. She always moved quickly and with purpose, and Martin was known to say more than once, "When it comes to certain jobs, sometimes I'm better off just to get out of her way."

Martin parked the car in the "old garage," a name he had given the grassless spot next to the house.

"I'll get the box of groceries," he said, "and we can leave the sacks of chicken feed in the trunk. Then I'll change out of my good overalls and get down to the barn right away."

Mary added, "I'll bring in the six-pack. It'll stay cool on the porch for tomorrow. Then I'll put away groceries, take some hamburger out of the chest freezer, change clothes, and still beat you to the barn."

Martin knew she was just conning him to hurry, but he didn't care. "You're on," he said. "I'll bet you a big kiss."

"Not fair," she said. "You know I never withhold a kiss unless you got snuff in your mouth."

They doubled down to move fast. In less than fifteen minutes they were both on their way to the barn. Mary stopped in the milk house to check that the strainer pad was secure and that the valve on the bulk tank was closed. As Martin opened the barn door, he met Jimmy carrying up a pail of milk to dump into the strainer.

"Hi, Dad," Jimmy said briskly. "We're nearly done with the east row but haven't started with the double rows on the main aisle." He continued the few yards back to the milk house, easily carrying the full four-gallon "shotgun" pail, which was designed with tall, straight sides and a cover to prevent debris from falling into the milk when the pail was carried a long distance.

Mom held the milk house door open for Jimmy. "If you haven't put a bucket on Valentine yet," she said, "I'll milk her by hand to hurry things along. She's hard, and it takes the machine forever."

"Haven't got to her yet," Jimmy remarked, turning away to hide his face from his mother, but both parents had already spotted his swollen eyes and lips.

"Going to tell us what happened?" Mom asked.

"I was talking when I should have been listening."

"I'll let that stand for now," Mom said, "but if this has anything to do with school, you'd better let me know."

They waited as Jimmy lifted his pail over the strainer's lip and dumped the milk, and they watched while the milk strained through it. Feeling his drinks, Dad asserted with a wink, "Look, son, if it was a teacher and you want me to come to school Monday and tune the guy up a little, just let me know."

"Shush, Martin. That won't help!" Mary exclaimed.

Jimmy held back a smile as he thought of his dad, wearing bib overalls that smelled like barn, confronting one of his teachers. Too embarrassed to tell them about being beaten by Jack Drude, he said, "No, Dad. It wasn't a teacher. Don't worry about it. I'm okay. Nothing anyone can do about it but me."

"You know you can tell us anything," Dad offered. "If it's some big guy bullying you, I want to tell you that it's never over. They keep at it, and the idea that a bully is a coward is just BS. He can be tough as hell."

"Yeah," Mom added, "remember we're on your side."

Jimmy shook his head to acknowledge but remained silent.

Mom hurried away, saying, "I'd better get down the barn."

Dad took the pail from his son and added, "Hey, Jim, there's a cold six-pack on the porch. Go get a couple cans and bring them to the barn."

"Mom's not going to like that," Jimmy warned gingerly.

"Let me worry about that."

"The machines are on Robin, Daisy, and Stella, in that order," Jimmy said before leaving for the house to do his dad's bidding.

Dad checked the three milking-machine buckets as soon as he returned with the pail. Mom was already perched on a stool next to Valentine, stripping out some milk to wet the cow's teats, which had dried since being washed half an hour ago.

Maggie prepared to carry up the partially full pail of milk Dad had recently poured from a bucket taken off a cow on the east aisle. She fitted the cover on the top and began her journey to the west aisle, thinking, *I don't need to wait till the thing is full. It's heavy enough with just three gallons in it.*

On the west aisle, heading toward the stairs, she passed Mom, who was seated on a foot-high milk stool next to Valentine, squirting thin streams of milk into the pail in a steady background beat to one of her favorite songs, "Home, Sweet Home." As her mother crooned, "Be it ever so humble, there's no place like home," Maggie stopped to listen, waiting for a moment to talk. Mom was an even better listener than usual when she and Dad had been drinking. In a moment, as expected, her mother said, "I know you're not here to listen to my singing. There's something on your mind."

"Two things," Maggie said. "First, will I ever be able to carry a full pail as easily as Jimmy?"

With the tireless consistency of a drummer in a band, Mom kept the rhythm of the milk squirting into the half-filled pail. "Probably not. Nothing beats strength and size, but you do what you can, and you learn to do it how you can do it."

"Can you do Dad's job?"

"Not the way he can, but I can do it my way. And I'm better at some things than he is. I can milk cows faster than he can. And when it comes to cooking and baking, he's lost."

Maggie nodded and turned to leave.

"Hold on, dearie," Mom ordered. "You said there were *two* things."

Maggie stopped reluctantly. Hesitating, because she did not want to hurt her mother's feelings, she chose her words carefully. "How can you be so happy during chores? I mean, the barn stinks, it's late, there must be hundreds of things you'd rather be doing, and yet here you are milking Valentine, one of the hardest cows in the world, probably, and you're singing as if you're the happiest person in the universe."

Mom stopped milking and smiled at her daughter. "I'll explain, if you really want to listen, but I don't like to talk just for exercise."

Maggie nodded. "I really want to know how you do it, Mom."

"Well," she said, "my way may not be for everyone." She inhaled and exhaled before she began her story. "You see, I was the youngest of nine kids. Your aunt Emma was a few years older and helped Mom with the housework—cooking, washing clothes, ironing, and all that stuff, which was a lot of hard work. I helped too, but there never seemed to be a real place for me. My seven brothers took care of the outside work, and I learned that it was really only the outside work that was valued, even by my mother. Inside work or women's work was just taken for granted. In fact, I learned that girls were not valued like boys were. My folks took me out of school early because my father said girls didn't need an education.

"Well, one time when the men were out in the field late and Emma was taking care of the dishes, Mom took me with her to milk the cows. I was about six and eager to learn. To make the story short, I'll just say I loved milking cows and became really good at it. In a few years, I was better than anyone in the family, and I had found my place and got a certain amount of respect for it. Doing milking gave me confidence that I was a valuable member of the family, even if I was a girl.

"As I milked cows at home, I dreamed of having a herd of my own. Well, here I am now, living that dream. We owe a lot of money, sure, but we're doing okay, and I know this is where I belong. I'm good at what I do, and I like it. Why should I be unhappy when I realize how lucky I am?"

Maggie was silent for a moment before she said, "Thanks, Mom. I think I kind of get it."

Mom smiled, began milking again, and added, "What I do isn't for everyone, but it is what I do. This is my station in life, and I like it."

Maggie began to leave but stopped as Mom said, "One more thing, Maggie. You have little control over your life now while you are home with us, but what you can control is your approach to it. Learn to like your station in life until you can change it. It'll make your life better if you do."

As Maggie contemplated the words of wisdom, Mom prodded, "What do you know about Jimmy's bruises? Did he get into a fight?"

Maggie looked away for a moment to say, "I don't know anything about that. He wouldn't tell when I asked him. But I know he isn't in any real trouble at school. And school has nothing to do with any fight. It's just all a result of his usual efforts to stir things up. You know Jimmy." She explained the details of Jimmy's conflict with Mr. Sutter, as Robert had explained them to her when he told her which books to get from Jimmy's locker.

"Sounds like my boy," Mom said, shaking her head. "He's so willing to do everything we tell him to do at home, but I don't know why he bucks authority at school. Now, go on and take up the milk, and I'll send Joey with you. Then the two of you can go to the house and get the table ready for supper. Joey seems kind of quiet tonight. See if you can find out what's wrong." She glanced over at her youngest, who was moving belts from milked cows to cows-to-be-milked. "He just isn't his normal chatterbox tonight. He said something to Dad about kids at school, and Dad talked about Rose, but I didn't catch it all. See what you can find out. You're a good listener."

"Sure, Mom." Maggie lifted the pail to leave and yelled for Joey to follow her. Then, as she climbed the stairs, hoisting the long pail high enough to clear each step, she muttered, "Everyone's always worried about Joey."

After she exited the barn, she met Jimmy returning from the house. Noticing the two cans of beer in his hands, she commented, "Mom's not going to like that."

"My words exactly," Jimmy agreed and stopped to face his sister, appearing frustrated. "But it isn't my call, if you know what I mean."

Maggie nodded. "By the way, I told Mom what Robert told me after school, about how you got detention. I knew you wouldn't mind."

"Too late for me to mind, since you already told them, little sister," Jimmy said gruffly, his frustration increasing.

"Sorry, Jimmy. But why is it you never hesitate to do stuff at home for Mom and Dad, but you go out of your way to be such a pain at school?"

"Jeez, Maggie, there's such a big difference. I get my folks' authority.

They made me. But why is everyone else trying to remake me into what they want? Rule me. Big guys rule, old guys rule, authority rules, and all I'm supposed to do is what they want me to do, at school or anywhere. When do I get to rule?"

"Teenagers don't get to make the rules. That's true for all of us, Jimmy."

"Look, I love working hard and accomplishing things. But at school, I work at classwork and accomplish things. I get good grades, only to have some asshole pulling my hair or worried where I hang my jeans on my hips."

Maggie felt his anger increasing and decided not to interrupt.

"Soon they're going to decide I have to wear some useless dress slacks instead of jeans. And then there's Sutter's gym class. The whole class is a lame attempt at physical fitness. What a joke. I should have an A in it because I am physically fit and I achieve in class. Yet, to qualify for an A, they concoct a rule that says instead of doing physical chores after school, I have to play around with a ball on a team with a bunch of town kids! It's such BS!"

"But you have to comply with the rules, don't you? I mean, wouldn't it be easier to just try to get along?"

"Oh, I'm all for obeying smart rules. It's the stupid rules I object to, and I think complying with stupid rules may just encourage rule-makers to make up more stupid rules. I'd like to be free to do things that are important. My schoolwork is important, and I do it. Kids need to be free from stupid rules."

"But we need rules in school, don't we?"

"Of course, but we need to be free to focus on learning! Give us a bunch of stupid rules and the whole thing becomes less serious. If they'd treat us seriously, we'd be serious." He paused, seeming to feel relieved. Then he added, "I'd better get down there with this beer, but I'll wait till you dump your pail and take it down with me."

Maggie dumped the pail, handed it to him, and then left for the house, a little confused about her brother's comments. Even though she agreed with him that many of the rules were stupid, she took less offense at them. As she hurried into the kitchen, she muttered, "No one puts up with stupid rules more than girls. Girls can't wear jeans or slacks to school. Dresses or skirts only for the ladies."

When Jimmy reached the bottom of the staircase, Mom and Dad were happily working, but the jovial atmosphere ended in a flash when Mom noticed the two cans of beer in his hands.

"Martin, that's for tomorrow!" Her words were sharp. "We don't need any more tonight."

The argument lasted through most of milking. Old moments of jealousy surfaced. Past differences that had been reconciled once again became issues of bitter contention. Unkind words were said, words they would later regret.

At one point, Martin said to Jimmy, "It's my fault, you know. We agreed we wouldn't drink any more tonight. But when I thought of those cold cans of beer and how good one would taste while I'm milking, I made up my mind. You know, Jim, if you decide to be a drinking man, you will know what I mean. And there will always be arguments. Your mother is good, though. She doesn't stay mad long."

Jimmy said nothing as he left to carry up a pail of milk. He hated it when his folks argued, and he had heard it all before.

CHAPTER 11

COMPLAINTS

Once in the house, Joey and Maggie cleaned themselves up and set the table for supper. Each wrapped in their own thoughts about school, neither spoke as they peeled some potatoes to fry. Finally, Maggie said, "You'd asked me about the meaning of a word before Mom and Dad came to the barn tonight. What was it again?"

"It's nothing."

"Come on, Joe. I know it's something."

"I guess I know what the word *heathen* means, but why do they think it's so funny to call me that?"

"Let me guess." Maggie smiled. "Mary Ryan, right?"

"Yeah, on the walk home from school."

"She wouldn't do that if her older brothers and sisters were around. What brought that on?"

"Well, it started in the morning. During the Pledge of Allegiance, when everyone paused before putting in the new words, I forgot and just continued on saying *indivisible* while everyone else was saying *under God*. I felt pretty stupid after I did it. Some kids started giggling right then, and at morning recess, even Ronnie accused me of being a heathen in front of a bunch of kids. Sometimes friends can be real mean."

"Sometimes, Joey, one may feel like one has no friends at all. Or like they've been just pretending. I hope they dropped it after that. I mean, you just forgot."

"No, they didn't drop it! Later, Mary said her dad said that we were not real Christians anyway because we don't go to the Catholic church. So, she's saying that's why I forgot to say the words *under God*, because I ain't a real Christian. I told her that we only started saying it last year. And she said that I had a whole year of saying it, and I said but I don't say the pledge much over summer and she said that maybe I should."

"I understand, but they're just pushing you to react. Kids can be mean," Maggie said.

But Joey was not to be consoled. "When do I get to push back? Being nice is getting me nowhere! They think I'm just a pushover. Good old Joey the pushover. I'm so outnumbered. When you and Jimmy were in the country school, I wasn't so alone, but now every one of the kids goes to the same church but me."

Maggie had never seen her little brother so angry at the other kids in school. His shoulders sagged, and she wondered how long he had held back his anger.

Joey added quickly, "Don't tell Mom and Dad. Or Jimmy either. They'll just get mad. I don't want you to get mad either. I shouldn't have said anything."

"Mom said you mentioned it to Dad," Maggie fished.

"I started to, but then he started talking about Aunt Rose. He said, 'Just like Rose. We grew up in the same house with the same religion, but somehow her religion made her better than the rest of us.' I didn't really get the connection. She's Lutheran like us, right? Anyway, don't tell them I'm being pushed around by a bunch of girls."

"Sometimes the words from girls can hurt more than blows from boys, Joey. But don't worry. You can tell me anything. You know I won't tell." Then she added, "I don't know much about it, but I think God would be very forgiving of anything a sweet boy like you did and less forgiving of kids bullying a child with their self-righteous crap." Sensing that he was not quite convinced, she continued, "I think I know how you feel, Joey, but don't let them make you feel that you don't belong. I used to feel that way at the country school too, sometimes, but now when I go to the high school, I *really* feel that I don't belong. I get to thinking that I don't belong anywhere, and—"

Joey broke in, "Me too!"

"But Joey, we *do* belong as much as anyone else does. No matter that we have different groups we belong to. We still belong *here*. And don't forget it. You, me, Jimmy, Mom and Dad—we are our own group, and I'm proud to be in your group."

Joey smiled and said nothing. He was a sucker for kind words from his brother and sister. He thought about two things—how good he had it now and how much better things would be when he was no longer just a kid. Being just a kid was crap.

Mom came in from chores first, explaining, "Jimmy and Dad stayed out in the yard to talk a bit. Seems your father has to give him some pointers on fighting. I wish he wouldn't do that. It only makes things worse."

"And Jimmy hates it when Dad does that," Maggie said.

Mom continued, "But I don't have time to worry about it. I got to get supper on the table."

"Was he telling stories too?" Maggie was curious.

"Yeah," Mom replied. "The one about the Torgerson brothers."

"The who?" Joey asked.

"I know that one," Maggie said with some pride. "One time when the Torgerson brothers were drunk and raising hell in the taverns in town and had left their Model A parked in the dark area by the feed mill, some of the guys were sick of their BS and snuck out with a jack to put blocks under the axle so one back wheel was less than an inch off the ground. When the brothers got into the car to leave town, they didn't know the wheel was off the ground and nearly blew the engine trying to get the car to move before they figured what was wrong."

Joey was puzzled. "But what *was* wrong?"

"Well, it only takes one wheel to spin, and the car sends the power to the one that spins because it's easier. It's the mechanics of the car. I don't really get it, but the car wouldn't go forward or backward, and the brothers couldn't see the problem from inside the car. Finally, Magnus got out to look while Arne tried to drive. When they discovered the blocks under the axle, they went back into the bar to get revenge on the guys who did it, but all the guys in there claimed they did it and just threw the Torgerson brothers out. Even beat them up pretty badly, according to some reports."

Joey's mouth hung open, and Maggie laughed. "I've heard Dad tell the story in a lot more detail, but Joey doesn't need to hear all that."

"I'll bet you were younger than I am now when you heard the story in detail," Joey complained. "You guys treat me like a kid all the time. I'm not a kid, you know."

Mom said, "Go out and tell those guys to come in and get cleaned up for supper, Joey. And don't get wrapped up in listening to Dad's stories." She turned to Maggie and said, "Joey, Jimmy, and your father. It's like taking care of three children."

Maggie allowed her face to smile, but her mind questioned the moment. *Joey and Jimmy and Dad. Three children. I'd like a piece of my day to be about me, not them. Is that too much to ask?* She wondered if her mom ever felt the same way.

Within half an hour the family was sitting around the table, eating loose chunks of fried ground beef, fried potatoes, home-canned green beans, and homemade bread. All was peaceful as Dad talked about old John spilling the spittoon in town and Mom told of the new feed-sack pattern she'd bought. With the late supper, there would be no buttered popcorn and chocolate milk before bed, but the kids didn't complain. Mom had given them each a couple of nickel candy bars, and the evening had offered them adventure enough. By a few minutes after nine, all five members of the Carlson family were nestled into their beds.

CHAPTER 12

THE STALKER

The November night provided gusts of wind that roughly swayed the trees, but shiny brown leaves that had clung to twigs through steady October gales held tight, and moments with no wind seemed to offer the smooth, lifeless leaves time to regrip. It was during one of those moments of stillness that Sport sniffed a familiar scent in the wind, and from his doghouse he gave a soft yelp of recognition.

"Easy, Sporty," rumbled an enticing baritone voice. Its owner approached from the south, keeping the round granary between him and the house. He knelt to let Sporty come to him before reaching out to unsnap the chain. Sporty gave the visitor's face a quick lick before bounding off to the west, keeping to the shadows of the trees as if he, too, understood the value of staying out of the sightline of the house. Reaching into the tool pocket of his jeans, the stalker produced a pair of pliers, which he used to damage the spring-loaded clip on the chain before he left it lying on the ground.

There was very little light from the moon, but he was careful to stay in the shadows as he crossed to the small shed where Martin Carlson kept his tools. The shed had originally been the two-hole outhouse on the farm, which is why the door opened inward and could be hooked from the inside. When the family had to upgrade their dairy operation to remain on Grade A milk, the required upgrades included switching from shipping milk in cans to using a bulk tank, setting up the milk house with hot and cold running water to facilitate cleaning the tank and milking utensils, and either installing plumbing in the house or erecting a state-approved outhouse. The milk house and bulk tank improvements had drained the family of credit and cash, forcing them to delay installation of indoor plumbing for another few years and proving once again that in every farm family, the word *farm* always comes first. Martin had bought a clean two-holer from a country school that had closed and set it on an approved foundation in a new location. Then he hosed out the old toilet and, without repairing the wide cracks in the walls, repainted it outside and inside before moving it to a new location and using it to store tools. He even had his uncle run a wire over to bring electricity to his very first toolshed. It was small, but it protected the tools from snow and rain. Jimmy joked afterward that he was the only farm kid whose dad told him to go to the toilet to get a crescent wrench.

Most doors remained unlocked in the farm neighborhood, even when they had locks, and this particular door was held closed by a simple hook that slipped through a large staple. The stalker lifted the hook, pushed the door open, stepped inside, and held the door closed as he flicked the switch on his flashlight to locate the small hook that hung on the inside of the door. After securing the hook through another staple on the doorframe to ensure the door stayed tightly closed, he shined his flashlight upward to locate the light fixture mounted to the ceiling and pulled the short chain, sending power to the hundred-watt bulb to illuminate the small space.

Positive that his presence would go undetected, the stalker carefully searched for the perfect item to pilfer. The bulb brightly lit the inside of the toolshed, but he needed his metal flashlight to search the corners and under the shelves. The item should be something not used in the winter, so that its absence would go undetected till spring. It should look new for a good resale value, and it should have a special use that would give it extra value. A tool that had not come in a box would be preferable because selling a tool without its box had a lower resale value. Most farmers did not keep the original boxes anyway.

The stalker stooped down to look among the tools spread out on top of the bench where the toilet-hole lids had been nailed down, but he decided an absence there would be too obvious. The stalker searched through items in rusty dishpans, small wooden desk drawers, and old cooking pots on shelves built above the bench, but he found only used bolts and washers, nothing worth taking. He knew he was better off leaving empty handed than risking suspicion for an item of little value.

In the space next to the closed door stood two rusty fourteen-quart pails. When new, these pails had been used for milk, but lacking the alloys used in the modern pails, they had rusted beyond use. Concerned that the bottoms might fall out if he picked them up, he left the pails in place as he eyed their contents. Spotting something of interest in the second pail, he picked up the prize: a shiny, red twelve-inch pipe wrench, too big to have come in a box, too new to have any of the teeth damaged, and too good to be true. He would keep it for several months before trying to sell it. He could hear himself making the pitch to old Ziton: "Yeah, I bought it as a Christmas present for my dad, but I discovered he had two of them already, so I kept it and got him something else. Should be worth a couple dollars?" If he could get a dollar fifty, he'd be glad. He could get over five gallons of gas for a dollar and a half, or maybe he could trade it for some of Ziton's cloth that Mary might fancy to make a dress, something that might help warm her feelings toward him. He shoved the pipe wrench inside his coat pocket, and although its size and weight strained against the seams, the heavy wrench stayed secure. He checked his other coat pocket to feel the necklace and bracelet set. He rubbed the large red stone between his thumb and forefinger. Satisfied, he pulled the chain on the light and left the farmyard.

Jack moved swiftly to his next nighttime appointment, where he arrived early and slipped into the shadows while he scanned the farmyard for any movement. He felt powerful stalking others, seeing them when they couldn't see him, discovering things about them while he remained a mystery. Few activities surpassed this feeling of control, but as he crept toward the big sliding door of Schroedlers' hayloft, he anticipated an experience that would.

CHAPTER 13

WHITE DANCER

Maggie lay silently in her single fold-up bed in her tiny room at the east end of the upstairs hall, waiting until she thought her parents were asleep in the room below her before she stirred. Then, wrapping herself in a heavy red-and-white woolen blanket, she left her bedroom. The long blanket dragged silently behind her as she aimed her flashlight at the floor of the hallway and crept toward the larger bedroom. There was no door on the bedroom where her two brothers slept, and she entered without hesitation. The room was cold—there was no heat register to let in warm air from the oil stove in the living room below. Joey was curled up in the small folding bed on the south side of the room. Jimmy slept in the larger steel folding bed on the north side of the room, but his bed was empty, just as Maggie expected. She sat on the floor near the window next to her brother, who was adjusting the dial of a small electric radio in search of musical sounds from distant stations. Late at night they could hear stations from as far away as Memphis and New Orleans playing music they had not heard before, music with a raunchy sound and lyrics that thrilled their youthful curiosity. Jimmy kept the volume low as he put his ear to the speaker, slowly turning the tuning knob, waiting for a tune or a voice to break through the squeaking airwaves.

Maggie scraped away some frozen condensation to look out the window toward the barren vegetable garden.

"Anything out there?" Jimmy asked in a sarcastic whisper.

Maggie glared at him before she muttered, "I'll let you know. You don't even believe in ghosts. You're just making fun of me."

"Am not," Jimmy protested. "I saw White Dancer just like you and Joey did. I just don't call it a ghost. Besides, it's been a while since we saw it."

"Well, it's early yet. He may still appear," Maggie hoped aloud.

"True," Jimmy whispered. "And it is overdue, you know."

Magically, a voice broke through the radio static with music recently familiar to them.

As the signal faded, Jimmy whispered, "That was him. Elvis Presley. We were lucky to catch it."

"What does it mean, anyway? 'That's all right, Mama.' Did you catch it all?"

"Not really, but I kind of like it."

"I like it a lot. The voice. Thrilling!"

"For girls, maybe. I like it too, but . . ." Jimmy let the sentence trail off unfinished as he went back to adjusting the tuner. "No more luck. May as well turn it off."

Maggie stayed to talk. They talked, as they often did, about everything, but tonight each knew their confidence was withering, for things were on their minds that could not be shared between brother and sister.

Maggie offered a topic first. "After Robert told me about your detention, I asked him how you and he became friends. He seemed to love telling the story about the two of you getting detention in ninth-grade general science."

"Did he?" Jimmy replied before casually adding, "Before that day, I had him pegged as a rich city kid. I was set to not like him."

"Without giving him a chance?" Maggie challenged him in a whisper.

"Well, his family moved here from the East Coast that year. His dad had a high-paid engineering job, so they had to move every couple of years. They had money, so at first he wore nice slacks, shirts, and sweaters. Outside of school, though, he wore jeans that hung low on his hips, black shoes, white socks, and a white T-shirt. One time when he wore those duds to school, Sutter sent him home to put on a shirt with a collar. He told Robert his long hair and clothing style was corrupting our local youths. Told him they marked him as a 'dangerous rebel.' Hard to believe when you get to know him, but even if it was so, some local town kids wear similar garb and have slightly shorter haircuts, but they have credibility Robert didn't have—they're locals, not imported from elsewhere, and some play football or basketball. He seemed so alone and yet full of courage. I got to like him."

Jimmy reached up to scrape some ice off the window. Then he touched her shoulder gently and pointed. "There it is," he said, backing away from the small clear area of the window so she could peek through. "See the dancing whiteness, near where the garden gate is?"

"Yes! Yes!" she exclaimed too loudly.

He placed his forefinger over his lips. "If we wake little brother, our vigil is over."

"Or if we wake Mom," she added ominously.

"It just started a minute ago." He pointed to his pocket watch, which he had placed face up on the narrow white windowsill. "Four and a half minutes is the longest it's ever stayed. Let's see if it beats that record."

Maggie whispered, "I wonder why Sporty doesn't bark. He's chained to the granary. His doghouse is right there."

"It faces south, though, away from White Dancer." Jimmy smiled to himself.

"You just won't call it a ghost, will you?"

They watched the dancing whiteness in silence.

"Last time it was a big lump of white. Tonight it seems like many smaller ones, but a duller white than last time."

Jimmy calmly noted, "And it's dancing more wildly."

"Are you going down there?"

"If it stays longer than usual, I will. But if I wake up the folks, I don't want it to disappear before they see it. That could be a bad break in a long night."

Faces close together, they watched intently through the small, clear space in the frosted windowpane, Maggie intermittently wiping away the condensation that gathered from their warm breath.

The dancing whiteness was spotty, not solid, and its movements erratic, bouncing from left to right, dancing as if enjoying a moment of freedom.

Mags whispered with curious enthusiasm, "Do you think it is released from confinement during a certain time of the night? Maybe from a bottle or something?"

He gave her his older-brother look. She knew the look, even though she couldn't see it clearly in the dark.

"You believe in ghosts and I do not, remember?" he said as if scorning her.

She knew he wasn't, though. They always pushed each other with their banter but seldom crossed the line. She added, "Well, I don't believe either, but there it is. We are both watching it. Yet you say you don't believe."

He said nothing. He had theories based on a list of observations in a notebook he kept under his bed.

In the next moment, the whiteness vanished.

"Gone!" Maggie exclaimed too loudly.

Joey woke up abruptly, and as he sat up, he bumped his head on the low ceiling that slanted down toward the wall near his end of his small bed. "The ghost?" he asked with fear in his voice that reflected honest terror in his heart.

The head bump was louder than his voice, loud enough so they knew Mom would awaken. A moment later, Mom yelled up from the bottom of the stairwell, "Quiet down! Get to sleep. Five thirty will be here soon enough!"

"Okay, Mom. We're sorry," Jimmy said sincerely. "We'll be quiet."

Mags scurried over beside Joey's bed to comfort him. "It's okay, Joey. The ghost is gone."

Still sleepy, Joey whined, "I think we should tell Mom and Dad about the ghost. Maybe they could get it to leave. Why keep it a secret from them?"

"They have more to do than worry about ghosts. Let's just keep it a secret for now, okay?" She knew that Joey's fear of ghosts and the dark was no joke to him. He was more embarrassed by his fears because he was growing beyond the age and size where they were acceptable to adults and his peers.

Maggie returned to the window, sat down on the floor by Jimmy, and whispered, "Joey will fall asleep in a sec. Mom said nothing about the radio. Maybe we can listen for a while?"

"No, I think we'd better go to bed. Mom sounded mad." Jimmy motioned for her to come closer as he whispered, "I want to tell you something before you leave, but you need to keep it secret. Don't tell Joey or the folks. They'll just worry."

After Maggie nodded, Jimmy briefly explained the circumstances of his fight with Jack Drude and the outcome, leaving out the part about how Mary had saved him.

Maggie murmured sadly, "Why don't you ever fight with someone smaller than you?"

"I don't want to hurt them."

"You know, brother, it's only in fiction where the good guy wins regardless of the odds."

"Maybe life needs to be a little more like fiction," Jimmy said.

"Not if the fiction is by Edgar Allen Poe."

"Or Mary Shelley." Jimmy smiled with his answer, returning to the playful one-upmanship the two of them enjoyed. "The main reason I tell you, though, is that I want you to stay away from him. Tell Mary to stay away from him too. He's more than just a bully. He's dangerous."

"Okay, don't worry," Maggie whispered.

"Yeah, and one more thing," Jimmy teased. "I think the main reason Robert wants to be my buddy is because he's kinda sweet on you."

In the dark room, Maggie couldn't see her brother wink, just as he couldn't see her blush. She decided to change the subject. "What are you going to do about the ghost?"

"I have a plan."

"You always do." Maggie smiled in the darkness and left for her bedroom. But after she crawled into bed, she was unable to sleep. She felt good about what Jimmy had said about Robert, but was her brother's concern about Jack just a way to get her to tell him more about the relationship between Jack and Mary? Jimmy's feelings for Mary were clear, even though he kept them to himself. As her mind cycled through thoughts about the ghost, herself, and the people in her life, the image of Mary Schroedler always surfaced. There was something Mary was not telling her, secrets she did not share with anyone.

After Maggie left, Jimmy stared out the window toward the garden where the dancing whiteness had been, wishing he could reach the area instantaneously when the dancer appeared. Then he checked that his windup alarm clock was set for four thirty in the morning, a full hour before his parents would get up for milking. That hour gave him time to work on his long-range exercise goals before he helped with morning chores. Today's events had depressed him more than he let on, but he would not let the beating he had suffered deter his resolve.

Pointing his flashlight under his bed, he retrieved a small yellow tablet and a pencil. He wrote, *Friday, 10pm, clear, windy, dark, danced for 3 minutes, not as bright as last summer, Sport did not bark.* Then, in another column labeled *MS*, in script that was intentionally barely legible, he wrote, *M in car with J. Seems against her will. Chance for me?* Before he slipped into bed, he replaced the tablet and pencil and set the alarm clock within easy reach under his bed. His thoughts took him in too many directions to sort, and despite the lingering pain, drowsiness took him quickly into deep sleep.

CHAPTER 14

THE RENDEZVOUS

In her upstairs bedroom in the one-and-a-half-story farmhouse, Mary Schroedler lay still under her blankets. Her father had left her bed a few minutes ago, but his stench of whiskey, snuff, and barn remained. Still terrified by his fists and his threats, she turned her head toward the wall and inhaled and exhaled deeply several times, trying to calm herself with a method that had worked in the past. It never got easier.

But tonight it was different. Worse. Much worse. Because there was more horror to come. She had not the energy nor the will to rise and keep the promised rendezvous with Jack, but if she didn't, her secret would become public knowledge and her shame would define her to others. He would tell Jimmy. She had no options.

Mary waited for what might have been ten minutes before she rose quietly. Then, making as little noise as possible, she put on a bib overall, pulled on and tied her work shoes, donned her winter coat, grabbed a shiny metal flashlight, and exited through her bedroom window onto the roof of the back porch. The November night was cold as her shoes gripped the wooden shingles, making a bit more noise than she intended at first.

Suddenly an idea struck her. What if her father *did* hear her leave? What if he followed her? Maybe that would be a good thing! Maybe she had an option. Without turning on her flashlight, she carefully hung from the eaves before jumping to the ground, landing with an unusually loud *thump*. Risky, but she had nothing more to lose. Scurrying through the darkness, she slowed to noiselessly pass the old chicken coop, where the dogs were locked overnight. Rousing the dogs was not part of her new, haphazard plan.

Reaching the barn, she paused to lean on the smooth fieldstone wall of the ground floor as her mind screamed at her to find some way to avoid going to the haymow to meet Jack. Glancing back at the house, she hoped to see a light. Maybe the noise of her descent had roused her father. *But that might make it all worse! Could it be any worse?* "Probably not," she whispered as she turned on the flashlight. "If Matt's looking, let him see where I am." She aimed the light above the fieldstone wall to illuminate the twelve-foot-high wall of the haymow, which reached up to the overhang of the large hip roof.

Lighting her way with the flashlight, she moved to the far side of the barn, where the dirt driveway rose to the top of the stone wall. After trekking up the incline, she stopped at the ten-foot-wide sliding door, which, when opened, led to an aisle between towering stacks of baled hay and straw. After storing her flashlight in her coat pocket, she put her muscle and weight to the handle, forcing the massive door to begrudgingly slide open with its usual noise—the dull grinding of small steel wheels on an unlubricated steel rail. She stepped into the darkness of the hayloft and strained to close the door behind her. She chose to not switch on the ceiling light located on the rafters overhead. *Too obvious.* Instead, she flicked on her flashlight and pointed it forward, illuminating the smiling face of Jack Drude a few feet before her. Although she'd been expecting him, she gasped, as if she did not want to believe the truth of the moment.

"You're late."

"I couldn't help it."

"For a while I thought you were maybe serious when you yelled that our visit was off, but I figured it was a lie so Jimmy would suspect nothing. I don't know why you care what people know, but I'm glad you do, so I got something on you."

"Wouldn't be here otherwise."

Jack backed up a few steps and bumped into the manure spreader. "I wish Matt would keep his damn spreader somewhere else. And he parks it too close to the ladder. If I fell, I could get hurt."

Mary tried to stall. "Got to put it somewhere inside. He uses it every day to haul the daily cleaning out to the field." Her mind flashed to the sledgehammer leaning against the inside of the doorframe. Her father used it to pound support posts into place in the barn below. She could picture herself swinging it over her head and guiding the wedged end into Jack's skull. "Parking the spreader inside keeps the snow off. When he drives the tractor and spreader in here, they fit perfectly."

"Well, start climbing, or do I have to smack you a good one? I'd sooner not have to slap you around like Matt does." He motioned to the makeshift ladder created by long boards nailed horizontally to the twelve-by-twelve-inch support stud. Mary climbed with exaggerated care, reluctant to reach the top rung. Jack followed, urging her to hurry. She filed the sledgehammer plan in her memory for another time.

"So, do you usually prowl around at night spying on neighbors?"

"Not all neighbors. You and a couple others, maybe. But like I told you in the car, I was outside of your house that night when I heard Matt pound at your bedroom door. I saw you crawl out the window onto the porch roof, and I saw Matt pull you down from the roof and smack you around. I heard him cussing you out, as he dragged you into the house and took you on the kitchen floor, saying, 'If you don't want a soft bed, you get the floor.'"

Resigned to the task ahead of her, Mary remained silent as they walked to the far end of the hayloft.

Before they settled among the bales in a far corner away from the ladder, Jack removed the heavy pipe wrench from his coat pocket and set it down nearby. Brushing his fingers over the necklace and bracelet, he decided to give them to her later.

Feeling terror in her heart, Mary mentally prepared herself to follow his demands, ready to let her mind go blank and her body numb, as she had with her stepbrothers when she was a child and, more recently, with her father.

But then a faint but familiar sound broke the silence, bringing Mary both renewed hope and renewed fear—a sound they both had heard less than ten minutes earlier, the dull grinding of small steel wheels on an unlubricated steel rail. They both froze as the overhead lights came on to dimly light their corner of the hayloft. In one fluid motion, Jack reached for the pipe wrench, rose noiselessly, and hurried to meet the intruder, who was nearing the top rung of the ladder. He swung the heavy wrench hard, splintering the top rung where Matt's hand gripped to hold his weight.

Mary and Jack watched as Matt fell backward toward the manure spreader.

CHAPTER 15

AFTER THE FALL

Giving Matt aid never entered Jack's mind. He scrambled down the ladder, pipe wrench in hand, with every intention to finish off the old man. But there was no need to deliver a blow. Schroedler lay still atop the spreader's beater bar, as if someone had fastened him in place, with his glassy eyes bulging and his mouth open but unable to speak.

Somehow, Mary reached her father's side only seconds after Jack. Looking at his face closely, she exclaimed, "He's done for! He's dead!"

Jack watched her back away from the body, only to move closer again to stare at his face. Then, turning slowly to face Jack, she proclaimed hysterically, "And now I don't ever have to see you again! Not ever again! Get out!"

He grabbed her with one hand and squeezed her thin arm between his thumb and fingers until tears gathered in her eyes. With his other hand, he shoved the cold steel of the pipe wrench jaw against her throat, nearly lifting her off the floor. Staring into her eyes, he grunted, "So Jimmy already knows, then? And you don't care if I fill in the details? I'll explain how you were *damaged goods* long before I got to you. And I guess you don't care if I do Jimmy some permanent damage next time I see him."

Jack enjoyed watching the defiance on her face melt into fear. He let her struggle to breathe until she waved her hand in the air for him to stop. He eased the pressure on the wrench, and she began coughing.

He released his grip and shoved her hard against the side of the spreader. "I can keep this up all day, you know!"

She gasped deeply several times before choking out, "Look, Jack, I have to find a way to explain this situation, and it's best if no one knows you were here. You have to leave. You were never here. The only way I can explain Matt being in the barn is to say we were milking. I'll say we finished milking, and he went to throw down some hay."

Her response seemed reasonable to Jack. A cover-up. He liked it. He checked his pocket watch. "It's only quarter to three. Isn't it too early to be milking the cows?"

"You're right. You're right. I'll wait a couple hours, but I have to milk before I pretend to panic and run to Rosinceks' to report the whole thing to them. I'll use their phone to call the sheriff."

Still coughing, she repeated, "You were never here! You have to go, now!"

Jack let her gently push him out the sliding door into the darkness of the early morning. Pleased at her willingness to cover up his part in Matt's death, he knew she was right. He had to leave. He began his trek home. He was not in a hurry, but he knew the sooner he left Schroedlers' barn, the better for him.

He did not run but stretched his long legs forward one at a time, creating a fast, steady gait down a path going east to his folks' farmstead. The rhythm of his stride induced reflection. She had said, "I don't ever have to see you again!" The words stuck in his mind. He repeated them to himself, then said aloud, "But she came around with a little persuasion." He smiled as he gestured in the air with the pipe wrench before tapping it into the palm of his other hand. She didn't dare disobey. He still had her. Proof was how she planned so quickly to cover up for him. Her plans included him. He was sure of it. He didn't know why it mattered to her what Jimmy or anyone else knew about her, but he was glad she cared. He'd use that leverage.

His folks' house was dark. He could see the window of the upstairs room where his older brothers slept and the single window of the drafty enclosed porch where he had slept in a single bed crammed against the wall until he was about ten. Why they wouldn't let him sleep in the big room upstairs, he never knew. Nor did he know why his mother hated him. His father, though, treated him okay, even insisting his mother let him eat supper with the family most nights. Otherwise, he was not welcome in the house.

He opened the personnel door on the lean-to of the barn, but he did not switch on the light. By the light of his flashlight, he walked to his makeshift bedroom, a vacant horse stall enclosed by stacked bales of straw. The stall's door could be opened to allow heat from the cows to keep the area at a comfortable temperature. Jack remembered the day he moved his bed from the porch into the stall as a happy time. For him, the barn was home, and he enjoyed the company of the cats and cows much more than the company of his brothers.

He moved a couple of bales aside to expose his store of pilfered items, which was organized according to value. He took a moment to admire his stash before setting the pipe wrench down among other valuable tools and restacking the bales. Then, after hanging his coat on a hook formerly used for harnesses, he sat on his bed, removed his shoes, and crawled under the quilt without removing his trousers and shirt.

He was tired, but his mind worked to reconcile recent events with a future plan. Maybe Mary would stay at the farm alone—but that would be too good to be true. She hated her two older brothers for the same reason she hated her father, so she wouldn't stay with them, but she might end up staying with Rosinceks, which could foil his attempts to see her regularly. He ached to go back to Schroedlers' barn, not only to see Mary but also to do whatever he could to keep her under his control. He was confident in his methods, but he feared his absence would embolden her. He was still undecided about what he should do next when sleep took him away.

After pushing Jack out, Mary had already begun to doubt the plan she had hatched just to get rid of him. Would the sheriff know she had waited to call just by looking at the body? If so, he would want to know why she had waited. What if neighbors had seen the hayloft light on? In a rush, she reached for the switch and cut the light. It was unlikely, though—the barn was among trees a couple of hundred yards from the road. If they had seen, it was too late to do anything about it. But she kept the lights off and switched on her flashlight. Exhausted, she leaned against the stack of bales behind her and slid to the floor. She needed to think. Putting her head on her knees, she closed her eyes and slowly inhaled and exhaled deeply several times, trying to sort her options.

Jolted awake by cats scrambling in the hay, Mary felt rested, but how long had she slept? Her pocket watch was in the house. She rose, exited the barn, and closed the sliding door behind her. Maybe the story she had told Jack was her only option, but was there still enough time to milk the cows before reporting the accident? As she ran to the house, she began creating the story she needed to tell the sheriff. She would need to pay attention to details that would back it up. She needed to be wearing her barn clothes. She needed to be done milking. She would leave the strainer on the milk can, because after seeing Matt, she had rushed away to Rosinceks' place without washing up the pails and strainer. The cans were too heavy for her to lift into the milk cooler—Matt always did that. Cats and dogs would not be fed.

Bursting into the house, she saw that the clock read half past five. She heated water to wash the cows as she dressed in her barn clothes. In minutes, she was off to the barn to milk. Nearly numbed by the early morning's events, she talked to each cow as she washed its udder. As she milked, tears streamed a familiar path down her cheeks, but she did not sob. She had work to do. She had to plan her strategy. Invent and rehearse her story. She saw no other option. She planned what she would say to Rosinceks. They were good people. She hated to lie to them. And she would have to lie to Maggie and Jimmy and the whole family.

By quarter to seven, she had finished milking the ten cows by hand. She checked the barn to ensure the strainer and cans were in place. Walking around to the outside door of the hayloft, she readied herself for the scene. She opened the door, flicked on the light, and gasped. She did not have to pretend to be horrified at the sight of the gruesome body of the man she hated. To make her pretend discovery more real, she moved closer for a quick check. Her story for the sheriff would be more believable if she actually checked. Then, with only partial pretense, she ran in horror to Rosinceks' place.

Jack awoke at six, about his usual time to begin morning chores. He liked doing morning milking alone, and he also didn't mind cleaning out the gutters daily and using a wheelbarrow to haul the cow dung out to a pile next to the barn. It earned him his keep, according to his father. Milking by hand gave him time to think, to review what had passed, and to plan his next moves. As he pulled on Veronica's long teats, he whistled a few lines from one of the only songs he knew:

She'll be coming 'round the mountain when she comes.
She'll be coming 'round the mountain when she comes.

An hour later, he poured the last of the milk through the strainer. Then he washed both strainer and pail and carried the cans of milk to the cooler, lifting them over the side and setting them down carefully into the cool water. He hurried through cleaning the barn, then washed his hands and face in a basin of cold water he dipped from the stock tank. Jack knew his father would feed hay before noon and even handle evening milking without his help if he returned late. After a light breakfast of milk from the cooler poured over Wheaties out of the box, he dressed warm, but before he headed out the door, he stuffed into his pockets a package of crackers and a block of cheese for himself and any four-footed friends he might have to bribe on his trek.

CHAPTER 16

PREDAWN RITUALS

Jimmy reached under his bed to shut off his alarm clock at four thirty before it dinged twice. Careful not to awaken Joey, he grabbed his clothes and walked softly down the hall and down the stairs to dress in the kitchen. The family knew about his exercise ritual, so if he woke anyone, they just rolled over and went back to sleep. It was Saturday, but he allowed himself only Sunday off when it came to his self-imposed training, and today he was eager to work on some new ideas he had picked up during the beating Jack had delivered.

He dressed in layers as he would for chores, starting with old flannel shirts and finishing with a chore jacket, which he would remove while exercising and later when he worked in the warmth provided by the cows in their stalls. Carrying a large flashlight, he exited the enclosed porch and felt the cold breeze, which had gusted throughout the night, slap his swollen face, waking him to a reality he had hoped to overcome—that Jack Drude had the power to dominate his world.

Instead of taking the route directly to the barn, he detoured over to the garden fence where the White Dancer had been. He examined the area carefully, first in the darkness and then in the glow of his flashlight. He shined the light around the base of the small tree that had grown up in the fence line over the last decade. Nothing. Turning his attention toward the doghouse, he wondered why Sporty was not outside, straining against his chain, begging to be let loose. Usually he took Sporty along with him to the hayloft, where the dog would lie on the hay and watch Jimmy train, so he was shocked to find him gone. He knelt to pick up the chain, shining his light on the damaged snap and contemplating the mystery: how had Sporty escaped the chain, and how had he managed to bend and scratch the metal clip? "Not done by a dog," he concluded aloud, "unless you can handle a pair of pliers, Sport." Realizing that an intruder had visited the farm during the night, he felt a chill run through his spine. Should he tell his folks?

He decided not to worry them. He'd record it in his notebook. Hesitating only briefly, he dropped the chain and headed to the barn. He opened the door and left it unlatched in case Sporty came home. The dog had learned as a pup to use his teeth to pull the leather strap to open the spring-loaded door if it was unlatched; after releasing the strap, he would quickly get his nose into the opening before the door slammed closed.

Jimmy set the flashlight's wide beam to illuminate a rope that hung from the rail in the highest point of the barn's roof on the far end of the hayloft, where bales did not extend to the full height of the barn. He began climbing, then dropping, then twisting as he dropped, trying to control his body more and more as he fell freely before he bounced on the hay below. Orange Tom, or OT, as Jimmy called him, often clung to his shoulders as he climbed, adding twelve pounds or more to Jimmy's weight, but the wise cat would jump off when Jimmy released the rope. He had learned much from OT, trying to imitate how the cat always seemed both relaxed and tense at the same time. Jimmy copied how the cat used his legs and shoulders to turn his whole body before he landed.

OT kept him company almost every morning, but on this morning, Jimmy felt lonely, as both his dog and his cat had abandoned him. "Well, they have lives of their own, I suppose," he muttered to himself. During the day, sometimes he could get Joey to run at him and try to knock him down, and Mags sometimes held the rope as he climbed. But this morning he was alone in the small illuminated world of the flashlight's beam.

After about twenty minutes of climbing and jumping, he heard a scratch at the door. A moment later, Sporty came slinking toward him. Jimmy recognized his guilty look, and as the dog entered the beam of light, Jimmy moved to embrace him, saying, "It's okay, boy. I'm glad you're back home now."

The dog whined a bit before Jimmy noticed some specks of blood on his front leg. Sporty's whine increased a little when Jimmy touched the area, and he concluded the dog had been wounded slightly by a shotgun pellet. Sporty licked at the area, but he seemed to be fine.

"Hate to do this to you, buddy, but I think we'd better tie you up. Maybe no one will notice the result of your travels tonight. I'm hoping you didn't visit Shaurels' cattle, but I'm afraid those blood specks may have been caused by pellets from his twelve-gauge." Jimmy grabbed his light and sprinted with Sporty to the shed, where he grabbed a pair of pliers and cut a short piece of wire to fasten the broken snap. Once he had twisted the wire tight, he took a few moments to converse with his dog as he stroked his head and neck. "I missed you this morning, and I was worried. I wish you could tell me the secret about the wrecked chain and how you got loose. Your friend and mine, OT, was missing too, but I'm less worried about him. He doesn't chase cattle with his girlfriend." Using his red handkerchief, Jimmy took care to wipe all the blood off Sporty's foot before he left the dog alone in his doghouse. Feeling rebuked, the dog moved to the back of the small space, curled up in a ball, and rested.

Jimmy looked at his pocket watch. Over half an hour had passed since his alarm had rung, and he eagerly sprinted to the barn to try out some new moves. As he set his light to project the beam, he saw OT atop a pile of bales. Neither the light nor Jimmy's presence seemed to deter him from his focus on a dark corner of the loft. With a steady, ominous growl, the old tom remained perfectly still, only twitching his tail slightly. Jimmy marveled at the control of his tail and recognized the familiar situation. A younger tomcat was in OT's territory, and a fight for control was sure to follow unless the young tom ran away. Defending his territory by chasing away and sometimes even killing young tomcats was a challenge that OT faced regularly. Jimmy knew it was only a matter of time before his companion would lose to a challenger. He could not protect him from his fate in a world ruled by survival of the fittest.

OT waited. He even looked vulnerable. Then the sudden rush of the younger tom streaked toward him. The interloper was a lighter orange than OT and a bit larger. The older cat met the onslaught with claws and snarls and a fury that would've frightened most cats. Jimmy could see them together as a massive orange ball with the young tom on top. Suddenly, young tom seemed to fly backward as OT righted himself and stood firm, ready for another challenge. When young tom charged again, Jimmy noted that OT purposefully went down on his back to fight from the bottom, a position he seemed to prefer. Clearly, OT knew what he was doing, and soon the young tom flew back once more. But he was fool enough to charge OT again, and the older cat manipulated his opponent into the same configuration, putting himself on the bottom. In a matter of seconds the young tom flew back yet again, but this time OT sensed his moment and, with an amazing swiftness, attacked before the younger tom got his footing. Biting and clawing, OT pounced upon the young challenger, who defended his ground only briefly before storming past Jimmy and out of the hayloft door. OT chased him partway, only to stop at the door, lie down, and pant for a few moments. Jimmy ran to his side to check if he was hurt. Astounded that OT seemed to have garnered no major wounds, he touched his old friend on his side and stroked him gently, and OT purred as if telling Jimmy that he was never worried.

Jimmy spent the next few minutes with OT on his lap, and as he stroked the animal, he verbalized his thoughts in a soothing voice that made OT purr even louder. "It hasn't escaped me, old friend, that you beat up the bigger cat while he was on top of you, a situation I find myself in when attacked by my nemesis. Fat chance I can beat up Jack while he is on top of me, but the idea is something to consider, especially since I usually have no choice of my position." Jimmy scratched OT under his chin for a few moments more before he heard the door open and knew his folks were coming to milk. Leaving the cat on the hay, Jimmy stood up, saying, "You are a wise cat." He left knowing he had a plan to make, and he looked forward to finding some martial-arts words in the dictionary when he got in the house. He decided then that he would follow up by checking the encyclopedias at school on Monday.

CHAPTER 17

BREAKFAST VISIT

The Carlsons were about halfway through breakfast on Saturday morning when George Shaurel knocked on the porch door. Martin hurried to open the kitchen door and the porch door and told him to come in out of the cold. George carried his shotgun with him.

George was a tall, wide man who moved about with catlike grace, despite his large stomach, which proclaimed his presence before his actual arrival. His face always bristled with wiry whiskers, and he was never without a big chew of snuff stretching his lower lip to the point where the black-brown lump was constantly visible.

Regardless of the subject, his voice boomed loudly when he spoke. He regularly exhibited a harsh, teasing humor, especially toward children, and his very presence had frightened the Carlson children when they were younger. As Shaurel stood in the Carlsons' kitchen, dressed in his blue denim chore coat and red wool earflap cap, with his shotgun in tow, his presence filled the room, even though his demeanor was unusually apologetic.

"Sorry to interrupt your breakfast, Martin and Missus, but I shot at some dogs in my cow yard early this morning. They were chasing my heifers that winter outside. I know I hit one, and it looked like your dog, but it was kind of dark outside yet and the yard light didn't reach that area of the yard."

As he spoke, spit gathered in his mouth and the urgency to expel the wad of moisture became evident. The humor of his efforts did not escape any of the Carlsons, but the seriousness of the message encouraged them to stifle their responses.

George rushed on, managing as well as he could his need to spit. "Although it was a bit early, I helped my daughters get started milking before I decided to come over and tell you, but when I drove through your yard, I heard your dog bark as he came out of his house chained. He looked fine, so I guess it wasn't him, but I thought I should stop in and tell you about it. That black-and-white female was one of the dogs. I think I wounded her, and I thought the other one was yours, but I guess it wasn't. I'll shoot any of them on sight now, and I hope you'll do the same. I'll let you get back to your breakfast." He hesitated, waiting for Martin's response.

Martin said, "I agree. You need to shoot the dogs on sight. Thanks for telling us, George."

George nodded and exited the kitchen door.

Jimmy had remained quiet, wondering if he should've spilled the truth about Sporty to his folks during morning chores. He decided to tell them as soon as George left, but immediately after he shut the outside door, Maggie and Joey burst out with their stifled chuckles as Maggie proclaimed, "Gawd, I thought he was going to drown in his own spit!"

The family sat back to resume their meal, but George knocked hurriedly and barged back in with an urgency that worried Jimmy.

"By the way." George spoke now with a clarity proving he had spit during his moment outside. "I think someone's been stealing gasoline from my barrel, so I put a lock on the hose valve and a lock on the top filling port. You might think about doing the same, Martin. And before I left for your place, my wife said the party line was humming with news that Matt Schroedler fell backward off a ladder as he was climbing up into the hayloft to throw down some hay this morning. I've seen that ladder when I bought hay from him. It's one of those straight-up ladders nailed to the support post. Seems a board rung split, and he fell and impaled himself on the beater of the manure spreader parked in the driveway aisle below. Hell of a way to die. I guess the girl was milking and Matt went to throw down some hay. She found him when she went up to see what was keeping him. Then she ran over to Rosinceks' place to tell them. No one else home at her place, and Rosinceks have the closest phone. The sheriff might be there by now. The kid is staying with Rosinceks for a while. Caroline was glad to take her in, and Emil said he'll help the girl take care of the cattle until they decide what to do. I know Matt had a couple sons with his first wife, but they never amounted to much. Don't know where they live for sure, but I think they're farming south of the lake where the land is cheap. I've got to go." And with that comment, he left.

The news hung like a heavy cowhide over the family as they sat in silence.

Mom ventured the first words carefully. "This is a tough deal for Mary. First her mother last March, and now her father."

At the thought of Mary's tragedy, Jimmy's eyes moistened, but he stayed silent, thinking only of how he could help protect her from Jack.

Maggie sniffled as she stifled tears, feeling how insignificant her own problems were and wondering how to help her friend.

Joey's expression was blank disbelief. Jimmy had told him never to throw down hay while anyone was milking. It made the cows jumpy.

Dad spoke after a thoughtful pause. "Jim and I will go over there to see what we can do. Not right away, but after chores, after they clear out the . . . body. We'll stop to see how we can help."

"Maggie should go with you, not me," Jimmy offered. "Maggie's her best friend, and I . . ." He left his sentence unfinished.

Mom insisted, "You and Maggie should go right away, Martin, to see if you are needed. We will take care of the barn cleaning and other chores this morning. It's important for a friendly neighbor to be there to help Mary now. Tell Emil our whole family will stop by for a quick visit after supper sometime. The kids want to see Mary, and I want to see how I can help Caroline."

They all nodded, and Dad said, "You're right, Mary. I'll be on my way right after breakfast."

Maggie, who seldom stifled a comment even when it might be inappropriate, added, "Mary hated her father and his sons. Hated them! I'm sure she is not wasting tears on them now."

"I know," Mom responded, "and I don't blame you for saying so, but don't offer those comments beyond this family. And, Joey, not a word of your sister's opinion to those gossipy friends of yours at the country school."

"Don't worry," Joey retorted. "They're not really my friends, anyway, Mom."

When Dad and Mom started picking at their food again, Jimmy took advantage of the serious moment and the distraction it presented by telling the truth about Sporty returning with blood on his foot. As he had hoped, neither Dad nor Mom was upset by his confession.

Dad joked, "Your dog must be a hell of an actor—to come out of his warm doghouse and bark at the guy who shot him and then never show a limp!"

Everyone laughed lightly at the comment.

Then he added, "You know we will have to keep him chained or shoot him, Jim."

"I'll keep him chained, Dad," Jimmy promised, still wondering how Sporty had gotten loose while he was at school yesterday and again last night. *Should I tell Dad about the damaged clip? And that we might have a prowler? Maybe someone is stealing gas from our barrel. If Shaurel put on a lock, maybe we should too.*

Amid the clank of forks and knives against plates and spoons against cereal bowls, Jimmy was about to speak when Dad broke the silence with an unexpected remark. "Be careful when you walk out the door this morning." With a serious face, he waited until he was sure he had everyone's attention. As they looked up with expressions that asked *Why?* he continued, "Somewhere, on the ground near the entryway, is a gob of George's snuff spit that is so big you might slip on it."

The entire family responded at once, as he'd expected.

Mom: "Honestly, Martin. That's disgusting. And at the table yet!"

Maggie: "Ech! I'm glad I'm done eating, Dad."

Joey: "I'm gonna look for it to see how big it is."

Jimmy: "We should pick it up before it freezes. Someone could hurt their toe on it."

Mom summarized, chuckling: "Kids, I hope you learn better manners than your father!"

Jimmy decided to say nothing on the matter of a probable prowler.

CHAPTER 18

ACCIDENTS HAPPEN

Mary arrived with Emil Rosincek to meet the sheriff at the Schroedler farmyard less than an hour after she had run to Rosinceks' home to report the tragedy and call the sheriff. Although strengthened by Emil's presence, her heart raced as the sheriff began the interview. She had rehearsed her story, but her mind filled with images that she must keep to herself: Jack shattering the rung of the ladder with the pipe wrench. Matt falling backward onto the sharp prongs of the manure spreader's beater.

Standing on the front porch facing the sheriff and his deputy, Mary kept her story simple as the deputy took notes. "We were milking the cows. My father went to throw down hay while I finished up. I waited by the chute, and when no bales were coming down, I yelled up to tell him that I was done milking and he could start throwing down the bales. When there was no answer, I went to check and found him. He was not breathing. I panicked and ran all the way to Rosinceks' place."

Looking at her with sympathy, the sheriff said, "I'm sorry this happened to your father." Then, to fill an awkward silence, he added, "Accidents happen, especially on the farm."

Relieved to see that the sheriff seemed satisfied, Mary struggled to keep her composure.

When her brothers came to take her home, Mary clung to Emil. Their persistence lasted only until Emil's solid voice proclaimed, "Mary will be fine with me and Caroline. We have a room she can use as long as she wants."

Her brothers said that they would take care of the cows for the next few days and then haul them to their farm as early as Monday. But they didn't want the dogs and cats.

Concerned about her dogs, Mary boldly asked Emil, "Can we take the dogs to Crossroads Tavern? Berris loves dogs and has lots of empty space to keep them in the old barns. Then I can go over to visit them."

"I'll drive over to see Berris today to check if he'll take the dogs. I think you're right. He'll take them in."

Mary sensed the moment was right to ask politely, "Can we take the cats to your place? Please?"

"Absolutely! We can always use more cats." Emil smiled as he spoke.

Her brothers left to go to the barn, where the coroner's men were removing the body, and Mary dutifully looked away from the scene while secretly feeling gratified that Matt was dead.

Hearing the sound of tires on the dirt driveway, Mary turned to see the blue Ford entering the yard. "Carlsons!" She pulled on Emil's sleeve as she let go of his arm to run toward the car.

Spotting Maggie in the car, Mary opened the passenger-side door. As Maggie got out, Mary grabbed her friend's hands in her own and said, "I need you more than ever right now."

Maggie dropped her hands and flung her arms around Mary, whispering, "Are you okay? Are you okay?"

Mary nodded, whispering, "I have so much I need to tell you."

Sensing Mary's needs, Emil said, "Martin, you and your family should visit us tomorrow after milking, about half past seven. I'm sure Mary wants to talk to the kids, and Caroline said before I left that it's been too long since we had you over, anyway."

After the body had been removed and Matt's sons had left, Mary urged, "Maggie, come into the house with me and help me pack a few personal things." Once inside, she said, "Maggie, I'm so glad you are coming over Sunday. Maybe you can help me settle in. Caroline and Emil are wonderful. They say I can stay as long as I want. I haven't told them about school yet."

Maggie spoke gently. "You seem a bit strange. Are you sure you are all right?"

Realizing her facade was too composed, Mary relaxed. "Jeez, Maggie, I don't know what I'm thinking half the time. It's been a big blur," she confessed as she let her shoulders sag. "But I'm so glad to see you."

They carried several boxes to the car before Emil assured her, "We can come back for the rest of it tomorrow or whenever you want, Mary. Let's go home now. You should rest."

Mary agreed and said her goodbyes to Martin and Maggie, adding, "See you Sunday."

Eager to discover any activity at Schroedlers' farmstead, after breakfast Jack ran down the path he had taken a few hours previously. But once he crossed the fence into Schroedlers' pasture, caution took hold. Maybe he should stay clear for a couple days? What if someone spotted him lurking around with binoculars? Doubts like these had never bothered him on his previous spying trips. Why now?

As he moved from tree to tree toward the farmyard, he heard the sound of engines and voices. Stopping to raise his binoculars, he peered out from behind a tree to witness a county sheriff's vehicle exit the yard. Rosinceks' car and Carlsons' car remained only a short time before they sped away. Jack wasn't cold, but he felt a shudder seize his spine for moment as he realized he had returned to the scene of a crime. His crime. He turned to leave, whispering to himself, "Best if I make myself scarce for the rest of the day." He'd wait until Sunday morning to check out Schroedlers' place and maybe sneak around Rosinceks' with his binoculars to discover where Mary slept.

Silent during the ride back to Rosinceks' house, Mary continued to sort out the hasty plan she had started to assemble the moment she realized her father was dead. Where some saw tragedy, she saw a chance at freedom. Freedom from her father, from her brothers, and maybe even from Jack! That glimmer of freedom in the distance had inspired her to cover up for Jack and, in doing so, to push him out, to take control. Her bruised arm and the pain in her throat were constant reminders of his dangerous intentions, but his threats merely served to steel her resolve. She was proud she had waited and planned and then milked the cows by hand while her father lay impaled on the manure spreader. She smiled at the success of her pretense of caring about him after running to Rosinceks' to report that the accident had just happened. She hated to deceive them—they were good people—but they had taken her in. And now, somehow, she would run away for good.

CHAPTER 19

SUNDAY VISIT

Preparing for the visit Sunday evening, Carlsons and Rosinceks milked their cows about a half hour earlier than usual. Although Rosinceks owned more land than Carlsons, their dairy operations were similar in size and in the use of modern methods. Both had around thirty milk cows, lots of heifers and calves, a milking machine with three units, and a bulk tank. When Emil and Caroline's only son, Al, had still been home, the milking had taken less than an hour and a half, but after he'd volunteered to be drafted into the army it took Emil and Caroline longer, mostly because Al had usually attended to other chores, like feeding the calves and bedding the cows down with straw in the evening, so by the time they finished milking, nothing remained to be done. Because he was an only son in a farm family, Al could have filed for an exemption from the draft, especially during peacetime, but like many farm families, Rosinceks had a strong sense of duty to country, and Al felt it was his duty to serve.

Martin drove the blue '52 Ford into Rosinceks' yard at about quarter to eight, and as the family disembarked, Caroline and Emil came to the porch to invite them in. Tall and lanky, with arms that seemed too long for his torso, Emil towered above the others, especially his wife, whose short, hefty appearance contrasted with her husband's shape. What the two had in common, though, were their wide, welcoming smiles and friendly body language, which made the Carlsons feel as if their visit were a most valued event. In his raspy baritone voice, Emil proclaimed that Mary had insisted on helping with the chores, enabling them to finish as quickly as if Al were home.

Small talk ensued as they each took a chair around the oblong wooden kitchen table. With quick, sure motions, the couple scurried to fetch and open a bottle of beer for each of the adults and pour a glass of Kool-Aid for each of the kids. After a short time, Mary led Jimmy and Maggie into the small living room, where she spoke softly about how much she missed her mom and how she liked the Rosinceks and hoped she could stay there. No one mentioned her father's death, and it was clear those in the room cared only for Mary's well-being.

Uncertain of how Jimmy felt about her riding around with Jack, Mary found looking at him difficult. Finally, she offered, "I miss you guys," and as she stole a side glance at Jimmy, she smiled, evoking a wide smile from him.

"We all miss you at school," he offered cautiously.

"I miss you all the time!" Maggie proclaimed. "But mostly, I hate phy ed without you there."

The pause lasted longer than was comfortable. Although they had known each other since grade one, now they found themselves reluctant to share their real thoughts.

Jimmy could think of nothing more to say, and he hated himself for his reticence. He was relieved when Joey burst into the room, exclaiming, "Dad says if you come to the kitchen, Jimmy, there will be enough people to play six-handed euchre and I can be his and Emil's partner!"

Everyone knew this was a big honor for a ten-year-old, and Jimmy knew instinctively that the tension in the small living room would leave with him. Although he ached to be with Mary, Jimmy said, "Sounds like fun, little brother. I get to be partners with Mom and Caroline, and you guys won't have a chance." He nodded to Mary and left the room.

Mary wasted no time telling Maggie, "Follow me upstairs." They ran up the stairs to one of the three bedrooms, the one Caroline had proclaimed was Mary's for as long as she wanted it. Caroline and Emil slept in the large bedroom on the main floor, and they kept one of the bedrooms upstairs ready for Al whenever he came home on leave. The third upstairs bedroom was mostly used for storage and Caroline's sewing, but the bed was available in case overnight guests might arrive. Intending to treat Mary as one of the family instead of a guest, they had given her the large bedroom located above the farm kitchen, which had last been occupied by Al's younger sister, Helen, who had been a year older than Joey when she died of influenza in the second grade. Caroline had no plans for the room, but she cleaned it regularly, even after she had given most of Helen's toys and clothes to her cousins.

Now, stacks of cardboard boxes occupied the room's center, leaving walkways to the dresser, the closet, a chest of drawers, and a bed, all located against the walls. Mary explained, "This afternoon Caroline and Emil helped me pack up and haul some things from the house. I was too tired to go through much of it yet. I'll get to it tomorrow." She motioned for her friend to sit on the bed.

Within seconds Mary's firm facade broke down, and she moved close to Maggie, whispering, "Jeez, I'm glad to see you." Resting her head on her friend's lap, Mary cried silently as Maggie's body absorbed some of her pain.

Finally, Maggie whispered, "What's going on?"

"There is so much I need to tell you. And I can't tell anyone else."

"Go on, then."

Mary sat up. "Honestly, I don't know what to do! Rosinceks will let me stay with them forever—they are both so nice, and generous, too. But I am afraid of what Jack will do if I refuse to see him."

"What will he do?"

"You can't tell Jimmy. Jack says he will hurt Jimmy and tell him that I am . . . he will tell everyone I am . . . *damaged goods.*" She choked the words out, breaking her heart with her own breath. "I can hardly say it aloud. You know what has happened. I can't bear to tell you details, but you know . . . generally. Don't you?"

"Not really," Maggie confessed.

"When I see people, I think everyone knows . . . knows everything, and I imagine them judging me as I judge myself . . . as filthy, as unworthy. I need to tell someone, but I've never said these things aloud. I guess I was hoping they weren't really true. But I will tell you now."

Maggie waited as her friend gathered her breath to whisper so she would not be heard downstairs.

Mary started with a memory. "Remember when you and I used to lie on our backs on the bed in your tiny bedroom, and we had our feet on the slanted ceiling . . ."

"Yes, on a Sunday, when we'd hear the rain on the roof in summer or hear the cold wind howl in the winter, making it too miserable to go sledding."

"And we'd talk about everything and make plans about who we'd choose first on our perfect ball team at school? You always picked Al."

"And you always picked Jimmy, even though he wasn't the best player." Maggie smiled at the memory.

"He was pretty good, though. Besides, he was so cute." Mary smiled too, letting her tears ebb, and for only a moment, the two girls allowed themselves to embrace the innocent times of their youth.

After a brief silence, Mary finally added, "Your folks' house, your folks, you, Jimmy, your room, they were my only refuge then. And Jimmy was always my hero. Being a hero is too much to expect from anyone, Maggie. I know that now."

"Funny thing," Maggie mused, "Jimmy always tells me that I've got to be my own hero. He says no one should depend on anyone else. I'll bet he never said that to you, though. He likes you a lot."

Mary repeated, "I've got to be my own hero," as she stared away and briefly seemed to occupy a place beyond where the two girls cuddled.

The long pause was unbearable for Maggie. She yearned to share Mary's pain, but she didn't know how to do so without asking questions she did not know how to ask.

Understanding her friend's dilemma, Mary turned her eyes down and away before she began talking quietly. "With my stepbrothers, I can't even remember the first time they forced me to . . . I was really little. On my back. No explanation. Just threats. I had to promise to tell no one. I didn't understand what they were doing. With my father, it started later. And Jack knows. He knows I'm damaged goods. He threatened to tell everyone if I don't . . ."

Maggie said nothing as Mary spilled her pain. She was not naive, but neither was she sufficiently schooled in the evils of mankind or the perversion of adults who would sexually abuse a child. Her imagination rendered no concrete images of the horrors Mary's stepbrothers and father had visited on her. *Damaged goods* was a term Maggie had heard from others, a term that referred to an unmarried woman who was no longer virtuous. Maggie's eyes teared up when she heard her friend use the term to describe herself. Longing for more explanation but sensing she knew enough, Maggie sniffled through her own tears. "I understand, but . . ."

Understanding Maggie's loss for words, Mary interrupted her. "The times we talk of now—when we talked on the bed—were kind of a break for me because my stepbrothers had both left home to farm on their own. Turns out they didn't get along with Matt either. I was so relieved. Then Matt started to . . . and though it was less often than my brothers, it was worse, far worse. Because I was older and I felt shame. And because he threatened to hurt Mom if I said anything."

Mary allowed a short silence before changing the subject. "Remember when Peggy Ryan pushed me into Brummer's electric hog fence on the way home from school, and you picked her up and threw her over the fence into the muddiest part of the hog pen? I marveled at your strength, and I knew then I never wanted to get you angry at me."

"And I've never been," Maggie said. "And I promise I never will. I am always on your side."

Mary blew her nose into a small handkerchief on which her mother had embroidered a purple lilac. "I need to go far away, where no one knows me and where not even you, my best friend, will know where I am. I need to disappear so Jack will know that hurting anyone to coerce me will be futile."

Maggie responded, "But you've got to write to me."

"No, I won't let anyone know where I am, not even my best friend. Otherwise, Jack will force you to tell."

"Jimmy will be heartbroken if you leave."

Mary breathed deeply before answering, "Jimmy and I are both already heartbroken. We must be safe, first of all. I'm not good enough for him now, anyway. I'm damaged goods."

Maggie did not have words to say aloud. She felt her friend's despair as much as she could, but the depth of Mary's predicament and shame was beyond her scope of imagination. She was too ashamed to stay silent, so she said, "Do you have a plan?"

"Sort of. Maybe."

"Can I help?"

"I'll need help, and I'm glad you're willing. There'll be some risk. The less you know now, the better."

"You can count on me."

"I'll send you a letter, and we will meet to plan things out. Maybe I can use Jack to help me get away."

"Is that smart?"

"He won't know what's going on. Maybe I'll tell him we're going to elope. Pretty funny, huh, me eloping with Jack? But I need him to believe it."

"Sounds risky. Too dangerous!"

"Don't worry. I'll plan it carefully," Mary assured her.

"But where will you go? And how will you get there?"

"I don't know yet," Mary whispered. Then, finding Maggie's eyes with hers and holding the connection, she said, "I've told you this already, but you must believe that you and Jimmy and Joey are my only friends and the dearest people I know. I miss Mom so much, and I cannot even bring myself to talk about what my life has been like since she died. Rosinceks really care about me, but I need to leave. I live in fear of Jack—and not just what he will do to me, but to you and Jimmy and Joey too. He has threatened all of you if I do not comply with his demands. I can put him off for a time—maybe even through the winter, but I'm hoping you can help me to come up with the plan."

"Of course," Maggie said.

"First, I need to go back to the house to search for some of Mom's things I missed. I must find them."

"It's too dangerous to go alone. I'll go with you."

"Yes, but we have to go in daylight. Jack prowls all over at night."

"How about if I come over on the Friday after Thanksgiving? We'll go sledding on Rosinceks' hill and then duck over to your house."

"It's a plan!" Mary exclaimed, without concern if those downstairs heard her.

An hour or more later, after euchre games had been played, after Mary and Caroline and Emil had walked out to the porch door with the Carlson family to say their long goodbyes, and after the blue '52 Ford had crawled out of Rosinceks' yard, Mary said good night to her temporary guardians and left for her bed.

CHAPTER 20

REVELATIONS

Alone in her bedroom after the Carlsons left, Mary still felt the pain of reliving the events she had confessed to Maggie. Although she pulled the chain on the overhead light to darken the room, she had no intention of going to bed. She'd be unable to sleep. Her mind was filled with images, and the pile of boxes in the room begged to be explored. She clicked on a small flashlight. Now would be a perfect time to look through the items they had hauled from her old bedroom that morning, but she had to be careful not to awaken Emil and Caroline, who would worry if they discovered she couldn't sleep.

Working by the light of her flashlight, she unbundled papers bound with old rubber bands that had lost their elasticity, many of them breaking when she disturbed their position. Most were old paid invoices for cattle feed and so on, used for tax receipts, no doubt. She found nothing useful.

In the last box she discovered a small photo album with thick cardboard pages meant to hold portraits taken at special occasions. In her mother's youth, and indeed, even now, personal cameras were rare and most photographs were taken by local professionals, who processed the film in their studios in nearby small towns. She paged through the album slowly, enjoying the photos of her mother's relatives, even if she didn't know their names. Heat from the kitchen below warmed the linoleum floor of the bedroom as the photos helped warm her heart, but they also intensified the fear she had felt at the loss of her mother.

Against her will, images of discovering her mother's body loomed in her mind. When she had come into the house from milking that morning, Mary had not been surprised her mom was not in the kitchen making breakfast. *Good,* she had thought at the time. *Maybe she's resting.* Mary had walked throughout the house, both upstairs and downstairs, calling, "Mom, Mom!" No answer. She had looked everywhere.

When she found herself back in the kitchen, she had glanced in the pantry and seen the broken hook on the wall used to hold open the trapdoor to the cellar. It had been broken for weeks. Matt was supposed to fix it. She'd hurriedly lifted the small door and kneeled down on the floor to flick on the light switch fastened to the cellar ceiling. The light had instantly revealed the horror of her mother, lying still on the dirt floor at the foot of the ladder. She must've fallen while backing down the ladder and reaching for the light switch as she balanced the hinged door on her head. She had probably been going to get some tomato juice for breakfast.

Mary said aloud what she had said then: "I begged her to let me get stuff from the cellar." Her mom had still been weak from her illness. Heart attack, they had said. She tried to blank out the image from her mind.

Mary refocused on the album in her hands. Her memory of its contents was dim. She recalled her mother paging through it with her nearly a decade ago, but Mom had preferred to keep it out of sight and especially out of reach of her husband, who liked to control his wife's past and present. Maybe Matt didn't even know the album existed, and that's why her mother had kept it boxed up in a closet instead of out on a shelf. Neither Mary nor Matt nor the boys had ventured to look through the boxes after her sudden death. The boys weren't interested, and Mary avoided sharing any memory of her mother with Matt.

Digging through her mother's personal things in the dark room, with only the flashlight illuminating her work, intensified every small discovery. One page of the album seemed thicker, warranting a search behind the photographs, where Mary found something that at first appeared to be just a folded piece of paper. Shining the light on the item, she read the words *In Remembrance* and recognized it as a memorial card for a funeral service. Inside she found a folded newspaper article, which she set down on the floor beside her as she viewed the card. In ornate and lovely script, the twenty-third psalm was printed on the left side of the page. Scrolled across the top on the right were the words *In Loving Memory of*, and printed below in larger letters was *Harold A. Hansen, Born October 5, 1920, Died January 30, 1939.*

Contemplating the information on the memorial card, she unfolded the newspaper article and smoothed the yellowed paper against the warm linoleum floor, revealing it to be a clipping about an accident. She scanned it first and then reread a piece: *Hansen was killed instantly on Monday, January 30, when the car in which he was riding accidentally hit a horse on the road about a quarter mile west of town.*

At the top of the article was a small photo of a young, hatless man, whose handsome face, light hair, and fair skin were apparent even in the low-quality black-and-white newsprint. Mary stared at the photo, searching her memory for any link to the name or the photo. Finding none, she muttered to herself, "Must've been a close friend." But she resolved that she and Maggie would search the house thoroughly when they next met.

Exhausted by her search and the emotional challenges of the day, she went to bed, but before she drifted off to sleep, a memory surfaced: She was walking into her mother's sewing room, discovering her mother intently reading a letter. "I'll read this to you when you're older. It's not important now," her mother had said as she tucked it under some cloth.

Mary vowed again to search all the remaining boxes in the sewing room. Then she let her fantasy of possible freedom take her into a tentative sleep, interrupted by visions of terror: Her father bursting into her bedroom, and the stink of his tobacco and sweat. Jack Drude lurking in the shadows of the night. Jack Drude's lust-laden face illuminated by a flashlight in the darkness. When her eyes opened to see only silent darkness, she breathed in and out deeply several times to calm herself, handling the horror of her dreams just as she had in the past.

Next to a small window in Rosinceks' hayloft, Jack rested comfortably among the bales of hay, his perch giving him a clear view of Mary's bedroom window. He had seen her light go out, but he was in no hurry to leave. Her window overlooked the front porch, making access from outside reasonably easy, but he knew surprising her was not a good plan. Not yet, anyway. As he stared at her window, the image of her lying in bed kept him from leaving for home, even though he was tired.

Jack had been busy all day. Using his binoculars to spy on the Schroedler farmstead early in the afternoon, he'd watched Emil, Caroline, and Mary carry boxes from the house to the car. He'd hoped for a chance to see Mary alone but realized she'd never return to the place without others. She was not about to stay or go anywhere alone. It would be hard for him to find a way to meet her anywhere. He ached to get her back under his control.

Before he left Schroedlers' place, he risked a visit to the hayloft where Matt had gasped his final breath. He opened the door carefully, and the grinding sound reminded him of the moment early yesterday morning when Matt had entered the barn, the moment that had changed everything. When he stepped into the hayloft aisle, the scene before him was much as he had left it, with the exception that Matt Schroedler's body, with its blank staring eyes and gaping mouth, was no longer impaled on the beater prongs. Jack closed the door before he left to begin the hike to a small group of trees north of Rosinceks' farmstead, where he had waited until they were finished milking before he sought shelter in the hayloft.

Discovering the location of Mary's bedroom had made the day's efforts worthwhile, and he felt gratified as he climbed down from his perch to exit the door facing away from the house. The family dog appeared from nowhere, but he didn't bark. As Jack knelt down next to the friendly canine, he whispered, "Good boy, Barney. Good boy." He let the dog take a small piece of cheese from his hand. "I'll see you again soon."

CHAPTER 21

LIBRARY

After the packed bus dropped the children off at school on Monday morning, Jimmy had ten minutes to check out the library for information on his new plan before his first class began. Library time was the only reason he sometimes wished he had given himself a study hall when he registered for tenth grade. But because there were so many classes he wanted to take, he didn't want to waste an hour with a study hall. Besides, he preferred to do his schoolwork at home, where he could spread out on the old wooden table in the living room or on the metal table in the kitchen.

Once in the library, he hurriedly grabbed the J volume of the *World Book Encyclopedia* and thumbed to the right page. He found the word *judo* and realized he had only five minutes to read it and take notes. He decided to ask the librarian, Miss Tennison, if he could check the volume out overnight.

Miss Tennison was young and had the kind of figure and personality that made her a target, behind her back, for crude remarks by some of the boys. Although she was about Jimmy's height, her high heels made her tower above him. She dressed impeccably, and her hair and makeup were always perfect, her lips delicately covered with the right shade of red to match her outfit. Though she was a thoroughly striking beauty, her professionalism as a librarian was even more striking. She protected her books and magazines as if they were her children, and she came down hard on anyone who abused books or library protocol. Yet, she had earned a reputation of being kind and approachable.

"Well, Jimmy," she started as if she were going to scold him, "I'm very picky about loaning our reference books. Losing one decreases the value of the whole set." She gave him a smile that allowed her white teeth to flash briefly between her red lips, an action that Jimmy found sexy though he wouldn't admit it even to himself. He listened to her voice, almost purring as she spoke to him, looking directly into his eyes. "But I know *you* are a responsible young man, and also one of the most avid readers in the entire school, as I see by all the novels and nonfiction *you* check out regularly. I would permit you to sign out the book overnight, but there may be a better option. What are you looking up?"

"Judo," Jimmy blurted before he realized he had said anything. For a reason unknown to him, he felt embarrassed at the thought of sharing his plans with anyone, especially Miss Tennison.

"We have some excellent books on judo. Follow me." And Jimmy followed her as she hustled gracefully to the nonfiction section, grabbed a book off the shelf, and handed it to him. "The book has excellent diagrams and explanations for beginners. If you want, we can check it out to you now. I'll write you a pass in advance so if you are late for first hour, you don't end up with detention."

Jimmy nodded. "Yes, I'll check it out now. Thanks."

She chattered easily as she stamped the book and wrote out the pass, asking, "Are you writing a report, or is your interest personal?"

"Personal," he choked out.

"If your interest holds"—she smiled at her own pun—"maybe you can take some classes. I did, and I found it fascinating."

Jimmy's mouth fell open a bit more than he expected as he visualized Miss Tennison throwing people around.

"Thanks again," he said as he grabbed the book and the pass from her hands.

He hurried off to first-hour English. He would have American history and geometry before lunch, and then typing, wood shop, and phy ed. There were just too many things to learn to give himself a study hall. Next year he'd take six classes again so he could fit in bookkeeping, biology, Algebra II, English, world history, and industrial arts. He was glad there was no phy ed in grades eleven and twelve, but he thought a health class to study the human body would be useful. He hoped they would study the human body in biology. He would've loved to take choir, but it involved too much travel outside school hours. Besides, the teacher was a jerk who felt obligated to pull on Jimmy's long sideburns. So juvenile. It was just Sutter and the choir director. The other teachers never mentioned his hair.

After school that day, Jimmy took fifteen minutes to read up on judo before he changed clothes in his room. He didn't remember where, but he knew he had heard something about judo as having to do with using the opponent's force to your benefit. Part of the definition from his own dictionary at home described it as using holds and leverage to unbalance the opponent. He doubted that he could successfully put a hold on a man with superior strength, like Jack, but using leverage and the force of Jack's own charge to throw him off balance might work. As Miss Tennison had promised, the book's pictures and diagrams displayed techniques for throws, holds, and strikes. The thought of trying to do to Jack what the diagrams showed was a bit scary, and he dismissed a few of the moves immediately because Jack was just too big. He knew the element of surprise would be on his side for only the first couple charges: he would need to get Jack down and then strike him. Risk for Jimmy was high. He wondered for a moment if he would be better off just lying there and letting Jack pound on him till he tired of it.

He read part of the book on throws and found the okuri ashi harai move appealed to him, because it depended on meeting a charge with a grab, a quick rotation, and a trip, while using the opponent's force and forward motion to throw him off balance. He could even use Jack's height against him. He studied the diagram, and he decided to practice the throw during his next morning training, although he was unsure how he would practice without a partner.

CHAPTER 22

HOLIDAY DINNER

"Don't fry an egg for me, Mom," Joey said. "I'll just eat cereal."

"Are you sure?" Mom responded. "It's only quarter to eight. Four hours till we eat dinner."

"I want to be really hungry for Thanksgiving dinner, Mom, so I don't want to fill up now."

"As you wish, son."

"But you've got it wrong, Joey," Maggie said with authority. "The idea is to keep your stomach stretched so it holds lots of food. Eat hearty now and you'll work it off by noon, anyway. By dinnertime your stomach will be all stretched out and empty and ready for more."

"She's right, you know," Jimmy said as he came from the small room by the kitchen, where he'd been slicing bread. As he set the plate of sliced bread on the table near the toaster, he added, "Eat lots and work it off. That's how to keep a good appetite."

Joey asked, "Is that right, Dad?"

"Don't know. Don't care," Dad replied bluntly. "I'm always hungry when your mom puts food on the table."

Skeptical, Joey said, "Maybe I'll eat another bowl of cereal."

Looking at the plate of sliced bread, Maggie complained, "Hey, Jimmy, what did you do with the trimmings you cut so the slices would fit in the toaster?"

"I put them in the old kettle for the cats like Mom told me to do."

"You know I like to trim my own and dunk them in the yolk."

"Cats gotta eat too, you know," Mom said. "I'll dump a little of Joey's leftover milk and cereal into the kettle, and the cats will have a feast."

"Maybe I won't leave any milk and cereal in my bowl," Joey protested.

"You always do." Mom chuckled as she dished out the fried eggs. "You say it gets too soggy." Then she sat down to eat with her family.

Silence lasted only a few moments before Maggie said, "It's going to be a quiet Thanksgiving with just Thorsons. I'll miss Dvoraks. Aunt Emma and Uncle Joe and the kids are so much fun."

"Yeah, Joe's accordion livens up the place, all right," Dad added. "And Dvoraks usually get here by eleven, and we open beers five minutes later."

"I mean," Maggie added hastily, "I like Uncle John and Aunt Rose too, Dad, but . . ."

"You don't have to explain, Maggie," Dad interrupted. "My sister isn't much fun. In fact, she's the opposite of fun. John's a good fellow, though, and Billy is always fun to talk and play cards with, although I'm not sure he'll be along. Maybe he's eating with Anna's family."

"No, he's coming too," Mom said. "I think Rose wants the romance between Anna and Billy to cool a bit. So does Emma. Rose doesn't want to lose her only son to a Catholic. Emma admits she doesn't want her oldest daughter to turn Lutheran, either, but she jokes that she has four younger daughters she can marry off to nice Catholic boys. She makes light of it, but I know my sister, and she's just as reluctant to have her daughter change religion as your sister is to have her son change."

"The two of them said some nasty things to each other when we got married, sixteen years ago," Dad said.

"I don't know who was worse, really," Mom added. "Emma told Rose I'd never change because Catholicism was the true religion, but when Rose found out I was going to change, she rubbed salt in the wound by needling Emma that I had found the true Jesus and didn't need a pope. I think they both called each other heathens."

Joey's ear perked up at the word. *Heathens*, he thought. *I guess adults use it too.* He continued to listen as he moved his soggy cereal around the bowl with his spoon.

Jimmy said, "But I remember the Thanksgiving you invited both families to dinner five years ago. I remember it so well because that was the first time Anna and Billy met. She was thirteen and he was sixteen."

"I had planned that as a time to heal old wounds," Mom said. "And it worked for a while, until Billy and Anna started to get serious."

Maggie smiled and added, "I think it was love at first sight for both of them. They started dating slowly at first because Anna was so young."

"I think they should let the kids work it out for themselves," Dad said bluntly. "But I understand Rose's feelings about losing Billy. After John Junior was killed in Korea, she became overly protective of Billy. She was clingy before he died, but she got even worse afterward."

"Yes," Mom agreed solemnly. "The death of a child is a tragedy a family lives with forever. She wanted Billy to try to get a deferment because he was an only-son survivor, but Billy was intent on going. I think he thought it was his duty to honor his fallen brother. He's such a fine young man."

"He is," Dad said. Then he stood up. "We got a couple hours of work to do, so we'd better get going, Jim."

"Right," Mom said. "Maggie and Joey, clear the table and do the dishes. I'll clean up the milk house and the milking utensils before I come back to the house to prepare dinner."

"Joey and I'll do the chickens after we finish in here, right, Mom?" Maggie asked.

"Right. Thanks," Mom said, and the family went to work.

Thorsons arrived about quarter to twelve. Although hugging was not a standard between the families, greetings were warm. John, a tall, soft-spoken gentleman, and Billy, a strong, good-natured man of twenty-one, smiled broadly as they shook hands with their hosts. All three Thorsons had light hair. Rose's hair had a tinge of red, but as a stern woman in her forties, she did not like to be called a strawberry blond. After the regular small talk, they sat down at the table to eat and Martin led them in a short prayer of thanks. "Well, you know, Martin," Rose teased after the prayer, "you needn't have neutralized it. There are no practicing Catholics here today."

"Come on, Rose," Martin said, "we gave thanks. That's what it's about."

Mary passed the chicken, then the potatoes, the dressing, and the gravy, and soon the table rang with the clinking of silverware on plates and voices praising the food and the cook. She took all compliments with grace and praised the help she claimed to have received from her children and her husband—help she grossly exaggerated.

John and Martin kept conversation during the dinner light and fun, though Rose's stern presence could stifle even the most pleasant topics. Billy remained unusually quiet, though he did praise the food as plates were cleaned and dessert was dished. Some chose blueberry pie, some chose pumpkin, and others chose apple, but each piece was heaped with fresh whipped cream. The family finished dessert, pushed their chairs back, and sighed with contented delight.

Clearly expecting sympathy from everyone, Rose announced, "I'm so glad Billy is back from his active duty in the army, but now he is breaking my heart."

Billy slumped a little in his seat. No one said a word. Everyone at the table looked at her except John, who looked away, seeming powerless to turn the conversation in another direction. He had said many times that no one could stop Rose from speaking her mind.

"Since we lost young John, Billy's my only hope, my legacy, my loving child," Rose continued. "And he's turning away from the church by courting your niece, Martin and Mary. Anna is a sweet girl, but I am afraid they are heading toward marriage, and I can't bear to lose him."

Hesitant to say anything, Billy ventured, "You didn't seem to be concerned when we first started dating five years ago."

"Oh, I was concerned all right, as your relationship progressed, but I hoped it would fade. And since Anna is the eldest of five sisters, I was hoping her mother would allow her to change faiths, relying on the other four to marry Catholics. Foolish of me, I guess."

Mary said, "They're a wonderful couple. I was hoping they could work it out."

Rose persisted, "It's my duty to see to it that my boy remains in the faith."

Mary asked, "What do you want, Billy?"

He answered with a bluntness that surprised his aunt. "I don't want to hurt my mother, but I want to be with Anna. We both want to be together."

As if on cue, Maggie and Jimmy rose to clear the table, and Mom began gathering leftovers. Maggie filled a basin with hot water from a kettle and set to washing the dishes. Joey was ready to wipe. The actions were quick and precise and meant to put an end to the conversation.

Martin said, "Let's feed the cows hay while they're handling the dishes. Jim and Bill can throw down the hay, and John and I will feed it. Let's go, guys."

John and Martin were out the door first. On the way to the barn, John confided to Martin, "Bill would like to propose over Christmas, but the only thing that has stopped him is that he knows his mother is nearly suicidal over the idea of him changing religions. Bill's worried about his mother. He's such a good kid, Martin."

"He sure is." They ambled down the stairway to where the cows were waiting in their stalls, taking refuge in farm talk while they waited for the boys to throw down the hay.

Billy and Jimmy hurriedly carried bales to the chute. Although Jimmy was eager to talk to his older cousin alone, he said nothing until his cousin broke the ice.

"Have you asked that good-looking blond out yet? I know her father had an accident and she's living with the Rosinceks."

"No, I don't have a license to drive. I don't know what I should do."

"Well, she likes you, right? Just walk over to visit her for a while. Bring her some candy."

"I've put it off. I don't want to start dating too young. Once I start, there's no turning back," Jimmy admitted.

"That may be true," Billy said, "but you can't pretend like you're still kids anymore. You aren't ten years old and in the country school. Any girl expects some progress in your attention, especially one as pretty as Mary. Believe me, if you wait, someone will beat you to it."

"May have already happened," Jimmy confessed.

"Who?"

"Jack Drude."

"Isn't that the guy who jumped you?" Then he added, "Maggie told me.

Are you afraid of him, Jimmy? There's nothing wrong with that. I hear he is a big guy."

Jimmy dodged the question. "No, I have a plan."

"Maggie told me that too. She said you were working out on the rope and reading up on judo. Look, I learned a few things about judo and karate during my army reserve stint. Sure, I was only gone six months, so I'm no expert. Mom didn't even want me to go in for that long, but anyway, the basic training was the same as the regular army. The important thing is that I kept working on the skills after I got out last spring. The key is to work on it regularly. Maybe we could work out together on Sunday afternoons."

Jimmy beamed like a kid. "Wow! You'd do that?"

"Let's see. Why not start this Sunday?"

"The sooner, the better. Last time, Jack charged at me, knocked me down with his whole body, and held me down while he punched me. I was helpless."

"Look, I know you can't make a fist with your right hand, but when you deal with a big guy like Jack, you can't box your way out of it anyway. Boxing doesn't work in your favor. Judo and karate, though, teach you to use your hands and feet in other ways—you chop or stab with the fingers extended, or you hit with the lower palm when the hand is open." Billy demonstrated as he spoke. "All your fingers can remain straight. Believe me, striking someone's nose with the flat of your lower palm is more likely to break it than striking with a fist. And poking your firm, extended fingers into someone's eyes or throat will cause more pain than the same blow with a fist."

"That sounds almost unfair!"

"Look, if you get a big guy like Jack down, you want to keep him down. You don't want to kill him or cripple him, or you could end up in jail, and yet, you have to treat every fight like you're in a fight for your life."

Jimmy remained silent as Billy continued. "Judo may be the best way to get him down, but throwing him down doesn't keep him down unless he hits his head on something." Billy laughed at that image. "If you are struggling with him standing up, I suggest poking his throat hard with your fingers firmly extended. It'll make him cough and have a hard time breathing. Then go for a groin or shin kick. Then, to keep him down, go for a heel stomp. Use your heel to stomp hard on an extended arm or leg. Try to break a bone. Do that, and the fight is over."

Speechless, Jimmy nodded as he felt Billy's reassuring pat on his shoulder.

"Don't worry." Billy smiled broadly. "We'll work on it. With your strength and speed, you'll be a natural. Hey, I hear our dads coming up the stairs. We should go. Let's keep this between us, okay? And take my advice about seeing Mary."

Jimmy, his head swimming with ideas, followed Billy out the door.

When the men returned, the kitchen livened up with good-natured razzing about who would win the inevitable euchre games, the men or the women. Maggie, Mom, and Rose played as partners against Billy, Dad, and John, with Jimmy sitting in for anyone who needed a break to visit the toilet.

The women won the first game, and the men rallied to win the second, but as Martin began shuffling the cards for the first hand of game three, Rose inquired, "I understand your neighbor came to a strange end?"

Jimmy looked down. Maggie looked at Jimmy. Joey watched the face of his mom and dad to learn what he could about the mystery.

Martin took the cue from Mary to field a question he knew couldn't be ignored.

"Quite a shock to the neighborhood." A pause followed, and Martin thought it best to fill it. "Not much more I can say, really. Matt Schroedler kept himself and his family strangers to neighborhood business. He raised mostly hay, so he threshed his few acres of grain alone and filled his small silo alone and hired Pete Dunn to bale his hay. One or both of his sons, who farm a few miles away, helped him haul the bales and stack them in the barn. He and his only daughter, Mary, milked their dozen or fewer cows by hand. He seems to have had no intention of getting a milking machine, and why would he with a herd that small?"

As Martin explained the details of the accident, Maggie's mind filled with images of Mary. Mary the beautiful, delicate child and Mary the tough teenager. Mary the silent creature who avoided talking about her life at home, and now, Mary, the abused child who shared her most intimate secrets with her best friend. Mary, who loved her mother and hated her father, and Mary, who, in the weeks before her father died, had been seen regularly with Jack Drude, a boy she hated. Maggie choked back her tears and remained silent.

Jimmy's thoughts covered a decade of thinking Mary was an angel, an angel his heart held close, an angel who had reached out to show her affection for him ever since he had known her. His unofficial sweetheart in the country school, even though it had taken Jimmy years to admit to himself how much he liked her. And now, it seemed, she belonged to Jack.

Joey knew that if he stayed quiet, the adults might talk as if he weren't in the room, and he might learn facts and stories that untangled the mysteries adults often kept from kids.

Martin was finishing his narrative. "The daughter is staying with the neighbors, Emil and Caroline Rosincek."

"Didn't the girl's mother die recently?" John asked. "And wasn't she his second wife?"

Martin answered, carefully choosing his words. "He and his first wife had two sons, Albert and George. They moved out years ago. They barely got along with their father, but I think they still helped him with haying."

"So, the boys are the girl's half brothers, then," Rose persisted.

At this point, Martin wanted to say as little as possible. "Maybe, but it's common knowledge that after his first wife died, Matt began courting Bess Erickson after she had just turned eighteen. They married a very short time after that, and she had Mary six months later."

Rose chuckled. "Six-month babies are not really much of a scandal. The world is full of five- and six-month babies. It just reflects the love the couple have for each other." In the short silence that followed, no one commented on her willingness to reconcile her approval of premarital sex with her stern religious faith.

Then Mary said, "From the beginning, Matt treated Bess and her daughter like they were dirt under his feet, just as he treated his first wife and all women. He taught his sons to be the same way. Matt Schroedler's disdain for women is well known." She looked at Maggie, who responded with a nod of approval.

Joey had been listening intently without comment, but now he couldn't hold back and blurted, "What is a six-month baby?"

The silence in the room was like the moment of death waiting to strike, but cutting the silence, Mom explained, "It's just when a baby comes earlier than expected, Joey."

Martin said, deadpan, "Right. I'll deal the cards, and then John and I will take a break to start the pump to run some water to the storage tank in the hay barn. Maybe we can let Jimmy and Joey play our hands? Are you ready, boys?"

Instinctively, Joey knew the explanation about six-month babies was lame, but he knew it was best to go slow with adults, so he exclaimed, "Heck, yes!" while he and Jimmy moved into place.

CHAPTER 23

HIDDEN LETTERS

On the morning after Thanksgiving, Jimmy rose at six with Mom and Dad, nearly an hour later than usual. After morning chores, breakfast, and after-breakfast chores, Mom started packing eggs in preparation for a trip to town. After they ate a huge dinner of leftovers at noon, Maggie left in the '52 Ford with their parents and Joey and Jimmy stayed home, Jimmy to work out on the hayloft rope and Joey to watch and serve as an opponent when he could. Maggie asked to be dropped off at Rosinceks' place to visit Mary, which was not out of the way if they took the less-traveled route to Newburg.

Mary greeted her friend, and they immediately set off, pulling Mary's sled behind them, toward a hill east of the farmstead. At the crest of the hill, Mary, who was the smaller of the two girls, sat toward the front of the long sled with her knees bent toward her chin. Maggie, after giving the sled a good running push, hopped on behind and settled into the steering position, with her legs on either side of her friend and her heels against the steering handles. Mary grasped the sled's sides tightly with her hands and clamped her upper arms against Maggie's sturdy legs. With less than two inches of snow cover, the short alfalfa on the thick sod made a perfect sledding surface, and soon the sled sped down the hill, giving a thrill to its riders. The swishing of runners against the slick snow and the feel of the damp, cold wind against their faces exhilarated their hearts and freed their minds from the serious task ahead of them. For a few lovely minutes they forgot about the complications in their lives.

But the fantasies yielded to reality as they neared the bottom of the hill. Maggie stuck her legs out to drag her feet in the snow, slowing the sled before bringing it to a halt a few yards from the fence that marked the property line between Rosinceks' farm and Schroedlers' wooded pasture. Without a word they each took turns holding the barbed wires apart as the other ducked between them. Then, parking the sled under a bush, they silently walked toward Mary's house, both on the lookout for the presence of anyone else, especially Jack Drude.

"I think Jack does all his snooping at night," Mary said. "If we spot him, we need to run for the road. We can outrun him on the road."

They stopped momentarily at the edge of the trees, scanning the yard for signs of anyone. After scurrying to the house, they noiselessly stepped onto the wooden porch and entered the unlocked front door.

Mary cautioned, "Let's not switch on any lights. The windows let in enough light. We'll use our flashlights when we need them, but we'd better keep the beams low so the light cannot be seen through windows."

They checked the downstairs and upstairs rooms to ensure they were alone in the house. Mary searched her room only briefly and returned to meet Maggie in the small hallway, saying, "I know there is nothing in my room. I took all the stuff I wanted."

"What makes you think there is anything to find anywhere? Did your mom say anything to make you think so?"

Mary explained her memory of her mother reading a letter, adding, "I've been curious about it ever since."

The closet in the small bedroom Bess used as a sewing room was crammed with boxes full of pillowcases ready to be embroidered, small pieces of material for quilt squares, and joined squares ready to be hand quilted. The two girls looked through it all meticulously, carefully returning things to their boxes after shuffling through them.

After about half an hour, Mary whispered, "I wish I knew what to do with it all. We took a few of the boxes that had papers in them already, but what do I do with all this material? And these quilts? I'd love to keep it all, but that is too crazy." As she caressed one of the finished quilts, she choked out, "I think I'll give it to Caroline Rosincek. Emil will come over to pick all this up if I ask him to. I think he knew we didn't get it all the first time."

Maggie was still, giving her friend time to work through the memories. Finally, she asked, "Where should we look next?"

"Well, there are only two rooms upstairs, mine and this one. The only way to get into the attic is through a hole in the hallway ceiling, but the cover over it has always been nailed shut. There's nothing up there. We need to look for hiding places in the hallway and on the stairwell before we take on searching the living room, the kitchen, and the downstairs bedroom."

"Should we separate?" Maggie asked.

"No, let's stay together and search. I've already searched the kitchen and the pantry. We'll start with the bedroom closet under the stairwell. That would be a good place to hide stuff." Mary gave a small forced laugh and added, "Matt never ventured in there. He never hung up any clothes in his entire life."

They found nothing in the closet, the downstairs bedroom, or the living room.

"May as well check the pantry again," Mary said as she led the way into the narrow room. Shelves covered the inside wall from floor to ceiling, and at the far end, a multicolored rag rug, crocheted in an oval, lay on the floor over the small trapdoor to the cellar. Looking at the rug, Mary said, "I never checked the cellar. Matt never went down the cellar. He could hardly fit through the trapdoor."

Maggie ventured a question cautiously. "Isn't the cellar where you found your mother?"

"Yes, and I'd prefer not to go down there now, but I think if we're going to do a thorough search, we have to check it." Images of her beloved mother lying at the foot of the ladder flashed, but she held her composure. "Besides, you're with me, and that gives me courage."

Maggie smiled and nodded.

Mary moved the rug, lifted a small hatch door, and shined her flashlight down so Maggie could descend the ladder. "I'll hold the door for you," she said. "I'll have to shut the door after myself. The hook to hold it open is broken."

Shining her flashlight around the space, Maggie noted the cellar extended only under the kitchen. The walls were made of fieldstone and concrete and were over two feet thick in some places. Exposed log joists in two-foot intervals extended from wall to wall, holding up the kitchen floor. The uneven dirt floor was the source of the constant smell of damp soil. Along the stone wall were makeshift shelves, stacked on near-flat rocks. Quart jars of tomato juice, pickled cucumbers, pickled beets, peach and pear sauce, and smaller jars of jams and jellies filled the shelves.

"Lots of good canned goods here," Maggie commented.

"I'll tell Caroline to take this stuff too. My brothers are too lazy to crawl down here to get it anyway."

Maggie marveled at her friend's apparent ease in visiting her mother's place of death, and she took it as a cue to remark casually, "Looks a lot like our cellar. Smells like it too."

The two girls checked each corner, finding nothing of interest on the floor. Then, shining her light where the logs rested on the thick wall, Maggie commented, "I noticed your mom stores the empty jars on the pantry shelves upstairs, which keeps them handy to get at when canning season comes. So why are those jars up there on the foundation wall in this far corner? They're those old, dark green jars you can't even buy anymore. We have some of them too. Mom said they keep the light away from the produce inside, but in a dark cellar, light isn't a problem."

The wall was a little less than six feet tall. Maggie reached up to one of the jars near the edge and shined her light into its contents. Nothing. She stretched herself to retrieve the jar that was farther back on the rock foundation and shined the light through the glass. "Hey, there's something in here."

In haste, Mary took the jar and screwed off the lid with little difficulty. Reaching her fingers inside, she pulled out several envelopes that looked like letters before she screwed the top back onto the jar.

At that moment, the two girls froze as they heard distinct footfalls on the kitchen floor. "One of your brothers?" Maggie whispered.

Then the visitor began whistling a tune, and not just any tune, but a tune with which both girls were familiar.

She'll be coming 'round the mountain when she comes.
She'll be coming 'round the mountain when she comes.

"Jeez, it's Jack," Mary whispered. "Sounds like he's right next to the pantry." She wondered if the rug had fallen into place as she had closed the cellar door.

Mary stuffed the letters into her coat pocket and motioned that the jars could be used as a weapon. With their flashlights off, the two girls huddled in the darkness of the far corner.

The footfalls indicated that Jack was near the pantry door. Trapped in the cellar, the two girls breathed silently, trying to imagine how they would possibly escape if Jack descended the ladder. Seconds passed like minutes and minutes like hours as their legs began to cramp from the tension of holding still. They longed to remove their coats as sweat began to gather on their bodies, making them feel even more tense and trapped. But they remained still.

They strained to listen for sounds coming from the pantry. What could Jack be doing? Was he eyeing the cellar door? What would they do at the first sound of the cellar door opening? *Wait for him to descend,* Mary thought. *Run over, surprise him, get him off balance as he climbs down the ladder? Go around him to scoot up the ladder? Shut the cellar door on him and run!*

At the creaking of the cellar door, their fears came true. A shuffle of Jack's feet told them he was kneeling by the opening. The light flicked on, dimly illuminating the basement near the door. Prepared to rush Jack if he descended, the girls pressed their backs against the wall. He was talking to himself, his deep voice musing, "I could use some of these canned goods. That's a job for a night visit, though. I'll bring a wire to fasten this damn door open when I return."

The loud slam of the cellar door brought silent sighs of relief from the girls, but they continued to wait in fearful silence.

At last Jack began whistling again, and the girls heard his footsteps move across the kitchen floor and into the living room. After a few minutes, his footfalls took on a different sound, leading Mary to whisper, "He's climbing the stairs—let's go! We must make no noise but hurry. There is no window looking toward the driveway from upstairs, so we'll go out the front door and run down the driveway until we get to the road. That's the safest way home. Once we start, we can't turn back. I can get the sled some other time."

Mary switched her light on, scurried up the ladder, and held the door open as Maggie soundlessly climbed out. After closing the trapdoor with care, Mary hurried with light footsteps to catch Maggie, who held open the front door for her. As Mary slipped toward the freedom of the porch, Maggie closed the door without a sound. The two girls softly shuffled off the wooden porch and onto the hard ground of the yard. Running toward the driveway, both girls cast a quick glance behind them to see nothing but a closed door and an empty porch. Now, all they had to do was hope Jack wouldn't see them before they turned the corner onto the road.

Once on the road, they ran all the way to Rosinceks' house.

THE READING

Emil had just come in from feeding hay and sat down to eat a few of the cinnamon rolls Caroline had baked for his midafternoon lunch. "You'll want to try one of these, kids," he said with his mouth full as the girls entered the kitchen.

Mary was burning with curiosity to open the letters, just as Maggie was burning with the uncertainty of whether or not she should leave Mary alone to read them, but both knew they should not refuse the rolls. They sat and ate rolls with cool milk, answering questions about how the sledding was and if they had fun, questions that would have started an enthusiastic discussion under normal circumstances. But now, everything but the letters seemed irrelevant.

Salvation arrived as the '52 Ford pulled into the yard and Mary exclaimed, "Gee, Emil, I wanted Maggie to help me with some schoolwork I have to make up. Can you take her home later?"

"Sure, I'll go out to tell Martin."

By the time he returned, the girls had already finished their milk and rolls, thanked Caroline for the snack, and headed upstairs to examine the letters.

"By the way," Mary said, "that's the last time I can use the excuse about schoolwork. I'm telling Caroline and Emil that I am quitting school. I'll tell them I realized I'm just too far behind."

Saddened at the news, Maggie said, "I wish you would stay, but I understand why you want to quit. I know it's not just the work. It's the danger from Jack."

"And the stigma once the word is out. I can't bear the looks," Mary said as she pulled the letters from her pocket.

Unsure of how she should proceed, Maggie said, "Look, I don't know how private those letters are, and neither do you. I can just wait while you read them to see if you want to share the contents with me or not."

"No, we will read them together. I am frightened of their contents as well as curious. I need you with me."

The first letter was addressed to Mary's mother as Bess Erickson, her maiden name. Maggie held the single page steady as the two friends read silently.

January 12, 1939

My dear Bessie,

This will be my last letter to you, my love, because I will be boarding a train for home tomorrow morning and I'll make it home for your eighteenth birthday. Let's plan to celebrate big time. Maybe we can get our marriage license during the day and get married in early February. The CCC isn't bad, and I know the money I sent to Dorothea every month helped her get through the winter, but all I can do here is think of you and how great our lives will be together. I don't want to ever leave you to go anywhere again. Once we're married, you are stuck with me forever and ever. My hugs and kisses are all for only you.

With all my love,

Harold

Mary glanced at Maggie before exclaiming in a whisper, "What does this mean? Mom was in love and going to marry this man only three months before she married Matt!" She glanced again at the full name on the return address on the envelope: *Harold Hansen.* "This is the same name on the memorial card I found in Mom's album! The man who died in the car accident."

She jumped up from the bed to fetch the box with the memorial card and newspaper clipping, explaining to Maggie, "I found these after you left on Sunday." Maggie examined the card and the clipping as Mary jubilantly raised one finger at a time, counting off, "February, March, April, May, June, July, August, September." Holding up her ninth finger, she exclaimed, "October! I was no six-month baby! Matt Schroedler, the rotten son of a bitch, is not my father! Harold is! Look at his light hair. Matt had black hair, and Mom's was brownish. My real father was probably a decent human being!"

Elated at her friend's excitement, Maggie shared Mary's joy, but with a calm voice she mentioned, "There are two more letters."

Mary scrambled to open the next one, addressed to Bessie Schroedler, and held it firmly, though her hands shook with excitement.

June 12, 1939

Dear Bessie,

Congratulations on your marriage. Forgive me for reminiscing about the old days. Ever since we first met while threshing at your neighbor's farm, you have been like a little sister to me, so I'm hoping you forgive me for speaking frankly. Mourning my brother's death forever is not anything I would recommend, and although I always encouraged you to move on with your life, you know my feelings on your quick decision to marry Matt. He is not a good person, and neither were his folks. They gave no value to girls. When Harold and I came over on the orphan train, Matt's folks tried to get Harold, but he hung onto me, his older sister by over two years, and I insisted we had to stay together. Small girls or orphans who were mixed blood had a hard time getting sponsors, or maybe worse, they ended up with farm families that worked them hard without really caring for them. I think it helped that Harold and I were Scandinavian, because farmers liked to adopt kids with a similar background. It helped that Harold looked strong, even at eleven, but Matt's folks would not take a girl, so they refused the two of us. Lucky us! Jakob and Else Pedersen took us in and treated us like the children they never had. They were pretty old already, and Harold and I ended up running the place by the time I was eighteen.

You already know the story, of course, and you know they willed the farm to us before they died less than a year later. I tell you all this now so that you know my offer isn't a "charity" thing. When I offer you and your child a life here with me, I am only trying to pass on the good luck I received. I did nothing to deserve being taken in by the Pedersens. Life hands out good and bad luck indiscriminately.

But dear Bessie, I understand your decision to marry Matt, even though I think you have made the wrong choice, and I understand the sentiments of your folks. But I'm afraid marrying to prevent scandal is never a good reason to marry. I sincerely hope you manage to live a happy life, but I will always wish you had accepted my offer for you and your child to live on the farm with me. If you change your mind, you will both always be welcome.

I had hoped we could exchange letters and even visit each other, but I respect your request for me to no longer communicate with you according to your husband's demands. I know we need to take his threats seriously.

Best wishes to you always,

Your friend,

Dorothea

Mary checked the envelope for a return address, but there was none. After a short silence, Mary breathed in deep and exhaled her comment:

"That's my real father's sister. Sounds like she probably knew Mom was pregnant with me, and she told her not to marry Matt."

There was no address on the third envelope. Mary opened it with fearful anticipation.

There was no date on the top. It simply began

My Dear lovely child, Mary,

Please, please forgive me for

The rest of the page remained blank. Mary crumpled the page to her face and cried in it.

Maggie said nothing but put one arm around her friend's shoulders and held her tight.

A half hour passed before Emil hollered up the stairs, "Time to go back, Maggie. I told Martin I'd have you home to feed the chickens."

"Be right down," Maggie responded. "See you Monday at school," she offered as a farewell before she remembered Mary was quitting.

"I'll write," Mary said before her friend hurried downstairs.

Maggie put on a happy face as she said goodbye to Caroline and thanked her for lunch, but in the car, she found it difficult to match Emil's optimistic tone while he talked of the weather and the upcoming Christmas season.

When Emil dropped her off in the yard, Maggie saw her mom returning from the chicken coop with some eggs in a pail.

"Don't worry, Maggie, I took care of the chickens, figuring time might get away from you while visiting Mary. I hope you had fun sledding."

"We did, Mom. Thanks for doing the chores."

"Hey, you do them for us when Dad and I are late." She smiled with her reply.

As they walked to the house, Maggie moved closer to her mother to assert, "Mom, I like my life. I wouldn't want to be anyone else in the world, because I'm the luckiest teenager alive."

Mom stopped to look at her daughter. "What happened to you? Tell me if you want to, but I'm not going to press you on what brought on that burst of joy. Knowing when to shut up is the height of all wisdom, especially for parents."

Maggie's silence spoke for itself, and Mom queried, "Is Mary all right?"

"Yes, nothing's wrong, Mom," Maggie lied, before smiling and adding, "And I want to tell you that I even like chores, sometimes. Yes, I really do. But I have a request. Could Jimmy and I swap afternoon and evening chores with each other on weekdays? I know he won't mind. Jimmy will still do morning milking and feed silage, but he and Joey will feed chickens and pick eggs, and I will throw down silage before supper. I'll help with evening milking while he and Joey empty chamber pots and slop pails and wash dishes. I think it will be good for Joey to spend more time with Jimmy. When he's with me, he talks about Jimmy most of the time."

Mom stopped. "Sure. But now I have to ask you, what brought this on?"

"Nothing. I want to embrace being a farm girl. I've been thinking on it a while. I don't want it to be permanent. Just for the rest of the year. We'll switch back on January first."

"All right. If that's what you want. Let's go in. I've got to get supper started."

CHAPTER 25

NEW YEAR'S DAY

"I hate it when we have school the next day after a big holiday," Joey lamented as the family sat around the table eating breakfast. "I mean, we get up even earlier than usual, rush though everything so we can have a big meal with company. Then the afternoon flies by, and soon we're doing evening chores later than usual and it's bedtime by the time we're done with chores."

"The time goes fast because the day is so fun," Jimmy offered.

"And then," Maggie added, "morning comes even faster, and my body goes to school, but my mind is still thinking about the fun we had on the holiday."

"I can't disagree with you," Mom said, "and that's why I was all for skipping church. If it had been at nine like it is every other Sunday, we could've made it. We'd just get up earlier. But when it's at eleven, it delays the whole day."

"Yes," Dad added with a chuckle, "and it always seems the minister is dead set on keeping us an extra fifteen minutes when it's a holiday. As if he knows we plan on drinking beer all afternoon. You can be sure Dvoraks will be here by eleven, and we'll be toasting to 1956 fifteen minutes after they arrive."

"I'm pretty sure our company will be coming in two cars," Mom said suddenly. She waited until the rest of the family looked at her curiously before announcing, with special satisfaction, "Because Anna isn't riding with her folks. Billy is bringing her in his car. Emma wrote to tell me last week so that I could arrange the table accordingly."

"But Aunt Rose and Uncle John aren't coming, right?" Maggie inquired.

"No, they will be visiting John's brother's family," Mom explained.

"Good planning," Dad said. "We don't need my sister turning the conversation into a rant. She really needs to let Billy and Anna do as they please."

After finishing breakfast, the family doubled down, rushing to their after-breakfast chores, which included barn cleaning, bedding the cattle with straw, feeding chickens, gathering eggs, and cleaning the milking equipment. Jimmy knew he would have to throw down silage for the next day either before dinner or in the afternoon when company was visiting. Despite the fact that all five of his Dvorak cousins were girls, he liked visiting with them, and he also liked playing cards with his aunt and uncle. Also, he looked forward to getting some advice about girls from Billy. All this motivated him to work particularly fast to throw down silage before he cleaned up for company.

The family was ready and the table was set when Billy drove his maroon 1949 Ford into the yard, with Anna sitting so near to the driver that they appeared as one. When they came into the kitchen, the couple's love for each other oozed from their every move. They made a lovely couple: Billy, looking more like a Nordic god every year, and Anna, with lovely red hair to complement her fine figure and complexion.

Less than a minute later, Dvoraks' green 1951 Chevrolet drove into the yard, and in a few moments, the house filled with the energy and joy of people glad to see each other and eager to celebrate the New Year.

As company and hosts boisterously exchanged handshakes and hugs, coats were quickly removed and carried to the bedroom by Maggie and Joey, who placed them on three separate piles on the bed—a pile for Uncle Joe and Aunt Emma, a pile for Billy and Anna, and a separate pile for Anna's younger sisters.

Maggie and her female cousins gathered in the living room to catch up. Unlike their oldest sister, the four Dvorak girls had dark hair, and the older two had fuller figures than Maggie, but with Marcella and Helen older than her and Janet and Josephine younger, Maggie's presence filled the gap, making them appear as five sisters discussing their common interests— boys, clothes, popular music, and singers, especially Elvis Presley. Maggie expressed envy when Marcella said she had received a phonograph for Christmas, while each of her sisters got to pick out a record. Maggie made a mental note to convince Jimmy that they needed to pool their resources to get a phonograph, but she expressed another plan to her cousins. "Maybe I can get Jimmy to agree to convince our folks to combine our birthday presents into one phonograph for the two of us!"

"Might work," Helen said in support. "Your birthdays are only a day apart, but that still leaves you waiting until April thirtieth."

"I'll try to convince Jimmy it's a good idea," Marcella added. "I know he likes music too."

Escaping from the adults in the kitchen for a moment, Anna stepped into the living room to whisper to Maggie loud enough for all the girls to hear, "No, he hasn't proposed yet, but I am hoping today might be the day."

As the living room buzzed with voices, Joey and Jimmy remained in the kitchen with the adults, who had wasted no time before opening beers and toasting to the New Year. Joey and Jimmy pushed into the group to talk with Billy, whom they had unabashedly admired since they were toddlers.

Billy said, "Jimmy, I have to skip this coming Sunday's workout with you, but I think things are going really well, don't you?"

Jimmy nodded. "Practicing with a guy who's as big as Jack really helps."

"But what I really want to know is why you haven't gone over to visit Mary yet. Remember what I've been telling you. Don't wait too long, or someone will beat you to it. Valentine's Day is coming soon. Time to plan your move. Don't be a coward."

Jimmy nodded, smiling at his cousin's advice. According to Mary's letters to Maggie, she had not been seeing Jack since she left home. There was hope.

Mom left the kitchen briefly to poke her head through the living-room doorway and announce, "Don't get too comfy in there, girls. We're going to eat right away, so come on and get seated at the table."

This seemed to be good news for everyone. Those already in the kitchen sat down immediately, taking the same places they had for other dinners at the same table and readying themselves for the grand feast they expected from Mary.

After the passing and dishing, quiet settled over the table, broken only by the faint clanking of forks and knives. As the eating slowed, compliments on the fine meal were given freely to Mary, who never failed to get embarrassed by any praise.

Mary nodded at Billy and Anna, saying, "So good to see you here together for dinner."

"Oh, they will probably be leaving to go to a movie or some such date thing," Emma proclaimed. "But Anna told me she couldn't miss a holiday dinner at her favorite aunt and uncle's place."

"Absolutely, but I also wanted to see my cousins and wish Joey a happy birthday. I will always remember we were born the same day, December twenty-seventh. Let's see, it was number nineteen for me, Joey, and if I remember right, it was number eleven for you."

"Yup!" Joey replied shyly. For all his talk of not liking girls, he had always been enamored with his older cousin. Her personal charm had the same effect on everyone.

"What movie are you going to see?" Maggie asked, trying not to show her envy of her older cousin dating.

"*East of Eden* starts at two, which means we'd better get started if we want to catch the beginning," Anna said, eyeing her beau.

"But you've already seen it, haven't you?" asked Maggie, remembering how Anna had raved about James Dean in the role of Cal.

"Yes, but I think we both want to see it again, right, Bill?" Anna said, smiling.

"Sure," Billy replied, "but I wouldn't mind seeing something a little lighter, like *Lady and the Tramp*." He added quickly, "But it's fun to see a good movie more than once. I catch so much more in the second time."

Seeing her sister get up from the table to serve the dessert, Emma said, "Let me help you with that, Mary." And the two of them went into the adjoining room to bring out the pies. As Emma cut the pies and asked guests about their choice—apple, blueberry, or cherry—Mom began whipping the cream with the new handheld electric mixer she'd gotten for Christmas, which led to a discussion of who got what gifts as they enjoyed their desserts.

Emma and Mary soon rose to begin clearing the table as all raved about the pie. Billy and Anna got their coats and prepared to leave for the movie, and Dad, Joseph, and Jimmy left for the barn to feed hay, a job that could only be done after the cows had cleared the manger from their morning feeding of silage.

Joey had a decision to make. Should he follow the men to the barn or stay and listen to the women talk? His experience told him that all adults talked more freely in a group of all men or all women, but especially women. He decided to stay and remain quiet as a mouse.

As soon as the leftovers were stored, everyone pitched in to organize the dishes in a manageable stack before beginning the chore of washing, drying, and putting them away.

Familiar with the kitchen as if it were her own, Emma asserted, "There's only so much room here at the sink. I'll wash for a while, and then one of you, Marcella or Helen, can take over. Janet, Josephine, and Joey can take turns wiping, and Maggie is the best qualified to put the dishes away. But first, Mary, I insist you sit down and sip on a cup of coffee or have another beer. Okay?"

"If you insist," Mary said, giving in to her older sister's plan.

Once everyone was in place, Mary said, "I hope the kids come back here after the movie. Might as well eat supper with us."

"I think they will," Emma joked, "because they know there's plenty of pie, and they know you will feed us again before we leave."

Emma added, nodding to her daughters, "So, what do you think of the young lovers, girls?"

Janet and Josephine just giggled.

Without reservation, Marcella said, "Billy is a dream."

"Yes, and Anna's stupid if she doesn't marry him," Helen agreed. "I'd flip to Lutheran for him in a second, if Anna passes."

"Don't talk foolishly, girls," Emma reminded her daughters. "I'm counting on each of you to find a nice Catholic boy."

Mom added, "Anna and Billy are a perfect couple, I think. Both kind and sweet. To have my sister's daughter and my husband's sister's son in love with each other is a beautiful thing. I'd like to see it work out."

"Yeah, me too," Emma admitted, "but Bill's mom holds onto him pretty tight. I'm bad enough that way myself, but she is beyond reason, if you'll forgive my saying so."

Mom nodded in agreement. Joey wiped another dish, mouth zipped tight.

Emma surprised everyone when she announced, "I maybe shouldn't tell you this, but in December, a few days before Christmas, when George Lange came back from six years in the navy, he stopped in to pay Anna a call. Clearly, the young man is interested. I think he was interested in her before he went into the navy, when he was nineteen, but Anna was only thirteen then, the same age as when she met Billy. Anyway, Anna agreed to go for a ride with him just to be nice, but she told him she was seeing someone. George is such a nice young man. And he is Catholic."

Janet said, "He's so old."

And Josephine agreed, saying, "I hope he doesn't mess things up between Billy and Anna. Billy is so much fun, and he's not exactly a heathen, Mom."

Joey nearly gasped aloud upon hearing his cousin say the word *heathen*, and in that moment, his mind shifted from the kitchen to the memory of his schoolmates calling him a heathen. They had laughed at him, making him feel so small and unworthy! Were his own relatives no different from the neighbors? And suddenly, what his father had said about Rose—that she thought she was better than everyone—started to make sense. *Does everyone think they're better than everyone else?* Calling someone a name was more about the name-caller. The discovery saddened him, but he did not get angry. He felt free. Jimmy was right. Being different was good.

"Yes, Billy is fun," Emma agreed, "but so is George. And I admire him for his courage and ability to roll with his station on life. You may remember, he was born out of wedlock, and his mother, Josie Novotlik, raised him on her own until he was about two, when she married Elmer Lange, and they went on to have some kids of their own. One hears, sometimes, how a kid with a different father is not treated well, but I think Elmer treated George okay, though, and even adopted him so his official name became Lange. I think Elmer realized he was lucky to marry a jewel like Josie."

Silence followed, indicating that enough had been said on the subject of George's past. Joey had some questions, but he had heard much of George's story before and so said nothing, hoping his aunt would continue to talk.

Marcella broke the silence, asking, "Maggie, how is your friend Mary Schroedler? I've only met her a few times when she was here while we were visiting, but she seems like such a kind person. I just can't imagine losing a mother and a father just a few months apart."

Maggie replied, "I think she's doing well. She's living with Emil and Caroline Rosincek, and they treat her like a daughter. I try to visit her often, but I haven't seen her for over a month. She seemed to be doing fine when I saw her last. We went sledding in November and had planned to visit in December, too, but she wrote to cancel. Said she had the flu. She quit school, so I miss her there, but she writes me regularly."

"She's lucky to have a friend like you, Maggie," Emma said bluntly. "She needs a friend her own age, I am sure. She has to be hurting inside, you know. Losing your parents hurts. The damage takes time to repair."

Joey had been listening intently, trying to stifle any comment. But when he heard his aunt say *damage*, he couldn't stop himself from saying, "Yeah, someone at school said Mary was 'damaged goods.'"

The silence in the room was like death waiting to strike. Maggie glared at him and demanded, "Where did you hear that? Who said it?"

Joey said defensively, "Caroline Shaurel said that she heard Mary was damaged goods. She seemed sad about it."

Maggie looked sad too—almost sick. Then Mom came to the rescue. "The kids all know about the possible damage to her heart because of the rheumatic fever she had as a child. They must be referring to that. Don't you think so, Emma?"

Emma replied, deadpan, "Right. I'm sure that's what they meant."

As if on cue, the men returned from the barn, and as they removed their coats, Martin said, "I see the table is cleared. I'll get the cards, and let's play a few games of euchre. I'll bet we have enough for eight-handed!"

Jimmy cornered his sister to whisper, "Billy and Anna turned west at the end of our driveway. The movie theater is east."

"Don't tell anyone," Maggie replied softly. "Anna said they were stopping off at her place first."

Meanwhile, miles away, Anna and Bill lay still and silent on her bed, their embrace no less passionate than earlier, when they were in the midst of lovemaking. Neither felt the need to speak, feeling the oneness that only sex between youths in the throes of love can provide.

CHAPTER 26

ANOTHER RIDE

On the weekend before Valentine's Day, overnight temperatures warmed to near freezing, and during the day, sunshine brought temperatures into the low thirties, making it perfect for hauling hay home. Many farmers waited until spring to buy hay, but Martin Carlson liked to buy it in the winter and haul it home before Valentine's Day for a number of reasons. First, roads were muddy in spring, but winter roads stayed frozen and fairly smooth. Second, in the winter he could stack the hay he bought outside without fear of rain, making unloading fast and easy. Third, he'd feed the boughten hay from the stack first, keeping his own hay safe and dry in the barn so he could feed it through the spring rains until the cows were sent out to pasture. Martin liked to buy hay from Emil Rosincek, who seemed to have a knack for getting the hay up without a rain, making it perfect feed for dairy animals. He always had good hay for sale because every summer he used his haying machinery to put up several of his neighbors' hayfields, with the agreement that he got half of the hay in payment for the use of his machinery. The families worked together to haul and store the hay.

On Saturday morning, as Jimmy drove the tractor pulling the empty hay wagon at full throttle down the dirt road to Rosinceks' farm, he turned his face to the side to avoid the force of the wind. The brand-new Ford Model 860 tractor had been delivered to their farm only two weeks earlier, and although Jimmy had been surprised when his father let him drive it on the road this morning, he was not surprised at his father's words of caution as he'd fastened the pin that bolted the wagon's tongue to the tractor's hitch.

"Be careful," his dad had warned. "Just because it can go over twelve miles an hour doesn't mean you have to go that fast. The road has rough spots, and if the tractor and rig start bouncing, you can lose control. Be ready to slow down."

As Jimmy hit a rough spot in the road, he throttled back a bit and admitted to himself aloud, "Yeah, Dad's usually right about stuff."

As he turned left at the crossroad toward Rosinceks' farm, the south wind hit him directly in the face, and he realized that maybe his dad letting him drive the tractor and wagon to get a load of hay wasn't such a sacrifice for him after all. Jimmy had dressed warm—standard long underwear, flannel shirts, bib overalls, long coat, earflap cap, and a wool scarf knitted by his mom—but he could feel the damp, cold air penetrate his body, despite the fact that the temperature was slightly above freezing. He pulled his scarf up to cover his face as he mumbled, "Glad Rosinceks' place is only about a mile and a quarter. I'm halfway there."

Jimmy figured they could haul two loads before dinner at noon and maybe get three more loads in the afternoon. At eighty bales on a load, Dad thought they could finish hauling the entire four hundred bales he had purchased today.

Jimmy slowed the tractor's throttle as he turned into Emil's driveway. He cruised through the yard and toward the barn in road gear, marveling at how the engine easily handled the slower speed in its highest gear. Barney, Rosinceks' dog, emitted a vigorous volley of barks before retreating to avoid being hit by the tires. He was an old dog, and with his age came the wisdom to know that a short outburst of barking was enough to warn the family that a visitor had entered his domain. Barney followed Jimmy's rig to the barn, wagging his tail to let him know he expected some attention.

Jimmy stopped by the barn, dismounted, and immediately knelt to hug and pet the old dog. He had known Barney since he was a pup. Martin drove into the yard with the car as Emil came out of the house to help load the hay. Jimmy eyed the front door carefully, hoping Mary would come out to visit as they loaded, but he was disappointed that he saw nothing of her during the entire time he helped Emil and his father load the wagon with bales.

After they finished loading, Dad cautioned Jimmy, as he mounted the tractor to drive home, "I'll follow in the car, but not too close in case you lose a bale. Drive slow. We don't have a new wagon with a solid bolster like Emil does. Our wagon won't trail straight, so watch it." Jimmy had heard all these warnings a thousand times, but he never resented his dad's repetition.

After the next load, they stopped for dinner. Mom fed them loose-fried hamburger, eggs, fried potatoes, and chocolate cake for dessert. The family listened to Dad rave about the nice green hay they had hauled from Emil's. "Smells like we're hauling it right from the hayfield," he bragged. "We'll put off grinding feed until tomorrow after church so we can get as many loads as possible this afternoon—three more for sure, but four if he'll sell us more. I'd like to get even more, but we don't have the cash, and I won't ask him for credit."

Later, while loading the first afternoon load, Emil teased, "If that new tractor of yours can pull two loads, why not load up my wagon and pull both loads home? Unless you think it'd be too much for your tractor going up the hill by the school. We can put over one hundred bales on my wagon."

"It'll handle it easy. I wouldn't want to go downhill with two loads pushing me, but pulling two loads uphill is not a big deal. Let's load them up."

The three men loaded two big loads in a short time and hitched the wagons together. Martin said, "I'll drive the tractor this time, Jimmy. I'm concerned how the wagons will trail, plus I want to see how my new tractor handles the hill in road gear. You follow in the car, but not too close."

Eager for a chance to drive the car, Jimmy sat in the driver's seat and watched as Martin pulled the loads slowly out of the yard. He had given up on seeing Mary when suddenly she appeared alongside the car, carrying a large shoebox. Wearing a bulky winter coat instead of her sleek navy jacket, she paused for a moment before hurrying around the front of the car to the passenger side. Pulling the door open, she teased, "Mister, could you please give me a ride to the Carlson farm to see my three best friends?"

Jimmy could feel his face redden, even after being out in the cold, but he mustered his manly voice to reply, "Sure thing, young lady. Just get in." Then he added, "I admit I don't have a license."

They giggled together for a moment, and Jimmy was in heaven.

"I've got my permit, though," Jimmy added hastily.

Mary chirped, "Then we're legal, because I've got my license! Emil has been letting me drive his car home from church since last fall and arranged for me to use it for my test in January. I passed the first time I took it."

Jimmy smiled. "Good for you! Getting a license to drive is a big deal. I'm hoping I can take my test before school starts this fall. I'll be sixteen this spring."

"Yeah, I know. On May first." Mary bragged, "Emil starts up his son's Model A once a week, and he taught me how to do it. When Al joined the army, Emil promised he would keep it running until he returned."

"I've never driven a Model A," Jimmy confessed. "Is it complicated?"

"Not really. You just have to remember to turn on the gas and advance the timing when you start it. It's not something I need to know or anything, but it's fun to help Emil. He even showed me how to use the heater." She paused a moment before she added, "He misses his son."

"Al is a great guy," Jimmy said, remembering the tall, strong, gentle kid from the country-school days. "No one bullied us when Al was around." Neither of them mentioned Jack Drude's penchant for bullying after Al had finished the eighth grade and started high school, but both of their minds filled with bad memories of him.

Jimmy noticed that her face seemed fuller than in the past. Maybe she was eating better at Rosinceks' than she had at home. Searching for more small talk, he added, "I didn't know those old cars had heaters."

Mary seemed eager to talk. "The car didn't come with it. Al had to buy it and install it. Emil said that anyone who wants to drive a Model A in the winter is sure to get one."

Unaccustomed to driving the car with a pretty girl by his side, Jimmy became self-conscious and took special care in trying to talk and drive at the same time. He was glad there was no pressure to drive faster than about eight or ten miles an hour. They followed a safe distance behind Martin, but as they gained on him, Jimmy stopped the car to allow his dad to get ahead.

He turned to ask Mary, "What's in the box?"

"It's a surprise," she answered coyly.

"I thought maybe you were running away," Jimmy joked, but he was sorry after he said it, noticing that Mary's smile faded as she looked down at the box on her lap.

In the uncomfortable pause that followed, Jimmy felt his heart beating in his throat. There were many things he wanted to say, but he really didn't know *precisely* what he wanted to say. As he looked at her face, he became enamored of her presence, her closeness, her smile. He knew he had to say something, but he was glad she spoke before he said something dumb.

"Okay, I'll tell you what's in the box. You'll find out soon anyway. I spent part of the morning making valentines for you guys. Thought I'd deliver them today, since I won't be seeing you in school or anything."

Delighted, Jimmy emitted a quick "Wow!" before he realized he had not yet prepared anything for her. Mary and Jimmy had been exchanging valentines since the first grade and special ones nearly as long, but with the Jack Drude issue hanging out there, he'd been unsure what he was going to do this year. He was glad Mary had broken the ice.

"I don't have . . . that is, Maggie and Joey and I don't have our valentines ready yet," Jimmy confessed sadly.

"I'm sure you can deliver them when you do, though. After all, you drive the car pretty well. When it's moving, that is."

Realizing they had been stationary all this time, Jimmy exclaimed, "Jeez, I'd better get going. Dad must be almost home!" He put the car in gear, revved the engine, and sped home to find Dad turning into the driveway with the loads. He parked the car and took Mary into the house while Dad parked the wagons.

Once inside, everyone greeted Mary with honest enthusiasm. Taking her coat, Mom told her to stay all afternoon while the men hauled hay. Maggie was ecstatic, and Joey even put down his comic books to enjoy the moment.

Mary insisted, "Before you go to unload, Jimmy, just take a moment while I give you and everyone your valentines." She took the lid off the box to reveal five large, pink cupcakes she had made, each covered with white frosting and with the name of a Carlson family member written with chocolate in a delicate, ornate script.

Jaws dropped at the beauty of the cakes. Always sensitive to the moment, Mom said, "Let me go get Dad to come in out of the cold for a bit. I'll tell him that Jimmy and I will come out to help him unload after we all have a short visit with Mary and a quick lunch."

The Carlson kids commented on the beautiful cupcakes before they turned their attention to the three envelopes with their names on them.

"Please don't open your valentines now," Mary pleaded. "Save them for after I leave."

"Okay," Maggie said, and she collected them to store on the wooden table in the living room.

After Dad and Mom returned, they raved about Mary's beautiful cupcakes. Dad and Joey decided to eat theirs immediately, and the group laughed as Dad teased the others that he would pilfer the remaining cupcakes if he had the chance.

The visit remained lighthearted and fun, for no one mentioned the passing of Mary's mother nor the tragic accident that had killed her father. Jimmy watched Mary's every move, noticing she seemed more jubilant than usual and more attractive too. The oversized green sweater she wore helped her hair and complexion stand out. He tried not to stare, but when she saw him eyeing the sweater, he looked away quickly.

Mary eagerly explained, "It's one of Caroline's old sweaters. When I told her I loved the green color, she gave it to me. Said it was too small for her, anyway. It's way too big for me, but I love it."

"It looks great," Jimmy managed to say.

Soon Jimmy and his parents went out to unload the hay and stack it next to the barn. Maggie hinted to Joey that he shouldn't follow the two girls as they climbed the stairs to Maggie's bedroom.

"I know when I'm not wanted." Joey gave his pretend-pout routine.

Maggie replied, "It's not that you're not wanted, dear brother—it's that you're not wanted at this time, when we talk girl stuff in my room."

"I'm not interested in coming, anyway," Joey muttered. And he really wasn't.

CHAPTER 27

DECEPTION

In her tiny bedroom upstairs, Maggie asked Mary, "Are you still planning to run away? I think Jimmy is planning a nice valentine for you."

Although this news moved her, Mary tried not to react, choosing to answer only the first question. "Yes, I'm going to run away, but I really don't want to leave any of you, especially Jimmy and you and Joey and your folks and Rosinceks. But I have to. Jack becomes more dangerous by the day. I spotted him lurking near the barn once."

"Did you tell Emil or Caroline?"

"No, I don't want to cause trouble."

"Have you decided where you will go yet?"

"Somewhere far from here and safe. A few days ago, I received a letter from someone I wrote to before Christmas. I won't tell you more than that because you will be safer if you know nothing. Anyway, she's eager to take me in, whenever I can get away."

"You won't tell me who it is?"

"Oh, my dear Maggie." Mary hugged her. "I don't want you to worry, so I'll tell you this much—she is the older sister of my real father. The lady who wrote the letter we read, remember?"

"I don't remember her name." Maggie sounded apologetic.

"Good! And don't try!" Mary exclaimed.

"There was no return address on that envelope."

"No, but I just used her name and rural route and sent it to the town where my father had the accident. As it turned out, that was the wrong place, but these post offices in small towns know everyone, and the letter bounced around until it found someone who knew where it belonged."

"Amazing luck," Maggie said as she filed the fact in the back of her mind—*These post offices in small towns know everyone.*

"So, you haven't talked with Jack?" Maggie asked hesitantly.

"God, no!" Mary blurted. "I hate him, but every moment I am outside at Rosinceks' farm, I'm afraid he may show up and force me into his car. I have nightmares about him sneaking up to kidnap me." She paused briefly before adding, "I'm pretty sure I've seen him lurking in the grove of trees north of the house, too. Barney was out there, and normally he barks, but you know how Jack can charm dogs."

"Except yours." Maggie smiled, trying to lighten the mood. Sensing her friend's growing despair, Maggie put her arm around her, and Mary, unable to hold her tough facade any longer, choked back a sob and scooted closer to her friend.

"I have nightmares about a lot of things," Mary confessed. "I know I will sleep better when I am far away from here, where neither Jack nor my brothers can find me."

"Your brothers?"

"I'm afraid they may not have given up on getting custody until I'm eighteen."

"How are you going to run away?"

"I've thought about it a lot. If I could trick Jack into meeting me somewhere and leaving his car to fetch me, maybe I could double back and drive it away."

"Steal his car?"

"I know it sounds terrible, but what else can I do?"

"Do you have any ideas how to get him to leave it?"

"No, do you?"

Maggie shook her head. Then she added, "Maybe I do. You should send him a valentine!"

"I don't have any more."

"We have a boxful. We could pick out a juicy one, and you could write something and give him directions on what to do. You could put some perfume on it to entice him."

Mary was skeptical. "I don't like leading him on so much. He gets serious."

Maggie was adamant. "Look, I don't like leading him on either, and it could be dangerous. Who knows how he'll react when he finds out you're gone?"

"And when he figures out that I took his car! I need to get far away from him, but I'm worried about you."

"He won't know I had anything to do with it."

"And I'll write a message to him that I'm gone forever and that no one knows where I am, not even my friends or Rosinceks."

Reluctant to deceive at first, the two girls soon started to enjoy planning the ruse. Maggie fished out a couple valentines and even brought out some candy hearts to put in the envelope.

"Jack always gets the mail," Maggie said. "Maybe you can mail it."

"I was hoping to get it to him sooner than that. Maybe I can put it in his mailbox after the mailman goes."

"Too dangerous," Maggie said. "But I can do it."

"Too dangerous for you too!" Mary exclaimed.

"I can get Joey to do it. If he gets caught, he can say you gave it to him and that you didn't want me or anyone to know about it. Hey, I think Joey will like it, even if he gets caught. I'll train him on the deception, and he'll enjoy keeping it from Jimmy."

Their enthusiasm dwindled as they looked at each other, realizing at the same time that they did not want to involve Joey.

"Bad idea," they said simultaneously.

"I got a better idea," Mary persisted. "I'll just mail it Monday. He'll get it Thursday or Friday, in plenty of time for him to follow my instructions."

With that settled, the two teenagers sprawled on the bed and began writing the valentine. Mary insisted she would write the note when she got home.

"I want you to be honestly ignorant of the details," she said to Maggie. "The less you know, the better for you." In truth, Mary had no idea what message she could send to get Jack to leave his car long enough for her to drive it away, but she knew for sure she did not want to risk getting in the car with him.

Meanwhile, in Rosinceks' barn, Martin was saying, "Emil, I'd like to buy the extra hay you are offering, but I don't have the money now. We should just load my wagon, and when we're done hauling today, I can pay you for the total."

"Martin," Emil said simply, "if you want the hay, take it home today and pay me later. I know you're good for it." Then he laughed. "If the milk price goes to hell, we'll all be in trouble together."

"Thanks. I know you could get more for the hay if you waited till spring to sell it, so I appreciate it."

"Don't mention it." Emil smiled. "Do we load two more trips with both wagons or not?"

"We do," Martin declared. "I'll pay you for four hundred today and the rest by May."

"Right, I'll come over with the pickup to pull my wagon home after the last trip. I'll bring Mary back too."

After Emil brought her home later that afternoon and she felt safe in her upstairs room, Mary relaxed the forced smile on her face. She breathed in deeply, exhaled, and allowed her shoulders to sag, relieved but sad to have deceived her best friends by not revealing her newest secret. Moving her hands to her belly under the large green sweater, she sighed. "Well, I think we fooled them. I haven't seen Maggie since I started getting sick in the morning, and she has no idea how much I wanted to tell her everything—to share our little secret with her. But I've burdened her with enough already. At least I know for sure that your father is my stepfather, not my real father. That's something."

Exhausted from the day's deceptions, she was eager to go to bed, but she forced herself to take up paper and pencil and compose two letters that had to be mailed Monday morning to ensure the success of her escape plan. First, she wrote to Dorothea, telling her of a possible arrival date. Second, she wrote a message to Jack, a message of enticing deception that masked her fear, even as she mused about the one great secret they shared together—his part in Matt's death and her elaborate coverup. She vowed never to burden anyone with the knowledge of those crimes.

CHAPTER 28

DILEMMAS

The next day, the Carlson family returned from church at eleven thirty, and by noon they were eating a dinner of wieners, fried potatoes, eggs, and homemade bread. Dad and Jimmy left soon after they ate to install a pulley on the new tractor so they could belt it up to the hammer mill, and Mom tended to cleaning. By one in the afternoon, Maggie and Jimmy were carrying tubs of cob corn from the crib to the hammer mill, where Dad fed the ears into the feeder to be ground up and blown into the wagon box, which was tended by Joey. When the box was full, they covered it with a canvas and parked it near the barn, ready for Dad to load into tubs each morning and put a scoop on each cow's pile of silage, like whipped cream on dessert.

At three in the afternoon, Billy came over to work with Jimmy on judo moves in the hayloft. Mom was baking bread and cakes, and Dad sat down at the kitchen table to work on his taxes.

Maggie sat at the small wooden table in the other room, contemplating her two dilemmas. Valentine's Day was next Tuesday, and although she knew she had to seriously think about what to send to whom, right now she was more concerned about a new assignment in English class. The blank notebook page glared at her, paralyzing her thoughts. Twisting short strands of her hair between the thumb and forefinger of her right hand, she finally scribbled a few lines of meaningless text on the dull white tablet with her left. Not much to show for a half hour's work. She sketched a lone tree and then wrote,

Sometimes I'd like to go inside a tree,

Where there would be no one but me.

I'd live happily inside the tree.

Holding her pencil in her left fist like a dagger ready to stab downward, she scratched it out, deciding it was too . . . She couldn't think of the word. She burst out, "Stupid!" and bore down hard upon the pencil. The dull end snapped.

Maggie glanced over to see Joey sitting on the couch, his eyes drilling into his Superman comic book. The red, blue, and yellow colors of Superman's costume shone brightly. Superman's muscled thighs and biceps strained the fabric, and the small red shorts worn over his blue tights to cover his privates made Maggie involuntarily snicker.

"Didn't you just read that comic book yesterday?" she teased her little brother.

"I like Superman. He makes things right."

Maggie and Joey both looked up as Jimmy barged into the room, smelling of sweat and hay from his workout with Billy. "Billy left right after we finished. His dad wanted him home for early supper and chores."

"Can Superman see through trees?" Joey blurted out.

"He wouldn't be very super if he couldn't see through a few trees, little brother." Jimmy seldom gave a straight answer to anyone, especially his two younger siblings.

"So, he can, then?" Joey persisted. "See through trees?"

"Well, you've watched the show. You've seen him do it, just like I have."

Glancing at Maggie's scribbled-out drawing, Jimmy teased, "Is homework not going well, Mags? I like the poem, though."

As Maggie tried to hide her broken pencil, Joey badgered, "But, Jimmy, Caroline says you can't believe everything you see on television. She says

Superman can't see through trees."

"She's just trying to get your attention, Joey. You know, she *likes* you."

"I hate it when you tease me about that! You know I can't stand her. She's always trying to talk to me and stuff. I try to ignore her, but we got in this argument about Superman, and I just want you to answer me. Can Superman see through trees?"

Jimmy moved toward him. "So, what's this really about? You know that Superman isn't real, right? That he's a comic-book character in a television show and the whole story is fiction."

"Of course, I know that! You always treat me like I'm some dumb kid. I'm not, you know."

"Hold on, little brother. I know. I know." Jimmy sensed his brother's short temper reaching its peak. "I just had to make sure that you know the stories are fiction, not real."

"Actually," Maggie chimed in, "the Superman series is more like fantasy fiction because fantasy has things that are impossible, like Superman's power to fly, to leap tall buildings, and to see through trees. And to enjoy the show, we suspend our disbelief of those things even though we know that they are not real, and we agree to believe them within the story."

"So we are suspenders of disbelief?" Jimmy chortled. "Ain't that snappy!"

"Come on, Jimmy. I'm trying to be serious with Joey. Trying to teach him something."

Joey giggled at Jimmy's suspenders joke in spite of himself. Then he complained a bit too loudly, "Yeah, Jimmy. Be serious!"

Jimmy ruffled Joey's hair. "Old Mags is three hundred sixty-four days younger than I am, and she thinks she's wiser, which I wouldn't mind so much if she weren't so obsessed with trying to prove it."

Maggie slapped Jimmy on the arm as she said, "It's Maggie to you, buster."

"So why all of a sudden are you an expert on fantasy and fiction?" Jimmy asked.

"We've been reading the novel *Swiftwater* in ninth-grade English," Maggie explained. "I really like it, and I told Mrs. Deem that it seemed so real to me. She told me that many of the characters and events were realistic and believable—like how the Calloway family was looked down on by most of the town folk."

"Yeah," Jimmy piped in, "I liked the story when I read it last year. Doesn't the boy end up winning the girl in the end? Tell the truth, Mags. That's what you really liked, isn't it? The love story part of the story."

Ignoring her brother, Maggie continued, "Then Mrs. Deem contrasted it with fantasy, where the characters and events can be totally unrealistic. They can do impossible things and have impossible powers. Then someone brought up the television show *Superman*."

Jimmy prodded, "You haven't answered my question . . ."

"So what if there is a little romance in the story? That's real, isn't it?" Maggie asserted.

Jimmy smiled, satisfied that he had roused his sister's feelings but dismayed that his little brother's feelings were heating up as well. Joey grumbled, "Why do they always have to put sloppy boy-and-girl stuff in a good story? Why does everything have to have love in it? Even *Superman* has Lois Lane getting sloppy about Superman. It's sickening. That's why my favorite television show is *Davy Crockett*. He doesn't get mixed up with any girls. He is a real man."

Maggie chirped, "And that's probably why it isn't on TV anymore." She stole a quick glance at Jimmy to share the joke. Then she added, "Anyway, Mrs. Deem said our next assignment was to write a fantasy story. I've got to get started tonight. I want to come up with a really good idea, because we have to revise it again when we get to the tenth grade."

"I suppose it will be real sappy." Joey pouted. "I bet you can't even write one that isn't sappy and about love. Everything is. They put it in every song on the radio and every story on television."

"No, it won't," Maggie said. "I already have a story in mind," she lied, "and it will have nothing to do with love."

"Really?" Jimmy said. "We will have to suspend our disbelief to enjoy it, then?" He glanced at her tablet. "Looks like you're keeping it hidden in your mind for now."

"Oh, shut up! I know what you're getting at, but it's not like I don't know about your secret love."

Jimmy's cheerful demeanor faded, and Maggie knew she had gone a bit too far. Jimmy did not like to talk about his feelings.

"You know nothing about me," Jimmy said firmly. "And to prove it, I'll go get my revised story. I got an A on it last year in ninth grade, and the revision isn't due until next month, but I finished it early because I figure we might be into spring fieldwork by the time it's due. When I read it to the two of you, you will both see that you can have love in a story without it being sappy or mushy. You'll see."

With that, he strutted across the floor and opened the door to the narrow stairwell. Maggie and Joey listened to his footsteps pound up the steep, narrow steps to the room that he and Joey shared.

Joey took out his favorite tablet, the one with Casper the Friendly Ghost on the cover, and proclaimed in his firmest voice, "I'm going to write a story too. And it will be better than yours or Jimmy's because there will be no love in it."

"No love in it, huh?" Maggie said sadly. "That will be a fantasy, indeed." She returned to her page with the scribbles, void of a topic or a plan. Thinking of Jimmy's positive comment about her poem, she reviewed it briefly before the scratching noise of Joey's pencil on his tablet began to annoy her.

"Great!" She confessed, "the eleven-year-old has a topic and I don't have an idea. Maybe I'll work on writing out valentines."

Joey's reaction was immediate. "That's another thing I'm worried about!"

"What's that?" Maggie asked. "Valentine's Day? What's there to worry about?"

"Jeez, Maggie, when you were at country school, you gave valentines to everyone. I mean, even people you didn't like much, you wrote out a valentine and signed my name along with yours. But what do I do now? Do boys do that too? Or is that just a big-sister thing?"

Maggie explained, "Jimmy used to give everyone a valentine. He gave a special one to Mary, of course, but no one really believes the message on a standard, store-bought valentine. I mean, they say something like *Be Mine*, or maybe *Be My Valentine*, but they don't even open up. It's just a card. It's a friendship thing. In the country school we gave everyone a valentine because if kids just gave them to someone they really, really *liked*, there would be many kids who would never get one. That would be too sad. It takes the pressure off if you give one to every kid."

Joey nodded but remained skeptical. "I really don't want to give a valentine to all those kids who think they are better than I am."

Maggie asked, "But how are you going to feel if everybody gives one to you and you don't reciprocate?"

"If I don't what?"

"*Reciprocate.* It means give them one too."

"I suppose you're right, but I really don't want to give one to Caroline. She's nuts the way it is."

"I suggest you leave no one out. And don't forget the teacher. Is there anyone you want to give a special valentine to?"

"You know there isn't. I'm starting to hate Valentine's Day. I liked it when I was little. But now, it seems the words might mean something different."

"Well, do as you wish. There are plenty valentines in the box."

Reluctantly, Joey began writing a card out for everyone, but he stopped when Jimmy came downstairs, proudly carrying his assignment.

Joey asked him, "Are you giving everyone in school a valentine?"

"No, I am not. That was a country-school thing because everyone in the school was friendly toward each other—well, mostly anyway. Even the bullies were part of the clan. It's so different in high school."

"Maggie told me to give one to every kid and the teacher."

Maggie jumped in to say, "Okay for you, little brother. My advice isn't good enough! You have to check with Jimmy. Since when did he become a social expert?"

"Slow down, Maggie. I agree with you totally. First, I am no social expert. Don't even pretend to be. I'm probably tied with Robert on the number of friends I have in school. Second, I think your sister gave you good advice. Give one to each kid and the teacher."

"Have you written yours out?" Maggie asked in a manner that seemed to add *to your special friend.*

"I have. And I'm glad Mary visited us to help me decide. I'd planned to give her one anyway, but her visit convinced me to do more. I gave her a really nice one and stuffed some candy hearts in the envelope too. I'll be running by Rosinceks' place after detention tomorrow. I'll drop the card off then. I'll admit to you, though, that I'm still really bothered about her riding around with Jack Drude."

Maggie gave a small smile that hid her guilt about knowing Mary's plans and then listened as Jimmy read his story, which was about a sickly boy who loved a garden statue that was really a beautiful fairy princess in disguise.

"Totally sappy!" Maggie exclaimed after he'd finished.

"There's love in it," Jimmy admitted, "but it's love between family members and unselfish love between others. It's not sappy. What did you think, Joey?"

"It was long. I liked it, though, especially the part about the Spirit of the Place. I liked his superpowers. It was a little sappy, but not like lots of other stuff."

"No, it's totally sappy!" Maggie gave no ground. "I like it, Jimmy, but don't you think unrequited love is even sappier than love shared? Anyway, I've got to go finish writing out my valentines." She hurriedly gathered her things and ran upstairs.

Once in her room, she giggled at how much she enjoyed teasing her brother, but secretly his story had inspired her, especially the character of the boy's sister and what she said about women wanting freedom in their lives. The ideas in Jimmy's story, combined with elements in the tree poem that she had written earlier, had sparked an idea for her own story. After jotting down notes, she turned to the more immediate task of writing out her valentines. She decided to give a nice one to Robert. He had become her best friend over the last few months.

**Fantasy stories written by Jimmy, Maggie, Joey, and other children in the neighborhood can be found in *Joey Meets the Ghost Elf and Other Stories*, by Gordon W. Fredrickson, forthcoming in 2024.

CHAPTER 29

SECRETS SHARED
AND KEPT

Maggie couldn't sleep. She had finished writing out her valentines, and she was eager to develop her idea for a fantasy story, but now her mind was heavy with Mary's problems. She had promised not to tell Jimmy about the plan, but she ached to say something to her brother to explain why Mary was riding with Jack. Thinking that Jimmy might be engaged in one of his late-night vigils, she eased herself out of bed and, with the blanket wrapped around her, crept toward the room her two brothers shared.

Sure enough, Jimmy was peering through the window at the garden gate. She sat on the floor next to him and asked, quietly, "See anything?"

"No. I sure wish I could see more than a few yards south of the gate, though. Maybe then I'd know how Sport gets loose."

Jimmy's flashlight created a dim circle of light on the floor next to him, and as Maggie watched, he casually turned over the tablet in his hands to keep the writing out of her sight. "You keeping a diary?" she whispered, half kidding. But she didn't wait for a response. Determined to say something before she lost her courage, Maggie rushed out, "Jack prowls the neighborhood at night. Mary's seen him outside Rosinceks' house in the evening."

Jimmy misunderstood and turned to face his sister. "She's still seeing him!"

Maggie sensed his anger. "No, no, *she has seen him* lurking outside in the trees at Rosinceks' place. He is spying on her. Mary hates him. She didn't ride with him willingly. He forced her to ride with him. Mary told me he prowls around at night and steals things. And he spies on people with his binoculars during the day and at night. She made me promise not to tell you. She worries about what he will do to you and her, and me, too." Maggie was relieved to get it all out.

Jimmy was silent as he rolled ideas around in his head. Finally, he spoke, as if relinquishing a big secret. "Some things are starting to make sense now." He turned over the tablet, adding, "I've meant to show you this for weeks, but I didn't want to worry you or Joey or the folks, either. So keep it between us." He picked up his flashlight. "I've been writing down events, curious events, as they happen. I wish I'd put dates in on all of the entries, but I did on a few. I've separated the events into two lists—one labeled *Dancer* and one *Other Events*. I've been trying to make sense of it. What you just told me about Jack may help."

Maggie saw a third column labeled *MS*, but she said nothing about it and, instead, focused on the other two columns. Of the four entries under *Dancer*, none had a date. Maggie pointed to the one that read, *Friday, 10pm, clear, windy, dark, danced for 3 minutes, not as bright as last summer, Sport did not bark.* She said, "That was the Friday you fought with Jack. I remember it because we hadn't seen it for a long time. Not since late summer."

"And the two listed above it are from the summer," Jimmy remarked. "They have the same description: *Near midnight, danced for 3 min. Sport did not bark.* And look over in the other column: *Saturday, going to hayloft in a.m., Sport gone, clip mangled. Pliers?* That was the next morning, when Shaurel came over and told us about Matt Schroedler."

"You didn't say anything about the clip being mangled," Maggie complained.

"Look," Jimmy whispered defensively, "I didn't want to worry everybody. Jeez, Mom and Dad have enough to worry about. Besides, I had no answers then, but now I'm thinking it's Jack who released Sporty. The way Sporty cuddles up to Jack makes me think he gives my dog treats. But how did he charm Mary?"

"With threats, Jimmy. Not with treats. And not with charm, either."

Neither spoke for a short time. Finally, Maggie said, "Jack's prowling might explain why we have fewer eggs some mornings. And it seems some of the heavy hens are missing. They're so tame and like to be picked up and stroked. I've missed them since last fall. He probably took a couple of them too."

Jimmy nodded and then confessed, "I suppose you figured out that the title of the other column stands for *Mary Schroedler*? I started noticing her strange behavior toward me during her mother's illness last March. I wrote down *M avoids me* several times, always adding the place or the situation. When she helped me after the fight with Jack, I felt hopeful. That Friday night I wrote *M in car with J. Any chance for me?* She was back to her old self, but after Matt died, things became twisted again. Everything was strained between us, but she seemed to grow even closer to you. I was happy for that, at least. But then her visit yesterday seemed to make things right."

Tortured about whether to encourage Jimmy or tell him the truth, Maggie said, "She really likes you, Jimmy."

"And I like her, a lot," Jimmy confessed. "Billy's been giving me some advice about dating when we train on Sunday afternoons. Well, you know how I don't want to start dating too young, but Billy said Dad gave him some good advice when he was falling for Anna but was reluctant to say anything because she was so young."

"Really? Our dad gave dating advice?"

"Yeah. Dad told him to never toy with a girl's feelings. If you think you like her, say something to let her know your real feelings. You can move slowly, but keep moving forward. That way you both keep interested and love grows."

"Good advice, I think." Maggie choked out her answer, wishing she knew how to warn her brother and still keep Mary's secret.

Jimmy smiled with enthusiasm and exclaimed in a whisper, "I'm going to take Billy's advice and ask her out to a movie. Dad told me I could use the car if they aren't using it."

Maggie stayed silent, disgusted that her own cowardice had led her brother into false hope. Sneaking out of the room, she noticed Joey sleeping with his blanket wrapped around his head. She envied his innocence.

Guilt followed Maggie to bed, where she lay thinking about her role in Mary's life. No one else in the neighborhood knew of Mary's abuse. No one else knew of her plan to escape. Would it be better to tell her folks? Jimmy? The police? But Mary had pleaded, "You mustn't tell anyone." Now, though, Maggie felt she was helping her friend toy with Jimmy's feelings.

CHAPTER 30

HAIRCUT

On the Monday before Valentine's Day, the last-hour bell rang at three ten, giving Jimmy five minutes to travel from his gym class to his locker on the third floor and then on to the first-floor detention room by three fifteen. He dumped his textbooks at his locker, put on his coat, and fished out the paperback novel he would read during detention and shoved it into his back pocket. With plenty of time remaining before he had to report, Jimmy decided to stop at the third-floor lavatory instead of the first-floor lavatory because it would be less crowded. Also, he would miss the immediate pandemonium that broke out in the second-floor hall and stairwells after the last bell. Approaching the lav, as the students called it, he thought, *Funny that Robert and I joked that we never mastered the art of the three-minute dump, and now I'm serving detention for being late for class for that very reason. Honestly, I don't know how other kids do it.* What he did know was that the subject was better left as a joke between friends.

The first of the two lav doors sprang back to close, as did the second. And then Jimmy froze, astounded at the scene before him. Robert lay face down on the hard floor, held in place by a big kid kneeling on his back and pinning his hands behind him. A junior named Gary, wearing a letterman jacket, was kneeling on the floor, using a scissors to cut the top of Robert's long hair.

Taking no time to think or plan, Jimmy grabbed the three-foot-tall metal wastebasket and crashed its steel-rimmed bottom into the big guy's side with enough force to roll him off of Robert. Jimmy's stomach turned over as he recognized Tom Ryan struggling to maintain his balance as he screamed in pain. Then, grabbing the wastebasket's open top with one hand and bottom rim with the other, Jimmy dropped it over Gary's head and shoulders, spilling wet paper towels around him. Gary slammed back against the metal partition around the commode. Robert sprang to his feet, and the two sophomores raced out of the lav.

"I took their damn scissors!" Robert exclaimed, holding the weapon high in the air. "I kyped the scissors from the self-appointed barbers of the lav. Your swing made Gary drop it! Nice shot!"

Robert's hair had been hacked to the scalp on top, and drops of blood oozed from a small cut near his forehead. Jimmy took out a white handkerchief. "Here, hold that on the cut. I've got to get to detention. Good thing I stopped in to take a leak. See you later."

"I'll meet you when you get to the railroad tracks." Robert gave his friend that incessant smile that proclaimed a challenge to the world and its inhabitants. "If I hurry, I can make it to Bill the Butcher in time to have him improve my haircut."

Hurrying to the stairs, Jimmy calculated he still had time to stop at the lav on the first floor. A minute later he was taking off his coat and settling into a desk in the detention room. He opened his book to the marker and stared at the page, unable to concentrate on the story as his heart raced. *Jeez! What the heck! Why did they do that to Robert?* Gary was capable of nearly anything, but Tom was a really nice guy. Was Sutter's BS getting to him? Jimmy felt like Tom had betrayed their neighborhood friendship, and like he had betrayed Tom by hitting him with the wastebasket. How would this work out? Would they be waiting for him after detention? If not, how long before they got their revenge? He and Robert were no match for the two of them. After countless battles with Jack, Jimmy knew he could face Gary with an even chance, but Tom? Though smaller than Jack, Tom was big. He was athletic. Would he and Tom ever be friends again? Having to choose between Tom and Robert was unfair, and he blamed Gary, but he wondered how much Coach Sutter's constant anti-long-hair rhetoric had led to their cruelty. Would they be waiting for him after detention?

CHAPTER 31

MAKING A DATE

Relieved that Gary and Tom were nowhere in sight after he got out of detention, Jimmy stopped at the variety store to pick up a small box of candy on his way home. With his purchase stuffed into his coat pocket, he had begun his run home when he spotted Robert in his mother's two-tone red-and-white 1955 Chevy parked on the railroad tracks. As Jimmy opened the passenger door, he heard the disc jockey introducing Pat Boone's "Ain't That a Shame."

"Get in the car, Bandit!" Robert ordered, enjoying the smile on Jimmy's face as he wasted no time climbing in the front seat and settling himself into the warmth of the cushions.

Jimmy demanded, "Does your mother know you have her car? And where did you get that haircut? It looks almost good!"

Robert turned the radio off to speak, but Jimmy urged, "Hey, leave it on."

Robert countered, "I've had enough of Pat Boone waltzing through Fats's song. Why don't they ever play Fats Domino on this station?"

"I hear it on late-night stations from the South," Jimmy said. "Sometimes I even hear Little Richard. They never play him up here. But if you're not playing the radio, answer my questions."

Robert tossed Jimmy's bloodied handkerchief to him and explained, "Bill the Butcher calls it a *Hollywood*. Says it's the first one he's done." Robert retrieved a comb from his back pocket and tilted the rearview mirror to look at his new haircut. He combed the long hair on the sides back to form his signature ducktail and propped up the half-inch-long hair on the top. "Crewcut on top with long hair combed back on the sides. Am I a leader in fashion or what? And the car? Well, you know I'd never take Mom's new car without her permission. Her idea. Mom felt sorry for you when I told her about your detention. I don't know why, but she thinks you're a good influence on me. Imagine that!"

"What? Me being a good influence?"

"No, me needing one."

"Robert, you're strange," Jimmy taunted.

Robert answered, "But not a stranger. You're gross."

Jimmy answered, "But not a grocer."

"Hey, that's a good one," Robert answered, and before Jimmy could continue, he bragged, "Say, I've got to tell you this before I bust a gut. I'm sitting in the chair, getting my buzz, when guess who comes in?"

"Haven't a clue."

"He can shoot like a champ but can't dribble or pass worth a shit."

"I'm starting not to care."

"Jerry Storch! The tall, skinny senior who made a basketball career out of bench-sitting."

"Still not caring," Jimmy assured him.

"Well, he steps in the shop to update Bill the Butcher because Bill likes to keep up on sports, like it's a professional requirement for a barber. Anyways, Jerry says, 'Guess my chance of starting in Friday's game has improved. Tom Ryan and Gary Snider fell down the stairs in school while they were horsing around. Tom is limping pretty bad and Gary has a cut on his right hand. Sure, I feel bad, but I won't shed too many tears if I get a chance to start.' Ha! What do you think of that, Bandit?"

Nearly speechless, Jimmy managed, "Jeez! I wouldn't have wished that on either of them, especially Tom."

"You are just too nice of a guy. Those guys didn't care if they hurt me. And what do you think they would've done to you if you hadn't got the best of them?"

"You're right, but Tom is my neighbor, and—"

Robert interrupted, "Hey, man, what's up with *the barbers of the lav*? What did I ever do to them?"

Jimmy smiled at the wordplay. He was no opera expert, but he had heard the title *The Barber of Seville* more than once. "I don't know, but it was pretty mean. Really, cutting your hair against your will! I don't think we've heard the last of it, though. I think I hurt Tom pretty bad with the wastebasket, and Gary never lets go of anything."

"I think the scissors ripped open Gary's hand when I snatched them away from him, and I know you nailed him pretty good too. But what are they going to do? Report us by whining to the principal? I can hear them bitching, 'Gosh, Mrs. L, we were just giving the boy a haircut against his will when a sophomore interrupted our fun and beat the shit out of us.'"

Jimmy smiled in spite of himself. "I guess I did, didn't I?"

"Yeah," Robert encouraged him. "I think you're ready for Jack Drude! Don't give me that dumb look. Maggie tells me you are training hard with your cousin, who is as big as Jack and probably a hell of a lot smarter."

Jimmy didn't deny anything but switched the subject back to what it had been. "Gary and Tom might be lying in the weeds for us to get even."

"I'm ready for 'em!" Robert joked. "But seriously, I don't think Tom is that kind of guy. He didn't seem to want any part in it in the first place."

"Hope you're right. Gary is, but he's the only mean one in the family. His sister is in our grade and really quiet. His kid brother, Jerry, is a go-getter. He's a town kid who really works hard. Gets up early for his paper route every morning and works evenings washing dishes at Frank's Café. And he's out for sports too. I'd sooner milk cows than do his chores."

"He's a ninth grader. How do you know so much about him?" Robert asked.

"He was helping Sutter put away equipment the Friday afternoon I was serving detention last fall. Sutter let the two of us work alone on the job. He knew where everything belonged. He and I talked for over half an hour."

As Robert began driving, both boys kept their remaining thoughts on the topic to themselves. Then Robert said, with enthusiasm, "I'll have you home in no time, Bandit."

Jimmy raved, "Wow, I love this car. It still smells new. I'll bet your mom made you promise to drive careful."

"Yeah, and I will too. Don't want to screw up my chance of getting a license in a couple months. I tried to get Mom to go with me to accompany her permit-son, but she had supper to make and Dad will be home soon. Personally, I don't understand what they see in each other," he joked.

"You're not supposed to. You're just a kid. You're a joker without a joke."

"Yeah, well, you're a bandit without a band."

"You're friendly without a friend."

"You're a jackass without a jack."

"Well, you're a donkey without a key."

They played the word game only between themselves, unrehearsed and unplanned. Nothing they shared with others. They had invented it, and there were no rules. Exchanging insults that made no sense was their unique way of bonding. Young men didn't hug. Once in a while one of them accidentally spewed a fun phrase, but no one tried to. It wasn't even a real competition. It was small talk without a subject.

"You're toilet paper without a toilet," Robert jibed.

Jimmy laughed. "Hey, that's truer than you think. We use it but have no indoor toilet!"

"But you have a toilet. I mean, you don't go in the corners of the house."

"Only if the two-holer is occupied. Of course not. We aren't total hicks."

"You're a hick without a hickey!"

Jimmy giggled. "Watch your driving or you'll be a driver in the ditch. A big wheel without a wheel." Then he added, "Hey, thanks for taking me home."

"Sometimes I think you only like me for my potential access to my mom's fine car," Robert kidded.

"What other reason could there possibly be?"

"Well, you get to rescue me from unwanted haircuts."

"There is that. But sometimes I think you're only kind to me because you like my sister."

"What other reason could there possibly be?" Robert asked. Then he began another story. "Say, when I stepped out of the barbershop, who should be passing by but Winston Washington—you know, the junior, the one in our typing class."

"I don't really know him, but I know who he is. Everyone does. He's the only Negro in school."

"Well, he sits next to me in typing, and we like to race during speed tests to see who shifts their carriage first. Sometimes he beats me and sometimes I beat him. Anyway, he saw my haircut, and his first reaction was 'Wow! Half military and half delinquent!' Cuz his dad is in the military—that's why they move around a lot."

Jimmy chuckled. "That's a good way to describe it, but now I'm jealous that you have a friend besides me."

"I sure do," Robert teased, "which means I have twice as many friends as you do. And ain't it funny, though, with him being a year older and all, we probably would've never spoken if we hadn't been assigned seats next to each other. As it is, though, there's not much visiting allowed in Mrs. Scharing's typing class."

"Zero to none," Jimmy emphasized.

Robert drove on in silence, ambling down the gravel road. As they approached Rosinceks' driveway, Jimmy said, "Turn in. I have to drop off a valentine and a box of chocolates for Mary. I can't stay long. I have to get home to throw down silage."

As they drove into the yard, Barney barked twice before retreating and waiting to see who emerged from the vehicle. Jimmy knelt to pet him before ramping up the courage to walk to the front door.

Caroline Rosincek answered the door. "Jimmy! Welcome. Come in."

"I have to get home for some pre-supper chores, but could I see Mary, please, Mrs. Rosincek?"

"She's outside with Emil. I think they're in the shed starting the Model A. Mary takes quite an interest in Al's old car."

Jimmy saw Mary exit the shed and wave as she exclaimed, "Jimmy! I wondered what Barney was barking about."

Jimmy crossed to her quickly and said in a cheerful yet serious voice, "Happy Valentine's Day, Mary."

Surprised, Mary exclaimed, "A card *and* a gift! I never expected this, Jimmy."

Her pleased expression encouraged Jimmy to add, almost too quickly, "Would you like to go to a movie with me next Sunday afternoon? I don't have a license yet, but you do. So, it's legal with my permit and all."

Mary's mouth hung open for a moment before she answered. "Well, yes. I'd like to, but I can't this Sunday. I'm doing a family thing with Rosinceks, and I promised them."

For Jimmy the pause seemed longer than it was, but in a moment, she added, "How about the next Sunday afternoon? I would love to go with you then."

Fleeting disappointment turned to joy as Jimmy replied, "I'll pick you up at half past one." Then he turned to leave.

Mary watched as Jimmy approached the car. She waved to him before he got into the passenger side. For a moment she regretted sending the letter asking Jack to run away with her. But she had mailed it that very morning. There was no turning back now. Her plan to run away was the best course to take. She had to be her own hero. Leaving Jimmy was something she had to do, but lying about making a date with the boy she loved left her numb. She had lied to his face, and she hated herself for it. She longed to be free of secrets. Free of lies. With shoulders slumped, she trudged to the house, preparing the facade she needed to fool her hosts until the time came to escape her past.

CHAPTER 32

CONSEQUENCES

Tuesday after school, Joey vowed to say nothing to Maggie and Jimmy about the problems he had encountered walking home. He wasn't about to whine how Valentine's Day was a mess and how others misunderstood him. He wasn't about to blame his brother and sister for their bum advice. So, when he heard the squeaking brakes of the bus slowing down to let them off, he made sure he was eating butter and jelly on a big slice of bread and reading the funnies as they burst into the kitchen. He gave them his best nonchalant act, showing how he barely cared they were home. He knew he could handle it on his own.

Maggie was first to ask, "How did Valentine's Day go, Joey?"

"Yeah," piped Jimmy, "how many hearts did you break?"

That was too much. "It was the worst day of school ever!" Then Joey choked on his snack because he had swallowed while he was yelling.

"Jeez, Joey. I'm sorry to hear that," Maggie said as she slapped his back to help release the bread from his windpipe. After a bit, he took a drink of milk to clear his throat.

"We're listening, Joey," Jimmy said with his best big-brother demeanor. "Tell us all about it."

"Why should I? You guys never listen anyway."

"Tell us now," Maggie said as she and Jimmy sat down with him at the table.

Silence worked on Joey, and sensing that he had a captive audience, he began his tale of woe. "Well, the school day wasn't so bad, but the walk home with those goofy girls was the problem. We had fun at noon, though. The weather warmed up and the sun made the snow slippery, so Ronnie and I worked up a good slide down the south hill where we could take a run and do a stand-up slide for thirty or forty feet. And nearly all the boys in grades six, seven, and eight are either Ronnie's brothers or his cousins, so we didn't have any trouble keeping off the kids who had new overshoes with good grips that would tear up the slippery snow.

"Anyway, right before lunch break was over, we let Mary Ryan and Liz Brummer take a couple runs on our slide. Mary's a pain, but Liz is lots of fun, even though she's a girl. I know you tease me about Liz sometimes, but I like her fine, but not as a girl. She is just a lot of fun and never cries like some of the other girls do. She never talks about girl stuff to me either.

"Teacher let us pass out our valentines about ten minutes before the end of the day. Some kids who were really stuck on someone made sure to hand that person the valentine, but most of us just went from desk to desk and put them out. If you were lucky, no one was at the desk because they were passing out valentines.

"So when school was over, I just stuffed all my valentines in my lunch bucket before we moved the desks to sweep the floors, and after we finished sweeping, I ran out the door as fast as a greased hog out of a loading chute. Somehow, I met up with Shaurels before I hit the road. No one said much until Caroline moved up by me and said in a weird voice, 'Thank you so very much for the valentine, Joey.' She was kind of blinking her eyes. I sped up a little and said, 'Sure thing,' but she was right next to me again in no time.

"Then Mary Ryan appeared from nowhere and said, 'Joey, you sure surprised me with that valentine!' Then she turned to Caroline and said, 'Joey gave me a valentine that said *Be Mine*.' She walked backward in front of me, and I nearly ran into her until I decided to stop and she said, 'You know, Joey, I don't mind that you are a whole year younger than I am because you are big for your age. Also, most of the girls agree you're sort of cute, but I can't be your girlfriend, you know.'

"I felt my chin drop to the dirt. I'm thinking, *Why do I care about this?*

"Then she said, 'You know why we can't be sweethearts, don't you?' I should've been able to give her about a zillion reasons, but I couldn't make a sound. She really wasn't waiting for a reply anyway. She just goes, 'It's because you're not Catholic, and Mom said I shouldn't even consider boys not of my own faith because they are all heathens.'

"I said, 'Jeez, I sure the hell am not interested anyway.' I didn't mean to throw in the *hell*. It just slid out. Ronnie says it lately, but I remember Mom saying, 'Don't blame on others what comes out of your mouth.'

"Then Mary started harping on my Pledge of Allegiance mistake again by shouting, 'Blasphemy is right down his alley! I can't tell you how many times I've heard Joey Carlson say *indivisible* while the rest of us remembered to say *under God* during the Pledge of Allegiance.'

"I yelled back at her, 'They only just changed it! I just forget sometimes!'

"She yells back, 'It's been a couple years, Joey, and forgetting about something as important as *under God* shows you're a heathen!' She was pretty sure on this point. I tried to walk around her, but I accidentally hit her lunch box. It fell open and all her valentines spilled onto the wet road. I swear I didn't mean it. She yelled something and stooped to pick them up, and I tried to help her pick them up before the wind took them too far. But then the Shaurels caught up and Caroline came up to me and her face looked kind of wet. She said, 'You gave Mary Ryan the same valentine you gave me! How could you do that!' Her face wrinkled up and she started crying.

"I said, 'Jeez, Caroline. I just wrote them out as they came out of the box.' But that just made her cry harder.

"Then Margaret put her arm around her sister and said, 'Don't let it bother you. He's just a heathen, anyway.'

"I wanted to smack the whole bunch of them, but since they were all girls, I just shut up and hurried home. But now I feel like a coward. I hate Valentine's Day!"

Maggie put her hand on Joey's cheek, a gesture he often rejected, but he warmed to it at the moment. "You did the right thing, Joey."

Joey smiled and let her put her arm around his shoulder and give him a half hug, like she used to do when he was little. Joey figured it made her feel good.

Then Jimmy said in his big-brother voice, a voice Joey loved to hear, "You did nothing wrong, little buddy. You did nothing wrong. In fact, you behaved like a real man."

Joey relaxed, satisfied. He loved it when Maggie hugged him and Jimmy called him little buddy, like they did in the old days when they were all just kids.

CHAPTER 33

THE MESSAGE

Getting the mail was Jack's one bit of control in his home life, which was otherwise dominated by his brothers. Mail was never addressed to him specifically, but looking at the bills and daily paper headlines gave him some sense of belonging. He enjoyed the walk down the driveway every day, even in foul weather, and he never drove his car just to get the mail.

The Drude mailbox was one of those country mailboxes large enough to hold packages from Sears & Roebuck or Montgomery Ward, so that foul weather didn't damage the contents before the resident got the mail. When Jack opened the hinged door of the mailbox on Wednesday, his nostrils caught a pleasant whiff of perfume, a familiar scent he immediately associated with Mary Schroedler. Aware of the fact that it was the day after Valentine's Day, he hurriedly dug through the contents to seize a letter addressed to him. Although it had no return address, he knew it had to be from her, the woman who had dominated his thoughts for months.

He crossed the road to the end of his driveway, sat on the snowbank, and opened the letter carefully, collecting all of the loose candies inside in his big hand. He read them aloud one by one: "Be Mine, Forever Yours, Sweet As Honey, My Valentine. U R Mine, U R Fun, I Am Yours." The candies were pink or green or white or yellow. Smiling, he popped one into his mouth and dropped the others into his coat pocket.

Next, he read the valentine, which was signed *Mary Schroedler*. The tablet paper inside was folded in half twice. He unfolded it carefully, read it twice, and then said, "I knew she felt that way all along." Proclaiming it aloud made it true, coloring his vision, obliterating any doubts that might have popped into his mind if he thought about the contents of the message objectively. It was the reality he wanted. He read the message again:

Jack,

Sorry this valentine is late, but I had to be careful no one discovered I sent you one. The Rosinceks are kind people and treat me well, but it's like a prison here. My movements are restricted, but it is better than being with my brothers, who I hate. I need to escape. I was hoping we could run away together. I know where we can go and live on a farm with a friend of mine far away. We can get jobs and be free of everybody else. I'm counting on you to do this for me. And for us.

Park your car below the first hill on Shaurels' driveway and I will meet you there about eleven thirty at night on Sunday, February 19. If I don't show up, it will be because I couldn't get away, but I am pretty sure I will be able to.

Be sure to have a full tank of gas and extra cans of gas in the trunk. We don't want to have to stop at any gas stations on the way because they might be looking for runaways.

See you soon,

Mary Schroedler

Jack began planning. He had a couple of days to decide what to bring, but he'd wait until Sunday to load all his stolen property into the Model A. On Sunday night he would bring his two-gallon gas can and take the one from Carlsons' shed and fill them both at Carlsons' gas barrel. Two smaller cans were better than a five-gallon can because it was hard to pour from a five-gallon can into the tank on the Model A. He'd make two trips from Carlsons'—one to fill the tank and one to fill the cans to take along, as Mary had suggested. He embraced the idea of not stopping anywhere. He decided he'd bring some cheese along to eat and swipe some crackers from his mother's cupboard.

When he stole gas from Carlsons or Shaurels, he normally limited the amount to a couple of gallons at a time so they didn't notice, but Shaurel had recently put locks on his barrel, so he would have to take it all from Carlsons. It didn't matter if they noticed because he would be gone. He'd park on Shaurels' driveway where Mary suggested and walk to Carlsons' farm as many times as necessary to steal as much gas as he needed.

Although he could feel his buttocks getting wet from sitting on the snowbank, he didn't care. In a few days he'd be gone from his thankless family, and he'd be with Mary. No one else would be around to distract her, either. He, Jack Drude, would be in control. Suddenly glad he had kept the necklace and bracelet, he reached into his coat pocket and let his fingers glide over the smooth stones. Rubbing the large red stone between his thumb and forefinger, he remembered Mary's softness firmly against him. He longed to feel it again, but this time, there would be no interruptions. As he anticipated the upcoming meeting, he was sure that nothing could stop him now.

When Friday came, Jack was eager to get started, figuring it was his last opportunity to shop the neighbors' sheds and barns and take anything worthwhile. Before midnight, he began combing the nearby neighborhood. He had intended to skip Carlsons' place, but he decided to check if they still had the two-gallon gas can. He entered the yard by way of the usual shadows, opened the toolshed door, and shined his flashlight to spot the two-gallon gas can in its normal place. Sporty gave a light yelp as a subdued greeting, and Jack strode over to the dog, knelt down to cradle his head in his hands, and whispered, "Here's your freedom for one last time." Using his pliers to unwrap the wire from the broken clip, he set the dog free. Sporty ran full speed to the northwest, making Jack smile as he uttered, "Tonight, you lose your dog. Sunday night, I take your girl."

CHAPTER 34

THE WILD

Jimmy rose at half past four on Saturday morning, his usual time to begin his training ritual. The morning darkness offered mild temperatures, just a few degrees below freezing, enhancing his usual positive morning mood. Like many farm kids, Jimmy was a morning person, although he never used the phrase to describe himself. For him, there was no other way to be but to look at the beauty around you and enjoy it all. It was, after all, free.

His bright demeanor faded when he saw that Sporty was not at the end of his chain. The wire he had used to fasten the broken snap had been untwisted. The heavy-gauge wire could not be untwisted by hand. It would take a pair of pliers. Was it Jack? "Not a good start to the day," he whispered to himself. "I hope you come back home alive, Sport. If you do, I'll lock you in the granary. Shaurel doesn't have to know."

Orange Tom kept him company as Jimmy exercised on the rope. Although he left the door ajar in hopes that his dog would appear, the time passed with no sign of him. Soon his folks arrived, and as they began morning milking, Jimmy told them Sporty was gone. Dad remarked that they should lock him in the granary when he came home. Then he added, "But he won't be coming home if Shaurel sees him in his cow yard."

The three of them carried silage to the cows, a tub each to thirty head, half a tub each to ten heifers, and several tubs divided among many small calves. After they finished, Mom left for the house to clean up and prepare breakfast, Dad carried tubs of mixed ground corn and oats from the grain box, and Jimmy climbed the chute to throw down silage for the next day, a chore he usually did after school during the week.

As Jimmy climbed the silo chute, he heard the *boom, boom, boom* of shotgun blasts to the northwest. Twenty minutes later he climbed down the chute, and as they walked to breakfast, Dad speculated, "Sporty's not home and shotguns are blasting west of Shaurels' place—not a good sign, Jimmy."

Jimmy nodded, but neither of them said any more about it as they washed up for breakfast. After eating, the family headed out to do more chores—Mom washed the milking equipment in the milk house, Joey and Maggie tended to the chickens, and Dad and Jimmy cleaned the barn, loading the solids and liquids from the gutters into a wheelbarrow that Dad wheeled out to the growing pile of manure east of the barn. By spring that pile would reach a size of about twenty yards by fifty yards and up to five yards deep, and the family would haul it onto the fields with the manure spreader in May.

Finished with the barn cleaning, Mom joined Jimmy and Dad and the three of them started putting fresh straw under each cow standing in a stall. Their work was interrupted by George Shaurel and Frank Droeser quietly descending the stairs, each carrying a shotgun: George a twelve-gauge pump and Frank a double-barrel twelve-gauge.

George was his usual gruff self, a perfect contrast to Frank, who was always lighthearted and ready to joke. Frank was older than most of the neighbors at about sixty, short, slim, and full of energy. In quick bursts in which they often interrupted each other, the two men told a grim tale of their early morning adventure.

After witnessing Sporty and the little black-and-white collie chasing his cattle that morning, Shaurel had followed the dogs west out of the yard, after first telling his wife to call Frank to help with the hunt.

Frank joked, "We nearly lost them trying to cross your fields, Martin. You see, I only got two feet to hold up my weight, but the dogs have four holding their slim torsos. I punched through the snow so many times I thought George would have to carry me!"

"We lost sight of your dog and the female for a bit as they ran over the far west hill," George asserted, "but then we heard yipping, and we figured she had her pups somewhere back there."

Frank described how they had split up, approaching the haystack from the north and east. "The pups were basking in the early morning sun on the south side of the stack. I didn't want to just shoot into the group because I didn't want to wound them and cause them to suffer. I wanted a direct shot. Well, then the female ran ahead of us, and George got a clean shot and took her down. Sporty ran across the river to the trees. Smart dog. He knew neither George nor I was about to follow him. We called the pups, and when they came, we were able to shoot them one at a time, even as some of them tried to run away. There were seven pups in total. We ain't proud of what we done, but it had to be done by someone. Those pups would be adult wild dogs by summer."

George added, "Yeah, we need to keep it safe for our animals around here. Safe for civilization. Martin, we're asking you to shoot your dog when you see him."

Martin turned to Jimmy as he addressed the two men. "It's the boy's dog, but I think he knows what needs to be done."

The three men looked at Jimmy, who made eye contact briefly with his dad. Then he nodded somberly, as if agreeing, but his heart held out hope. He could make a pen for Sport in the hayloft. No, it would have to be the dark granary, and Sporty hated to be locked in the granary. Why did the neighborhood have a right to take his dog?

George and Frank, satisfied, turned to leave, pleased to have eliminated a four-legged threat to the safety of cattle and chickens and squelched seven future threats before the pups became a problem. In a parting comment of reconciliation, Frank added, "I know it's hard, Jimmy, but imagine a year from now if all those dogs had grown and multiplied with pups and such. We would have to hunt them all down, and there would be many more of them."

The two men left.

Jimmy heard his mom say, "He's right, you know. George shot his own dog a year ago because it was chasing O'Kerans' cattle."

"I know, Mom."

During a dinner of fried potatoes and loose hamburger with macaroni and cheese, Dad explained his plan. "We all know the hay in that stack was spoiled when we took it off the field. We only stacked it there because I don't like to burn ruined hay in the summer. It's too risky for fire to spread to trees by the creek. What I want you kids to do is drag those dog carcasses to the stack this afternoon. Leaving them lie in the open would attract varmints. I'd help, but I promised Emil that I'd help him castrate his hogs this afternoon. Then tomorrow, if it ain't too windy, I'll douse the stack with some gasoline and light it up. The snow cover will keep the fire from spreading."

The three kids nodded in reluctant agreement and after dinner headed out toward the old haystack before one in the afternoon. Their job was a grim one, but they knew their father was right.

Once clear of the yard, Jimmy led his siblings west on the road. "If we take the road until we get to the creek, we can follow the high bank where there will be less snow. Frank said the snow and ice on the field made their trek difficult where they crossed the field to the haystack. I hope to avoid that. We will have to cross the river, but it's shorter than going up Shaurels' driveway and cutting across our field the way he did."

"Why are you bringing your sled?" Joey asked.

Maggie answered flatly, "Because we have to move eight dead dogs to the haystack. Shaurel said some of the pups are big. Carrying them in the snow would be tough." She avoided mentioning that the carcasses might also be bloody.

"Oh," Joey responded.

"You should stay home," Maggie urged him. "You really don't want to see this, Joey. It's dead puppies, mangled by shotgun blasts."

"Yes, I do!" Joey asserted. "You know I hate being treated like a kid. I want to be a grown-up, like you guys, like Mom and Dad. People think being a kid is all fun and stuff, but it ain't, you know."

Jimmy stayed silent, understanding his little brother's needs. He had been there. And so had Maggie. Silence ruled as the three youngsters easily covered the distance to Spring Creek, where they left the road to head north through an uncultivated wasteland where the small creek that flowed north through their land dumped its water into Rock River, which flowed east through the Carlson farm. The land surrounding the area was called the Wild.

"Instead of staying with the creek elevation," Jimmy told his siblings, "we'll take the higher route with less snow. Plus, if we stayed at the creek level, we'd have to climb back up a steep hill to get to the haystack. Better to not descend the hill in the first place."

Maggie countered, "But going this route, we'll have to cross the wide gulch, which is about twenty-five feet above the river! Mom and Dad tell us to stay away from this area."

"Not a big deal," Jimmy explained. "Besides, we have to have some adventures. It's safe if we're careful. There are wide logs across the two separate gaps to make the crossing. I'll crawl across and push the sled ahead of me."

When they reached the log over the river, Jimmy stopped. The three youngsters took a moment to enjoy the majesty of the place.

They sat on the snow-covered ridge, gazing down a long slope where huge rocks protruded five feet or more into the air and oak trees that had kept their leaves for the winter formed a ceiling that blocked some of the sun. Where the slope met the river's edge, huge elms and cottonwoods reached higher into the sky than the ridge where they sat. Full of ice and snow, the place seemed clean and silent.

"Everything looks so pure!" Maggie exclaimed and, with some reverence, added, "It's easy to see why this place is called the Wild."

Jimmy agreed, saying, "Isn't this place something? It's rugged and beautiful! Nothing is more beautiful or more powerful than nature."

"It's like a North Pole adventure." Maggie chuckled.

"I'm glad we don't have to farm it," Joey admitted before he could stop himself.

Jimmy and Maggie laughed. Then Mags added, "Dad won't even let the cows in here when he fences in the rest of the fields for fall grazing. He always fences around it, doesn't he?"

"Yes," Jimmy said. "Dad told me that the first year he and Mom were here, they fenced it in and let the cows here in the fall. Then one day they found one of the milk cows on her side against a huge rock. She was dead when they found her. She must've lain down to rest. When she tried to get up, the hill was too steep and she rolled against the rock. Dad says that the dairy cattle can't take the weight of their own bodies if they lie on their side too long. I mean, look at the sizes of their stomachs!"

"I wonder how Shaurel does it," Maggie inserted, and everyone laughed at the thought of George Shaurel lying down on a hill and trying to get up.

"I saw Little Collie and Sport here last fall," Maggie said to Jimmy, as if confessing a secret. "Before school one morning, when Joey and I stood guard on the road while Mom and Dad and you chased the cows across the road to pasture the fields, we yelled at the cows, and Sporty appeared from nowhere to help. And, as usual, he made it worse by chasing the cows at the head instead of nipping their heels. About the time they were running in all directions down the road, Little Collie showed up and nipped Sport a few times until he followed her lead. The two of them rounded up the cattle and ran them through the gate just like they knew exactly what to do. It was amazing."

Jimmy added, "Do you remember how Dad praised that female? He said he'd never seen anything like it. He thought she was probably part border collie."

As Jimmy rose from his perch on the snowbank, he assured them, "The log is still solid and wide, but don't try to stand up. Stay on all fours and don't look down."

"Didn't you walk across standing up last summer?" Joey wanted to know. "Why are you crawling now?"

"It wasn't slippery then," Jimmy answered. "Besides, I'm not your circus act. We have business to attend to. If I fell, you'd be hauling dog carcasses on your own." He mentioned nothing about what would happen to him if he fell. "I'll go first. Then Joey, and Maggie last. Okay?"

Maggie and Joey nodded. Jimmy crawled slower than he would have if his younger siblings had not been watching. He did not want to make light of the risk. When he reached the other side, he waved his arm for Joey to start.

Joey took a slow pace without looking down, but he didn't want to look frightened either, so he managed a few faster spurts. Suddenly, his foot scraped a piece of loose bark that fell down to the creek bed. Everyone held their breath until it bounced on the ice below. Joey stiffened up.

Jimmy started crawling toward him, saying, "Hang on, Joe. I'm coming."

Joey moved forward again. "Heck, Jimmy, I'm okay. I was just cleaning off the path for Maggie."

Maggie did not appreciate the humor. "Very thoughtful of you, Joey. I'm right behind you."

Jimmy turned around, Joey and Maggie crawled forward, and soon all three were safely on the other side. Joey admitted he felt a little weak-kneed. Jimmy told him to breathe deep and walk around a bit.

"We don't have far to go," Jimmy said, "before we head west toward our fence line and the haystack." He walked a couple steps across the snowpack and jumped up and down. "I think it's good. Let's go!" They forged ahead, bracing for the tragic scene they expected to see once they approached the haystack.

Pulling the sled behind him, Jimmy started to trot. Then, he pulled the sled up even with himself, jumped on, and rode the sled while standing. The rides were short, lasting only until a runner broke through the snow, stopping the sled and sending Jimmy crashing over the front. But he jumped on again and again, because nothing deters youthful energy from fun, even if the fun seems more like work.

Maggie had no trouble keeping up, and Joey managed it too. In some areas, shallow snow cover on the meadow made trotting easy, but the children slowed their pace when the bodies of the dead puppies appeared as lumps of color against the pureness of the white snow. Each of them stopped to stare at the small, mangled bodies and the bloodstains nearby. Jimmy remarked solemnly, "Let's count them to check if any are alive."

CHAPTER 35

A FAMILY TRAGEDY

Maggie and Jimmy ran from each body to the next, easily finding all seven and confirming all were dead.

"I'm glad none are alive," Maggie confessed. "I don't know what we would have done if one had been alive."

"Right," Jimmy agreed. "Though I know what we would've had to do."

Joey asked, "What? What would we have to do?"

Neither Maggie nor Jimmy answered the question.

Kneeling by a pup that looked like Sporty, Maggie suddenly sobbed, "Never had a chance. Poor little doggies never had a chance!" Looking around, she asked, "Where's Little Collie?"

She and Joey walked to the other side of the stack, where Jimmy, kneeling by Little Collie's body, silently wiped tears away.

Seeing Maggie cry had made Joey's throat tighten a little, but seeing his big brother's tears hurt him more than seeing the dead puppies. Feeling overwhelmed, Joey exclaimed through his own tears, "It's just not fair!"

Jimmy screamed at the sky, "No, it's not fair! She was such a great dog. The way she handled the cattle. The way Sport seemed to worship her. It's such a damn shame to see her end up like this. Now, she is just a pile of cold, bloody hair in the snow. Her body's already stiff."

Maggie came over to stand by Joey, putting her hand on his shoulder. Neither of them had ever heard Jimmy spill his thoughts as he did now.

"These were Sport's pups. Now they're all dead. Little Collie and her pups were Sporty's family. I wish I could've protected them all." Jimmy paused as he stood up to look around. "I wonder where Sport is. I sure wish I could've kept him home."

Maggie and Joey had stopped crying, but Maggie worked herself up to it again as she exclaimed, "Jimmy, it's not your fault! Look at this mess. It's a tragedy. Sporty's whole family is dead! But he couldn't have had a family if he'd stayed with us. What dog would give up a family like this for people? It wouldn't be natural."

The kids didn't use the sled; they just dragged the bodies over and laid them gently against the haystack. After taking a last look at Sporty's family, they turned to walk home the way they had come, but before they made twenty yards, Sporty came running toward them.

Jimmy knelt and held the dog's head between his hands. "Bad dog. Missed you. I thought you were dead. Stupid mutt." Mags and Joey rushed over to pet him too, but Sporty didn't give them much attention as he pushed his body tight against Jimmy's chest.

After a time, Jimmy stood up and said, "Come on, Sport. Let's go home!" Sport ran circles around him as they walked few more steps toward home, but he stopped about ten feet behind the kids and sat on his haunches. Jimmy called, but Sport stayed put. Jimmy commanded, but Sport whimpered and lay on the ground with his head between his paws. Jimmy's shoulders slumped as he and Sport looked at each other across the short distance.

"Please come, Sport. Come home." Sport didn't budge. Jimmy took a step toward him, and the dog turned and ran a few feet away before he stopped and looked back at Jimmy, who tried calling him again. "Please come, Sport. Come home with us."

Sport stood still for a moment before turning away and trotting to the haystack without looking back. Jimmy called, but Sport only turned once to gaze at him. The dog and the boy looked at each other for a while. Then, as before, Sport put his head down, turned, and trotted away.

Jimmy choked out, "Well, Sport, I guess this is goodbye. Can't blame you much. Why should you trust me? 'Come home,' I say. Home to what? The best I can promise you is imprisonment. The worst is death, and George

Shaurel can give you that." He turned away to begin the trek home, hiding his tears from his siblings.

"There's nothing we can do, Jimmy," Maggie consoled him.

"That's the bad part. If I could do something, I would try."

Joey exclaimed, "Maybe we can get Sport and hide him!"

Jimmy laughed before running over to Joey and slapping him on the back. They both giggled lightly, like they used to, and Jimmy said, "Maybe we'll try that. You're quite the little brother."

The gesture seemed to lighten the mood, making Joey feel warm all over and making Maggie smile, but Jimmy groaned. "Maybe I should have locked him in the granary instead of chaining him up."

Joey yelled, "He hates that! He used to howl all night when you did that. And who wouldn't? Nobody would like to be locked in the dark granary all night where you can't even feel the wind or see the sun come up."

"Jack would've probably just opened the door to let him out instead of unsnapping the chain," Maggie stated, before she realized that maybe Joey didn't know about Jack's night-prowling.

Joey stopped and asked, "So, the ghost didn't free Sporty? It was Jack?"

"Sorry, Jimmy," Maggie said quietly.

"Don't worry about it, Mags," Jimmy replied. "I'm so sick of all these secrets we keep from each other that I don't even know who knows what anymore. We're not sure who it was, Joey. That's why we didn't tell you." Turning back to Maggie, he added, "And you're right. Whoever let Sporty loose could've just as easily let him out of the granary as unsnap the chain."

What hurt Jimmy most, though, was something that he couldn't say to anyone. He couldn't say that it was Jack Drude, not Sporty, who had upset the rules of the neighborhood. And yet, he had to get rid of Sporty and had no way to get rid of Jack Drude. Maybe Joey was right. Maybe they could hide Sporty. He thought hard about it but said nothing more for a few steps, then lamented, "But he is my dog. I should've done something to save him. Now it looks like all I can do is sacrifice my dog's life for neighborhood peace. And Sport has already sacrificed his whole family."

Maggie added in earnest, "He's your dog, Jimmy, but we all love him."

The use of the word *love* bothered Joey a little. He didn't understand. Mom and Dad liked Sport too, but would they say they loved him? Maybe love wasn't all just sappy stuff. Lots of kids said they loved their dogs and even their cats, which was hard to figure, but Mom and Dad said, "It's just a dog. Don't get attached." Was it love that messed up everything? Seeing Jimmy angry and helpless bothered Joey even more than seeing Sporty lose his dog family or not come when his master called. Jimmy was always able to figure things out. Now he was troubled. Joey wanted to do something to help, but all he could do was imagine a better world for dogs and people, and maybe ghosts, too.

CHAPTER 36

DOG STORIES

When they got to the dirt road, Jimmy started picking up small stones from the road and throwing them at the base of the electric poles, his shoulders still sagging. No one was in a hurry to get home.

As the three of them trekked down the road, Jimmy said, "I remember when we got Sporty after what Dad called our dog drought, when our family didn't have a dog for about five years. Mom said it was because after Shep died, they didn't want another dog. I guess Dad and Mom really liked Shep. Mom talked about how he would go with her out to the dark pasture in the morning to get the cows. Shep would know right where the cows were in the big pasture. 'Without Shep,' Mom told me once, 'getting the cows in the morning would've been like trying to find your shadow in the dark.' And the bull never bothered Mom when Shep was along. He tried once, and Shep went after him so hard the bull ran way into the deep water of the slough, but Shep jumped on his back and chewed on him until he ran out the other side and bucked him off. Shep could get pretty tough if you messed with Mom. I was really young yet, so I had to ask Dad why he needed a bull in the pasture anyway, and he said to 'protect the cows.' I asked him, 'Why not just use Shep?' Dad got really serious and said, 'Well, I would, son, but I want the cows to fear Shep, not be friends with him.' Dad had an answer for everything.

"Anyway, we picked up Sport on the Friday after Thanksgiving. We had spent the day cleaning calf pens and hauling wood, so we were all really tired. But that night after chores, we all got into the car and Dad drove to Skluzaceks' place and drove the car right up to the barn. They were finishing the milking and carrying the cans to the cooler. Albert hollered a big 'Hello' but didn't give us his usual big wave because he had an eight-gallon can of milk in each hand. He's not that big, but he's got arms like Popeye the Sailor Man. We stayed in the car until he came to greet us with a big grin. I'll never forget that. He poked his head through the open window of the car and said, 'You decided to take one of those pups off my hands, then?' We followed him into the barn, and Lulu and Joan showed us the pups. Lulu said she wanted to keep them all, but her dad said they had to give away all five pups. When we got close to the mother's box, the cutest one came running over to me because I had squatted down. Seems the little guy wanted to come home with us. I named him Sport because he was so friendly and because Joan told me he wanted to play all the time. We had a lot of fun together. I just could never get him to stay home. It's my fault poor Sport may die today."

Mags used her bossy voice as she exclaimed, "Don't say that! Dad says you can't control nature. You have to roll with it." Trying to lighten the mood, she continued, "On the way home that day, Mom told the story of Laddie, a dog that she had when she was a girl. It wasn't her dog, though, because only her brothers could have a dog. She had seven brothers, and she and her sister had to wait on them because the men were more important in the family than the women."

"Yeah," Jimmy interjected, "but she told Joey and me that we'd better not try to pull that line on you, Maggie, even just for fun."

Maggie laughed. "Dad says things have changed for the better, even if only in some places. Anyway, Laddie was so good with cattle that when Mom was a little girl and herded the cows on the grassy strip by the cornfield, all she had to do was sit on the grass and read. Laddie kept the cows close together and away from the corn, so Mom got to read all these really good books like *Anne of Green Gables* and *Little Women*. I read them too, and so did you, Jimmy, even though they were books about girls. Maybe it taught you about girls and that's why they all like you. You have to admit, you did say that Mary Schroedler is a little like Anne in the book."

"And I wish I'd never told you that," Jimmy said. "I liked *Anne of Green Gables.* It was pretty funny, and I liked Anne because she was a tough girl. She reminded me of Mary because Mary is tough, and I like her for that, plus a lot of reasons."

Joey said nothing, but his mind raced. Jimmy usually said it was better not to let anybody know what you feel inside, but Mom told him to let people know his feelings. Dad had told him, "It's something you have to learn for yourself. It's always best not to spill your guts, but you have to learn for yourself when to keep your trap shut and when to open it." Maggie's answer was best. She'd said, "Look, Joey, you're lucky you don't have to learn this the hard way like I did. Only tell people stuff if it will do you any good. Otherwise, keep your mouth shut!" She had seemed mad about something.

They walked in silence for only a few yards, before Jimmy blurted, "On Monday I asked Mary to go to the movies with me this Sunday, which is tomorrow, but she said she was going with the Rosinceks to a family thing. She agreed to go the following Sunday, though." Jimmy grinned at his brother and sister. "So, there's some good news."

Maggie's heart skipped a beat, and her mind raced. Seeing her brother smile about an upcoming first date with Mary should've made her ecstatic, but why was Mary not free this Sunday? Was it her friend's day to escape? Jimmy would be heartbroken. She hated herself for keeping the secret from him. Now that she knew the day Mary planned to escape, should she tell him? She wasn't sure. No, at this moment, all she could do was bury her secret even deeper.

They turned into the driveway and hurried to the house. Once in the kitchen, Jimmy explained that they had piled the dogs by the stack. Dad said he would burn the haystack early the next morning if it wasn't too windy. Maggie and Joey took turns describing the horror of seeing all the dead pups, but they refrained from dwelling on the subject. They knew too much talk about it would put them back at the scene, ready to cry.

Dad asked, "Did you see Sport?"

The pause was longer than it would take to just tell the truth, but Jimmy's mind was racing. He finally said, "Yes. I called, but he wouldn't come home with us. With all his faults, the dog isn't dumb. Fact is, I think he is probably smarter than most dogs. He knows his fate now, and he knows that even his own home is a danger to him."

Dad said, "If we see him, we'll have to shoot him, if we get a good shot. It's our responsibility. It'll be better than if Shaurel does it, and we know he will shoot him if we don't. You know I'm right, Jim."

Jimmy nodded as Dad continued, "I'll get the twelve-gauge ready and set it by the door, but it won't be loaded. The shells will be on the table. He might come home just from habit around suppertime."

Mom told the kids to wash up for an early supper. As Maggie went to the sink, she peered out the window and saw movement in the yard. She yelled, "Sport!"

Dad went for the gun, but Jimmy stood up suddenly and said, "He's my dog. It's my responsibility."

"Okay, Jim. I'm sure you'll only get one shot, but I'll be right behind you with another shell."

Jimmy rushed out the front door with Dad and Mom behind him, none of them taking time to don a coat or cap. "Kids, stay here," Mom instructed before closing the door. "You don't need to see this."

But Maggie and Joey followed the others out the door and ran toward the road bank. Sport ran down the driveway and turned east at the road, while Jimmy ran to the edge of the bank, which was about twenty feet higher than the roadbed where it met Shaurels' driveway. Jimmy, standing high on the edge, raised the twelve-gauge, leveled the long barrel at the dog, and took only a second to give his running target the appropriate lead before squeezing the trigger with his middle finger.

The blast shattered all hope on a sunny afternoon. Maggie, Joey, and Mom had stopped only a few yards behind Jimmy, and the five of them watched as Sport buckled to the ground, his body skidding on the icy surface of the dirt road for a couple of yards after the impact. Then he was still. No one had ever seen him lie so still.

Dad stepped forward to offer Jimmy another shell, but he didn't reach for it. He knew he hadn't missed. Dad handed Maggie the shell, and Jimmy handed Mom the gun. Dad said, "Let's go get him, Jim. We'll get our coats and take your sled. I think if we shovel some snow away from the east side of the barn, the ground may be frozen only a foot or so. We'll get the pick and the shovel and we'll bury him properly before supper."

Mom added, "Let's all help. He was our family dog."

Jimmy breathed in deeply and exhaled, his shoulders rising and lowering as they always did when he made up his mind to do something impossible. Joey and Maggie began to cry a little, but Jimmy was all cried out.

CHAPTER 37

THE GARDEN GHOST

Unlike those whose jobs required them to work only Mondays through Fridays, dairy farmers get no reprieve from the daily demands of rising early for work. Still, Saturday and Sunday nights held the aura of the end of a work week. Fun-loving farmers, willing to sacrifice sleep for fun and suffer on Monday mornings the consequences of late nights filled with card-playing and beer-drinking, eagerly looked forward to the weekend. Mary and Martin Carlson were two such farmers, and despite Saturday's horrendous events, they were eager to attend a Sunday-evening card party.

But first there was the gruesome task of burning the haystack. Jimmy helped Shaurel and Dad carry gasoline to light the stack early on the windless morning, and the carcasses burned quickly along with it. They tended it for several hours before piling snow on the ashes.

The burning of the stack made church attendance impossible, but it left Maggie and Joey with time to work on special projects. While Mom baked bread and cakes in the kitchen, Maggie, inspired by her short poem about going inside a tree, worked on her fantasy assignment for Mrs. Deem on the table in the living room. Joey, who seemed unusually secretive, stole away to work in the cold silence of his bedroom.

After dinner, Jimmy and Dad cleaned a calf pen while Mom cleaned and packed eggs. Maggie was still writing, but she noticed that Joey was not reading his usual comic books or western novels. Instead, he continued to work alone upstairs.

Around five in the afternoon, everyone gathered for an early supper so they could begin evening chores early, and by seven thirty that evening Mary and Martin had left for the party. Their three kids sat down at the kitchen table to play some games.

"I vote we play euchre," Jimmy said, "but whatever you guys want to do is fine with me."

"I agree with playing euchre, but first, I think Joey has something to show his big brother," Maggie said. "He's been working hard on it all day, and he showed it to me to see what I thought. It's pretty good, Jimmy."

"I'm waiting," Jimmy said. "What is it?"

"I wrote a story for you, Jimmy!" Joey exclaimed. "I said I'd write a story and it would be a good one without mushy love in it. What happened to Sporty gave me an idea. I worked on it all day. Can I read it to you now?"

Jimmy laughed. "I'm sure I don't deserve it, but I am tickled. Let's hear it!"

Joey stood up and began to read.

The Dog and the Garden Ghost

By Joey Carlson

February 19, 1956

A shy, kind ghost lived in a large vegetable garden on a farm during the summertime because he liked seeing all the birds and insects in the garden. Garden Ghost did not enjoy the company of other ghosts, but he liked watching the family weed and hoe the garden. He especially liked to watch the family harvest green beans, peas, tomatoes, and cucumbers in the summertime. In the fall, he watched them dig potatoes and pick the large golden pumpkins off the ground, but he knew that after the pumpkins were picked, winter would be coming soon. In the winter, nobody came to the garden because it was covered with ice and snow, and the harsh winter wind blew across the garden. No birds or insects or people came to the garden in the winter, and Garden Ghost mostly stayed hidden near the buildings by the edge of the garden or in the small attic of the chicken coop, where he could lie down in the darkness on the straw-covered ceiling.

He knew that the three children watched for him to appear in the garden from the upstairs window at night, but Garden Ghost was too shy to come out of hiding. Other ghosts might have teased little boys and girls by appearing and disappearing in front of them, but Garden Ghost did not enjoy playing those games. He was too shy and sad and lonesome. He needed a friend who he could spend time with and who was loyal to him and not mean. But it is hard for a ghost to make friends because when a ghost shows himself to people, they run away screaming.

One day he found a friend who didn't care that he was a ghost. The friend was the family dog named Sporty. Sporty spent his nights chained to a stake by his doghouse near the garden in the summertime. When it was really cold in the wintertime, the family would shut him in the steel granary where it was dry and out of the wind. Sporty did not like being locked up, but when it was really cold, the family locked him in the granary for protection. He knew they were doing it for his own good, but he did not like the dark, lonely place.

Sporty wanted to be free from being locked up and free from being chained at night, but the family didn't want Sporty to visit the neighbors and chase their cows at night, which Sporty usually only did with other dogs.

Sometimes Sporty would hear noises outside when he was locked in the granary. If they were common noises, like the scratching of tree twigs against the steel granary or the wind rushing around the outside of the round granary, he did not mind. But sometimes, if the noises were strange, like chickens being frightened by an animal, he would growl a warning. If the chickens were making noises, Garden Ghost would awake too, because he slept on the straw in the ceiling of the chicken coop and could hear the chickens if they became restless.

One night before midnight, the chickens started to make a lot of racket. Garden Ghost looked around to see if there was anything threatening them, but he found nothing. Sporty kept growling even after the chickens settled down, and Garden Ghost decided to enter the granary through the walls and try to settle down the dog. He did not appear as visible at first, but he tried to watch Sporty a while to see what was wrong. Sporty could not see in the granary because there was no light, but Garden Ghost could see clearly, and he noticed a large rat that was near the dog. Sporty was unable to kill it because of the darkness, so Garden Ghost allowed himself to spread his light into the granary, which made it so Sporty could see the rat. In seconds Sporty pounced, killing the rat without much effort. In the same instant he saw the rat, Sporty saw Garden Ghost, too, and he associated Garden Ghost with the light. Immediately, he was grateful, and he wagged his tail and whined to make friends. Garden Ghost was happy to have a new friend, and after that Garden Ghost and Sporty always spent their nights lying on the soft oats in the granary where Garden Ghost created a soft nightlight that made the granary more comfortable for Sporty. In the summertime, Garden Ghost spent his nights nestled near the doghouse, unseen by anyone but Sporty. From then on, the two friends were always together.

Joey looked up from his story, announcing with a wide grin on his face, "The end!"

"That is the best story I've ever heard," Jimmy said. "I mean it."

"A happy ending but not mushy," agreed Maggie.

Joey felt proud. "I think Sporty needed a friend. One who isn't mean."

"Don't we all," Maggie said.

"You know what, Joey?" Jimmy teased. "If you think about it, I'd say Garden Ghost would have given Sporty a valentine."

Fearing a negative reaction, Maggie scolded, "Come on, Jimmy. Why bring that up?"

Joey giggled. "Believe it or not, I thought about that, and I agree."

"Probably not a mushy one, though," Jimmy said.

"I found out that they are all mushy, if you believe what they say. I thought a lot about what happened at school, and I'm glad I gave everyone a valentine. But every valentine I gave was just a card with a message on one side and blank on the back. A one-side card. Kids who had a special friend, a mushy friend, gave them a card that opened up and had a message inside. The valentines I gave had no inside. They weren't meant to be mushy."

Maggie gave Joey a good-natured slap on the arm. "Well, aren't you the young detective! And you're probably right! Did the card you gave Mary open up, Jimmy?"

"Heck, yes. We've been giving each other valentines that open for years. How about you and Robert?" Jimmy shot back in fun.

Maggie blushed. "Let's get back to Joey."

Happy to regain the center of attention, Joey said, "I've been thinking. Maybe I should feel good about those girls liking me. It doesn't hurt anything, not really."

"That's true, little brother," Jimmy agreed. "Just be kind to them. Maybe the others will slack off being mean."

"Or not," Maggie said.

The three of them nodded and smiled.

"I don't even mind being called heathen by a bunch of jerks," Joey said proudly.

"Atta boy, buddy. *Joey the Heathen*," Jimmy repeated. "Sounds like a mobster."

The three of them broke out into laughter at the image. Maggie hit Joey's arm lightly, and Jimmy playfully tousled his little brother's hair.

"I'll get the cards to play euchre," Maggie said as their laughter subsided.

CHAPTER 38

EUREKA

Maggie plopped the deck of cards on the table, sat down, and asked, "Hey, Jimmy, what took you and Dad so long in the barn after milking tonight? Mom was already in the house for ten minutes before you came in." Before he could answer, she teased, "Was he giving you some pointers on fighting? I thought he usually only did that after a party, not before."

"Nothing like that. Nellie's drinking cup was leaking and Dad was trying to close that old valve in the water line—the one that takes a pipe wrench to turn it—and the frame that holds the adjusting nut on the pipe wrench actually broke. He asked me to get the new one we gave him last Father's Day, but I couldn't find it in the shed. He eventually turned the valve with the big crescent wrench, though."

"I know where that new pipe wrench is!" Maggie hollered, jumping up from the chair and grabbing her coat off the wall hook at the end of the kitchen. "Come on, Joey. Grab the flashlight and follow me, and we'll show big brother how we store tools where we can find them."

Jimmy stayed seated until Maggie urged, "Come on, Jimmy."

"Okay, okay," Jimmy agreed, but the two younger kids were out the door before he got his coat on.

Once out the door, he saw Maggie and Joey rounding the corner of the toilet-toolshed. Confident that he had thoroughly searched the shed, he entertained how he might tease Maggie about being wrong, which was her most dreaded fear.

Jimmy paused to enjoy the evening, although his heart ached at the absence of Sporty coming out of his doghouse to greet them. The moon gave some light, but they had not switched on the powerful yard light, so shadows prevailed in the small farmyard. The mild weather before and after Valentine's Day had melted some ice on the road and shrunk the snowbanks a few inches. Temperatures dipped only a few degrees below freezing at night, making the night air and its breeze almost pleasant. As his siblings entered the toolshed and pulled the chain on the light fixture, Jimmy stopped to survey the clear night sky as the wind teased his face with soft gusts of cool air.

Then he saw it! The white light danced near the garden gate, fewer than ten yards from him. He smiled as he casually walked toward it without hesitation or fear, saying with the conviction of Sherlock Holmes, "Well, Dancer, you've been discovered." He reached into the dancing whiteness to grab it by a limb, and then he reached in further to grab its narrow trunk and shake it gently. The light streaming from a large crack in the toolshed reflected off the leaves that the small tree had held onto all winter, and the wind propelled them to a dance.

"If I had cut the volunteer trees and bushes growing in the garden fence line as I had planned to do last summer, you would never have existed," he said to White Dancer as if it were a real being.

Just then, the dancing stopped, and in a moment Maggie and Joey came running toward him. "We couldn't find it," Maggie groaned, "but I know I put it in the old pail. I know it."

Jimmy, having lost his taste for teasing, reassured her, "You probably did put it there, but someone took it. I'll show you why I think so. Go back and put on the light. Leave it on and come back here, and I'll show you what your resident detective has discovered."

When Maggie returned, the three of them watched White Dancer in silence.

Then Joey said, "So, for sure, there's no ghost. I feel better knowing there's no ghost."

Jimmy explained, "I didn't know the ghost was simply light reflecting off leaves that moved in the wind. I just knew it was not a ghost. I only discovered it because you put the light on, Maggie. And now we have something more concerning than a mere ghost. We have a burglar. And if we surprise him, he could become dangerous, like a cornered animal."

Without a word to his brother and sister, Joey ran into the house and slammed the door behind him.

"Well, at least one of us has some good sense," Maggie said. "I'm going in too."

"Good idea," Jimmy agreed.

In the kitchen Maggie asked, "Who put on the light? Who was in our shed in the middle of the night those times we saw the ghost? Someone stealing our tools? I think I felt safer with it being a ghost."

"I agree," Jimmy offered. "Especially if the prowler is Jack."

"You think it's Jack?" Maggie whispered with earnest concern. "Suddenly I'm not real keen on being home alone when Mom and Dad are gone. Now I wish we would've told them."

"We know Jack prowls at night, and he probably put the light on in the shed to look for tools to steal," Jimmy explained. "Jack Drude was our ghost, and I'm sure he released Sport so he wouldn't make any noise while he was prowling."

"So, do you think Sporty might still be alive if it wasn't for Jack Drude?" Joey asked.

Jimmy wanted to say yes, but instead, he said, "Maybe, but I probably couldn't have kept him home anyway."

Maggie disagreed but kept it to herself. Instead, she suggested, "Let's lock the doors, pull the shades in the kitchen, and close the drapes in the living room."

"Yeah, we can do that," Jimmy said, and he began pulling the shades in the kitchen.

After Maggie locked the east and west doors, the three siblings met in the living room, where Joey said, "Hey, it's only nine. Let's watch television."

"You would think of that," Maggie teased. "But I agree. I want to watch it too. Folks are gone. We can watch TV as long as we want."

Jimmy added, "And if there's nothing good on, we can go upstairs to listen to the radio without worrying about it being too loud."

They enjoyed watching *General Electric Theater*, but halfway through *Alfred Hitchcock Presents*, Maggie said to Joey, "Is this going to give you bad dreams?"

Joey said nothing.

"It's just a television show," Jimmy said. "Let's just finish the program and go upstairs and listen to the radio."

"I'll feel safer upstairs," Maggie admitted.

By half past ten the three of them were in the boys' room. With the lights off, they sat on the floor by the west window, staring into the darkness near the garden fence. They talked reverently about the nights they had seen the White Dancer, treating the moments as supernatural even though they were now privy to the mystery.

Maggie whispered, "I get chills just thinking about how we were actually witnessing a crime in progress. What if he had seen us?" She inadvertently backed away from the window.

Jimmy tried to show more courage than he felt at the moment. "I'll go down there now if I see the dancer. He should fear us, not the other way around."

"I hope we don't see it!" Joey exclaimed in a whisper.

"Me too," Maggie added.

In silence the three stared into the darkness, and as if it had been conjured, White Dancer appeared before their eyes.

"Oh, shit!" Jimmy let slip a little too loudly.

"Are you going out there?" Maggie asked.

"Not out the front door," Jimmy responded thoughtfully. "Watch the dancer while I get dressed. I'll go out the back door and scoot around the granary and try to spot him as he exits the shed."

"I'm coming with!" Maggie and Joey exclaimed at the same time.

"Okay, but if I let you come with me, you have to follow my instructions, not argue with everything I say like you usually do."

The two nodded and dressed hurriedly, but Maggie's mind flooded with the realization that Jack was probably stealing gas tonight because tonight was the night Mary planned to escape. She tortured herself with the question of whether to tell Jimmy the truth. Saying nothing about Mary's planned escape would mean he would find out the moment Mary drove away. How could she be so cruel to her own brother! But if she told him, would he try to stop Jack? And if Jack discovered Mary's lies, what would he do to them all?

"Don't switch on the yard light!" Jimmy warned. "But each of you should bring a flashlight. Don't switch it on unless I tell you to."

They crept out the back door, around the house, and into the dark shadow of the steel granary. Their hearts sank to see that the toolshed light was off, but Jimmy heard faint clanking by the gas barrel.

Jimmy whispered to his accomplices, "He must've gone into the shed to take our two-gallon gas can and is filling it from the hose."

"What are we going to do?'

"Follow him. I'm sure he'll take the dark shadows through the orchard and then to the road."

He didn't. In a frantic moment, Jimmy signaled them to back up and go around the granary as the intruder came toward them, carrying not one but two gas cans. Jimmy figured he must've brought one along with him. The three kids moved counterclockwise around the granary, keeping its bulk between them and the intruder.

They circled back around the granary until they saw the burglar carry the cans toward the trees east of the house.

"I'll bet he's parked in Shaurels' driveway. He'll be lugging those cans through the snow among the trees. Still, I doubt I can get to his car before he does. Stay here." Jimmy went into the shed and used his flashlight to find an old bumper jack and a set of wheel chocks connected by a short rope. Back to the granary in less than a minute, he said, "Let's go. We'll run down our driveway and hide along the road until we see him."

The three sprinted down the driveway, slowing down only when they reached the trees about twenty yards from Shaurels' driveway. From their hiding place in the shadows of the roadside trees they watched the burglar cross the road, carrying the cans of stolen gas.

Jimmy snorted and said in a whisper, "That's Jack, all right." He could feel the hair on the back of his neck stiffen. "I'd recognize that walk anywhere.

I'll bet he'll be pouring that gas into a Model A. And that's why he isn't using a five-gallon can. The gas tank opening is way up near the middle of the windshield."

"What are we going to do?" Maggie asked.

Jimmy didn't hesitate. "You and Joey take the road east and wake up Frank Droeser. Tell him the situation. Tell him to telephone Shaurel and that they should bring their shotguns to catch Jack Drude parked on Shaurels' driveway stealing gas."

They left immediately, without any questions, but after Jimmy had disappeared into the darkness, Maggie stopped and, with her hands on Joey's shoulders, faced him, pleading, "I need you to do me a big favor, and I don't have time to explain. You go on ahead and wake Frank. Tell him what Jimmy said. Tell him to telephone Shaurel and that they should bring their shotguns to catch Jack Drude parked on Shaurels' driveway stealing gas. I have to do something else. Sorry, Joey. I know it's dark and it's scary, but can you do it?"

Joey nodded and said, "Sure, I can." He left without another word.

Intent on stopping Mary on her way to her rendezvous with a Model A, Maggie hurried west to where she expected Mary to emerge from the pasture shortcut. She had to convince her to return to Rosinceks' house tonight.

Joey trekked east through the dark night, the moonlight reflecting off snow giving just enough light to show his path. His mind conjured images of ghosts and bogeymen in the thickets on the road banks. He grasped his flashlight firmly but kept it off. A flashlight would just call attention to him. Without a light he could move silently through the dangers hidden in the darkness. He began trotting, and in rhythm with his steps, like a platoon of soldiers singing a marching cadence, his mind repeated, *I can do this. Yes, I can. I can do this. Yes, I can.* When he had less than fifty yards to go, he began smiling with confidence, a confidence that he could overcome darkness, a confidence that darkness was neutral toward him.

Droesers' big, black, shaggy dog growled and barked as Joey trotted into the yard, but when Joey called out, "Easy, Rover, it's just me," the dog wagged his tail and his bark became less threatening. As Joey pounded on the door, the dog's muzzle drooled against his glove, searching for a friendly pat on the head. Joey petted the dog even as he pounded on the door, yelling, "Mr. Droeser, Mr. Droeser! Frank! It's Joey Carlson. I need your help!"

A call for help from a neighbor was never refused in farm country. Frank came to the door and pulled Joey into the house even as he began relaying his message. In minutes, Frank was on the phone with George Shaurel and then dressing. As he directed his wife to call the sheriff, Frank grabbed his shotgun and shells. Joey followed him out the door.

Maggie waited in the shadows of the trees near the road. She must convince Mary not to run away tonight. What if she confronted Jack? Or what if she met Jimmy, and he thought she was running away with Jack and grew angry with Mary for lying about the date? How could Jimmy understand? The whole plan was too complicated to explain quickly. She wished she had told him the truth about Mary's escape plan. But when? From the beginning? Or tonight after they spotted Jack? There hadn't been time. And she had promised Mary not to tell.

She paced back and forth quietly. All the secrecy angered her. Why had she agreed to it? But the secrets she had borne were small compared to Mary's burdens. She scanned the distant darkness for her friend. What was keeping her? Suddenly, she turned to run toward Shaurels' driveway, whispering, "I'll bet she's already there!"

After Joey and Maggie left him, Jimmy steeled his resolve and cautiously moved up Shaurels' driveway. He hoped Jack was planning to go back for two more cans of gas. If he didn't, Jimmy would have to stop him from driving away. But if he left for a second trip, Jimmy had a plan. He would replicate the prank played on the Torgerson brothers, the details of which his dad had told him many times.

He hurried, but he had to be prepared to duck into the shadows if Jack came back down the drive. Coming over a slight hill, Jimmy saw Jack pouring the gas into the Model A. He moved as close as he could without getting spotted. Preparing either to duck into the shadows if Jack went back for more gas or to charge him to prevent him from driving away, Jimmy closely watched his quarry's every move.

After emptying the second can into the tank, Jack picked up the other one and hurried back down the road. Jimmy stepped off the driveway into the shadows of trees. He remembered Al Rosincek had said his Model A held less than twelve gallons. He muttered under his breath, "Taking a couple cans along on a trip, Jack?"

CHAPTER 39

PLANS COLLIDE

Waiting in the trees not more than twenty feet from Jimmy, Mary Schroedler sat on her small suitcase, eager to drive Jack's car away into her future. She had spotted Jimmy when he took refuge near the same group of trees. Seeing him now, she withdrew farther into the darkness and held her breath, smiling ruefully at the fact that Jimmy's presence might thwart her plan. For only a moment, she fantasized about stepping out of the shadows and convincing Jimmy to steal Jack's car and run away with her now.

No, he was too good for her. She was determined not to ruin his life. She remained still as Jack crossed the road toward Carlsons' place and Jimmy left his hiding place to hurry toward the Model A. Her opportunity to speak to Jimmy had slipped away as quickly as it had arrived.

Suddenly, Mary saw another friend appear behind Jimmy. Maggie! Did they know she was escaping tonight? Were they going to try to stop her? Feeling helpless to take any action to save her plan, Mary could only sit still and listen, though she was able to hear only bits of the conversation.

Once Jack was out of sight, Jimmy rushed into action, but stopped when he heard Maggie softly call his name.

He turned to ask, "Did Jack see you?"

"No, I easily avoided him. He ducked into the trees across the road to go back for gas."

Jimmy had questions, but he simply said, "I don't have much time," and headed up the driveway.

Maggie grabbed his arm, turned him to face her, and explained, "Jimmy, I'm sorry to tell you this now, but Mary plans to run away tonight. She lied to Jack to get him to park his car out here, and while he stole gas, she was going to steal the car."

Jimmy felt his knees go rubbery. So many questions, but he blurted just one. "And our date?" His mouth hung open after he said it.

"Mary loves you, Jimmy, but Jack has made threats to hurt us all. She thinks she has to leave for the safety of everyone."

Masking the pain he felt, Jimmy breathed deeply several times, making up his mind once more to do the impossible.

"What can we do?" Maggie pleaded.

"I might have a plan," Jimmy asserted abruptly. "No time for details."

"You always have a plan. Do you want me to find Mary to warn her?"

"Don't know where she is. Hold the flashlight for me while I set up the Torgerson trick."

After jacking up the Model A, Jimmy crawled underneath and stacked the two chock blocks on their sides, placing them directly under the axle near the right side of the vehicle. He crawled out from under the car, let down the jack, and checked to see if the right rear wheel touched the ground by trying to wedge his gloved fingers under the tire. He decided it was perfect. From the driver's side Jack would not see the wheel, and if he stopped the engine to come around to look, the gap between the ground and the tire might be too small to see. With Maggie holding the flashlight, he had completed the tasks in record time.

"All done," he said to Maggie. "Now, go to Shaurels' and see if you can hurry George along. I don't want you here if I have to confront Jack."

"Are you sure?" Maggie protested. "I could hit him with the bumper jack."

"And do time for manslaughter!" Jimmy gave a muffled yell. "No, please do as I ask. The Torgerson trick will delay him."

Reluctantly, Maggie left for Shaurels' place, and Jimmy ran to the trees for cover.

Mary remained huddled behind the trunk of a large elm, not ten yards from where Jimmy hid behind a tree. Having seen Jack go for gas and Maggie run off, she had no clear understanding of her friends' plans, but now she was sure her own plan to escape with the Model A was impossible to carry out. What could she do? Jimmy was close. The temptation to reach out to him pulled hard. She could run to him and explain, and maybe he would help her leave before Jack returned. Or maybe they could escape together before Jack came back? No, too much to explain. Not enough time.

Suddenly, she saw the man she hated move swiftly up the driveway.

Jack finished filling the tank with part of one can and stored the two cans in the back of the car. Pleased with his work, he checked his pocket watch. It was time to move his car to the rendezvous spot, about fifty yards ahead, below the next hill. To prepare for Mary's arrival, he fished the necklace and bracelet out of his pocket and placed them carefully on the passenger seat, arranging them as seductively as he knew how, with the red stone prominently facing up.

The old vehicle started perfectly. He put the Model A into gear and let out the clutch. Dismayed at the lack of movement, he pushed the accelerator harder; when that failed, he tried reverse. Nothing. Clearly, he was stuck, but how could it be? He got out and walked around the car to see what he could see with his flashlight. Spattered snow and gravel on the fender and running board told him the tire had been spinning, but for a moment he could not understand why. Then he remembered the story of the Torgerson brothers. He straightened up and hollered, "Damn it! Who's out there!" And he began rocking the car to tip it off the blocks.

Jimmy knew the power and anger of Jack Drude would soon topple the chock blocks. He stepped out of the shadows to the front of the vehicle and said, "Transmission troubles, Jack?"

"You're a dead man, Carlson," Jack yelled as he charged.

Jimmy tried to relax as he readied himself to grab Jack and use his forward movement to set him off balance and throw him to the ground, just as he had practiced with Billy. There was no time for doubt. The moment had arrived. As the man and the boy clashed, Jack slipped a bit on the refrozen surface of the road, helping Jimmy to tip his balance. Jack went down hard.

Jack used his hands to get up, offering Jimmy a target. He stomped hard on the closest hand before moving away quickly to the center of the road, near the car. Jack raged in pain, and although he didn't slow down, he took a more strategic approach as he circled to put Jimmy's back to the driver's side of the vehicle.

Jimmy feared he had spent the element of surprise. Had Jack figured out his move already? Doubts began to haunt him as Jack moved in fast and threw a hard punch with his right fist. Jimmy ducked to his right, taking the blow above his left eye and bouncing off the side of the Model A behind the open door. Without regard for the pain in his left hand, Jack swung his left fist, which glanced off Jimmy's left shoulder, forcing him to the ground. Jimmy felt Jack's boot kicking his ribs again and again, stealing his breath and weakening his resolve. He rolled under the car for protection. Crawling beyond Jack's reach, he remembered Billy's words: *You have to treat every fight like you're in a fight for your life.* He prepared to roll out from under the car when he had the chance.

"Come out, you damn little coward!" Jack screamed as he put his strength and weight to the side of the car, furiously rocking it on the chock blocks.

Sensing that Jack was about to topple the blocks, Jimmy lied, "You've toppled the blocks! Stop rocking the car! I give up! You win. Just get out of here and leave me be."

"No surprise. You never did amount to much. Stay there, then. I don't care. I got better things to do than screw around with a punk like you." He opened the door and stepped into the car with his right foot.

Jimmy rolled out from under the car in a flash, grabbed Jack's left foot, and pulled as hard as he could, dragging his opponent out of the car and onto the ground. But Jack broke free and got to his feet. Once again, Jimmy realized what he'd always known—he could not stand toe to toe and trade punches with an opponent of superior size and reach. Finding no opening to strike, he retreated out of range on the other side of the open door.

Slamming the car door shut, Jack teased, "I guess I'll have to wipe the road with you if you won't let me leave." He charged as Jimmy scrambled for a strategy and moved to several feet in front of the Model A, hoping Jack would follow.

Jack yelled, "You ain't gonna get away, you little weasel!"

Jimmy turned abruptly to meet his charge and used Jack's redirected momentum to bring them both to the hard surface of the driveway, rolling over once together away from the car before Jimmy broke free. He won the race to stand, but not in time to deliver a blow.

Jimmy raced toward the front of the car with Jack a step behind him, leaning forward and reaching toward Jimmy, who suddenly pivoted, grabbed his opponent, and, while slipping his own body under him, threw Jack forward and smashed the burglar's face into the front bumper of his own vehicle. Jack's large frame crumbled against the car. Jimmy had landed hard on his back with Jack's knees in his face, but, unscathed, he jumped to his feet to face Jack. His lifelong opponent lay half dazed on the frozen ground. Was he dead? Then, as Jack moved to get up, Jimmy remembered Billy's words: *If you get a big guy like Jack down, you want to keep him down!* Seeing Jack's forearm outstretched at a weird angle, Jimmy jumped high to deliver a crushing blow, his foot making contact above Jack's wrist. He heard a muffled *snap* before Jack's holler disturbed the night.

Then, something strange happened, something that ripped Jimmy's heart in two. Stalling for time to recover, Jack sat up, leaned against the bumper of his Model A, and yelled, "I don't have time for this shit, Carlson! I could stay and beat you to a shit pile. You know that I could, but I'll give you this round. You see, I've more important things to attend to. I'm meeting your girlfriend here tonight, and she's running away with me. Do you hear that! With me! Jack Drude and Mary Schroedler. And it was her idea, not mine. So, while you're left in this screwed-up neighborhood, I'm off living with your old sweetheart. Looks like the best man got the girl, punk."

Trying to reconcile Jack's proclamation with Maggie's story of Mary's plan, Jimmy's legs weakened and he nearly fell to the ground. He wanted to believe Maggie, and he did, but hearing Jack's lies ring out loudly in the night felt like a cannonball to his stomach.

Ka-boom! The sound of a shotgun rang out from behind the car, freezing Jack and Jimmy in place as the booming voice of George Shaurel shouted,

"That's enough, boys. Jimmy, if you don't mind, I'd like to talk to the Drude boy about what he might owe me for gas while we wait for Sheriff Kaeler to get here." Maggie followed him at a safe distance as he approached Jack.

Within minutes, Joey and Frank Droeser arrived from the other direction. Frank carried his loaded double-barreled twelve-gauge. All had stories of the night to share quickly as they listened to the siren of the sheriff's car approach. He parked a safe distance from the scene before the siren went silent.

Of medium height and built solid as a brick, Sheriff Kaeler stepped out of the driver's door to take command of the situation. Seeing Jack on the ground and the men with shotguns slung over their shoulders, he barked, "Looks like the situation is under control. Good. Good." His bass voice boomed with confidence and authority. "Frank, George, you want to tell me what's going on?"

After hearing their brief explanation, the sheriff directed his tall young deputy to cuff Jack. "Put him in the back seat, Deputy Schultz, but be careful with him. Then, you can drive the Model A back to the office."

As the deputy cuffed Jack, he commented, "He won't give us any trouble, Sheriff. I think his wrist is broken."

The deputy tried to confiscate the Model A, but when it seemed stuck, the sheriff told him to just collect the stolen property from Jack's car. They would send someone after the car later. Neither Jimmy, Maggie, nor Joey told him about the Torgerson brothers.

After checking that the Carlsons were okay to walk home, George left the scene, eager to get back to bed. "Morning will come too soon," he said in parting.

Jimmy and Maggie thanked him for helping out before they wished him a good night.

As Frank walked to the end of the driveway with the Carlsons, he asked, "He had his car loaded with stolen items. Did he steal all of that loot tonight? Why the extra cans of gas? Was he going on a trip?"

Jimmy said, "Maybe so. I'm sure the sheriff will figure it all out tomorrow."

"Yeah, I'm too tired to worry about it tonight," Frank said as the four of them reached the main road. "Good night, kids." He turned to walk east toward his place.

"Good night, Frank," the three kids said at the same time as they headed west toward home.

"Thanks for helping me out," Joey yelled in parting.

"Anytime, son."

"Yeah, you came at just the right time," Jimmy added.

"Oh, I don't know," Frank joked. "You seemed to have everything under control. But, you know, Jimmy, you should've just let him go. He's a dangerous guy. Nothing in that car was worth risking your life for."

"Not yet, there wasn't," Jimmy whispered to no one. "Not yet." And the three kids waved to Frank as they continued up the hill.

Moonlight had dimly lit the scene around the Model A. Mary had witnessed the fight between the two rivals with concern, resolving, if necessary, to step out of the shadows and to plead with Jack to let Jimmy alone, giving her and Jack more time to hurry off together. She was willing to sacrifice her future to save Jimmy, but she had hesitated as circumstances altered, and a moment later she had enjoyed hearing her champion get the better of Jack. Then her heart had broken when Jack told Jimmy about how she had planned to run off with him. She wanted to jump out from her hiding place to tell the truth, but she knew no one would benefit from it at the time. She had stayed in place through the arrival of the neighbors and the sheriff, and she had even laughed lightly when the deputy could not move the car, realizing she might yet get her chance to run.

Now, after everyone had left the scene, she smiled, even as tears were icing on her face and the cold had penetrated her layers of clothing. Ecstatic, she ran out of the shadows, eager to climb into the car.

Like the deputy before her, she did not notice the jewelry on the cushion. As she threw her small suitcase on the passenger seat, the tokens of lust slid between the cushions and out of sight. She rushed to the spot where Jimmy had left the jack, and after lifting the car with it, she crawled under to drag the chock blocks out and set them along the road. Then she let down the jack and dragged it next to the blocks.

Suddenly, a familiar voice startled her.

"I decided to come back for the blocks and jack tonight," Jimmy said.

Speechless, Mary opened the car door before she turned toward him.

She winced as Jimmy softly accused, "So, you planned to run away with *Jack Drude*? Jeez, Mary."

Mary knew Jimmy would not stop her from leaving, but she did not want to leave like this. "I would've never run away with him, Jimmy. My plan was to run away on my own after he went back for the second trip to steal gas. And I would have, too, but then you showed up. I've been watching the whole time, and what he said to you is only true in his mind because I wanted him to believe it."

Eager to hear more, Jimmy quietly listened.

"I have to leave here and go far away, where no one knows me, to a place where Jack and no one else can find me, not even my best friends, not even someone I care for, someone I love, like you. Otherwise, Jack will always try to hurt those I care about. He will always try to control me with threats. If no one knows where I am, we will all be better off."

Jimmy found his voice. "But I won't be better off. Not with you gone. I don't want you to leave. I want you to be here, with me. We have a date next Sunday, remember?"

"I'm not good enough for you, Jimmy. I am damaged goods, not just physically—I have dreams, nightmares, flashbacks. I'm terrorized. I've got to leave this place!"

Jimmy said nothing at first. He had great respect for a woman's resolve. He breathed in deeply and admitted, "I have a confession to make too. While we were jacking up the car, Maggie told me about your plans. I don't want you to leave, but I came back to help you escape."

Mary darted toward him. Placing her hands behind his neck, she pulled him toward her, holding his head as she kissed him hard on the lips. Startled only briefly before he understood the moment, Jimmy responded in like manner as his arms embraced her body. They shared a long-awaited moment of passion before she broke away.

"I've got to go, Jimmy."

"Wait till tomorrow. Things will look better," he pleaded.

"I can't. I've never had a tomorrow. It's always been the same damn day. And life's been rocky for me every day. I've got to go. I've got to make a tomorrow for myself. And my leaving will make a safer tomorrow for everyone. You've got to forget me."

He could see her tears through his own. He watched her turn, climb into the Model A, and drive down the driveway.

Feeling his own passion, he lamented to the night sky, "Yeah, like that kiss is going to help me forget you!"

He wanted to chase after the car, but instead he watched it turn west, and then he lost the headlights among the trees. Sure that no one was watching, he let his tears come as they would.

Walking home, his thoughts were all about Mary. Her voice, her words, and her presence, a presence that had been in his life for over ten years. His mind filled with images of Mary smiling at him, laughing with him, and looking at him in a way he loved. He remembered how he had enjoyed driving her from Rosinceks' place. How they had giggled. Unable to accept never seeing her again, he knew had to find her. He would need a plan.

The '52 Ford was parked in its spot when he returned to the yard, and although the kitchen light was on, everyone, even his folks, was in bed. Jimmy cleaned up quietly as he reflected on his luck during the fight with Jack. He smiled at a revelation the night had brought. Perhaps there was yet another element to fighting: *Nothing beats dumb luck.*

After ascending the stairs, he stopped at Maggie's room to pull the chain on the light fixture. As he expected, she was wide awake. He put a finger over his lips and took a seat on the foot of her bed. "Mary left in the car per her plan," he whispered.

Maggie sat up in bed. "I'm glad."

"How long did you know about her plans?"

"From the beginning, but I didn't know it would be tonight until we saw Jack stealing gas. After you left to follow him, I ran toward the west, trying to head off Mary, but she must've already been there. I wanted to stop her. I wasn't sure how she would get away. She made me promise not to tell anyone, especially you."

"I get it," Jimmy said. "You promised to keep her secret. She was your best friend. And her secret will remain safe for a little longer. I'll tell everyone the car was still there when I went back for the jack and blocks. Technically, that's true. It was. It just wasn't there when I left."

Although they both had more to say, they stayed silent. Finally, Jimmy whispered, "If you ran west after we split, did Joey walk to Droesers' place alone in the dark?"

Maggie smiled and nodded. "He didn't even hesitate."

Jimmy smiled with pride. "We have a courageous little brother."

Maggie added, "Tonight, he turned the light off in his room and went to bed without either one of us there. He's never done that before."

Jimmy said, "I'll bet he'll be able to handle the bullying from his so-called friends at school a little better after dealing with the mess this weekend."

"Back to school for all of us tomorrow," Maggie said. Then, hesitating, trying to find the right words, she added, "After the killing of Sporty and his family . . . and after being in the middle of Mary's . . . situation and escape and all of the pain that goes with it, school seems like another planet, or even another universe."

Jimmy groaned. "Mary must've felt like that every day. I miss her already, but her safety is more important than anything."

"Did you talk to her tonight?"

"Yes. She told me about Jack and her plan to escape. I asked her to stay, but—"

"Look, Jimmy," Maggie broke in, "there's more to it. You deserve to know her past horrors." Maggie took a few moments to explain what she knew about Mary's abuse by Matt and her brothers and of Mary's discovery that Matt was not her real father.

Jimmy's face lost color as he listened. After Maggie finished, he gave a short sigh. "Jeez. I don't see how she could bear it all."

"She said telling me helped her, but she didn't want you to find out. She only told me after Matt's death." After a short pause, she said, "We have a lot to talk about, Jimmy. Mom and Dad got home after you left to get the jack. I told them about the ghost and Jack and the neighbors and the sheriff. I told them about everything except Mary. I'm sorry about Mary leaving, but I'm relieved to be rid of all the secrets. I hope she can feel relieved to be rid of them too. Mary's been tortured with secrets all her life."

"But she still carries the horrible memories with her," Jimmy said.

Suddenly, they heard Mom holler gently from the bottom of the stairs, "Keep it down, kids. Lots to talk about, I know, but save it till morning. Go to bed. Good night."

"Okay, Mom. Sorry," Jimmy said.

"Some things never change." Maggie smiled and added, "We're a pretty lucky family."

Jimmy said, "Yes, we are." His heart ached and his head pounded, but he managed to say, "You did right, keeping Mary's secrets. It must've been hard. Maybe we should've trusted our folks more from the start. But it'll be okay, Mags. We can talk in the morning. Good night." He switched off the light and left for his bed.

EPILOGUE

Mary and Martin Carlson slept until half past five on Monday morning. Mary reasoned that the kids were even more tired than she and Martin were, so she let them sleep until breakfast. Jimmy heard Mom's call and shook the sleep from his head. He purposely hadn't set his alarm for his exercise routine, but now he was embarrassed that his mother had let him sleep instead of waking him for morning milking. He dressed quickly, woke Joey, and called down the hall to Maggie.

Breakfast was a flurry of questions and truthful-but-limited answers. The kids had nothing to hide, and other than Jimmy's technical truth, there was no deception. Mary Schroedler's name never came up, although her presence was in the hearts of Maggie and Jimmy.

Eager to talk privately, Jimmy and Maggie left the house to wait for the school bus a full five minutes earlier than usual.

About halfway to the roadside, Maggie asked, "Do you think we should've told the sheriff about the abuse?"

"I don't know. It's not our secret to tell."

"I know, and I even promised not to tell, but if no one knows but us and Mary, there's no justice. And Jack goes unpunished."

"Guys like Jack never seem to get what's coming to them," Jimmy grumbled.

They arrived at the roadside and could see the school bus coming from the east.

"The bus is early," Jimmy said, as he slipped his comb out of his back pocket and slicked his hair back.

"Let's not tell anyone about Mary or this weekend," Maggie said.

"Agreed," Jimmy said, "but the neighbors already know some of it, and other people will find out. They always do." He smiled and looked directly at Maggie as he added, "My concerns about my treatment at school—you know Sutter, my long hair, detention—it all seems petty after this weekend. Real, but petty."

"I know what you mean," Maggie said as the bus stopped next to them.

Martin and Mary left the house for after-breakfast chores just as Emil and Caroline Rosincek drove into the yard. Distraught, Caroline showed them the note Mary had left.

> *Dear Caroline and Emil,*
>
> *You have treated me as if I were your own child, and I am very grateful. The entire Carlson family has always treated me like I was theirs too. I love you all, but I need to get away from here to escape all the terrible memories and the danger to me and those I love. Please do not try to find me. I will be safe with a friend far away from here.*
>
> *Love,*
>
> *Mary*

After much discussion, the adults agreed they should show the note to the sheriff. As if on cue, Sheriff Kaeler drove into the yard, eager to ask about the location of Jack Drude's Model A. Of course, no one knew it was even gone.

After reading the note, the sheriff said he'd follow up with a search and keep them posted. When Martin asked about Jack Drude's status, the sheriff replied, "The value of the stolen items in his possession only amounts to a misdemeanor, and although your kids witnessed him stealing some gas, there is no way we can prove he stole gas at other times. We interviewed Berris at Crossroads this morning. He was sure Ziton did not know that Jack was trading stolen goods to him. I've known Ziton for twenty years, and I'm sure he wouldn't knowingly deal with stolen goods. He said he is willing to testify. But adding several dozen eggs and some chickens to Jack's stolen loot will not make it a felony. The judge will probably give him probation and require him to pay retribution. You'll get your tools back after the hearing. One thing, though, his broken wrist may take a while to heal and leave some permanent damage."

Sheriff Kaeler left; Rosinceks left; and Mary and Martin went back to chores.

Only two people knew the present location of Jack's Model A, now parked where it would remain for decades. Notified by Mary's letter, Dorothea Hansen, a single woman in her thirties, had prepared a spot in her shed the day before Mary's arrival. Before dawn on Monday morning, when Mary drove into Dorothea's dark farmyard, the wiry lady was waiting to direct her niece to drive into a wooden prewar structure. Unlubricated steel rollers squeaked on the rails as Dorothea tugged on the heavy sliding door to let the Model A into its resting place.

A moment later, Dorothea opened the driver's-side door of the Model A, and Mary felt the strength of her hug as she whispered, "Mary, you and I will stay here forever and be safe. No one will know you're here but me, and your being here will make my joy complete. Your child will be safe here too."

In the embrace of her aunt, Mary's heart filled with love and joy. She felt a natural bond with Dorothea, whose love would help ease the painful loss of her mother. But never seeing Jimmy or Maggie again created a heartache that made her doubt if she could bear the sacrifice of her own decision. Trading being with those you love for the safety of those you love. Was that a good choice?

But the trade had given her a degree of freedom she had never known in all of her sixteen years. Freedom from being controlled by others and freedom from the secrets she had borne for most of her life. Maybe there *was* life without the terror of threats. Maybe there *was* sleep without horrific dreams.

Hand in hand, Mary and Dorothea strolled through the open sliding door. The steel rollers squeaked again on the rails as Dorothea closed the door, but before the door blocked her view, Mary caught a glimpse of the Model A, a lingering symbol of her dark past. She felt instinctively that as long as Jack Drude lived, he would remain a danger to her and to those she loved, including the child growing in her womb.

The End

FARM COUNTRY TALES

The earlier adventures of the characters in *Discovery* can be found in Fredrickson's Farm Country Tales, a series of family stories that depict what it was like to be a child on a small farm in 1950, five years previous to the action that takes place in *Discovery*. Below is a list of those books.

FICTION
Picture books that take place in 1950, when Jimmy is ten, Maggie is nine, and Joey is five.

A Farm Country Picnic
A nighttime rainstorm gives the Carlson family a break from putting up hay the next day, and the parents plan to take the children to a nearby lake where they can have a picnic and fish. When they discover their cows are in the neighbor's corn, their picnic plans are thwarted, and they spend the morning chasing cattle and the afternoon fixing fences.
Characters: the five Carlson family members and the Watkins salesman

A Farm Country Halloween
The Carlson kids trick-or-treat in the farm neighborhood, but Jack Drude turns their innocent fun into a brief nightmare with his extreme tricks.
Characters: the five Carlson family members, Mr. and Mrs. Droeser, Mr. and Mrs. O'Keran, Mr. and Mrs. Ryan, Jack Drude, and Mary Schroedler

A Farm Country Thanksgiving

Mary and Martin invite Thorsons and Dvoraks over for the noon Thanksgiving meal. The cousins go sledding, and a good time is had by all. *Characters:* the five Carlson family members, John and Rose Thorson and son Billy, Joseph and Emma Dvorak and daughters Anna, Marcella, Helen, Janet, and Josephine

A Farm Country Christmas Eve

The entire Carlson family goes to the barn to milk cows during their regular chore time on Christmas Eve, leaving the house vacant for Santa's visit. Although the kids are worried Santa Claus may not come, Mom keeps them busy with the chores to make the time fly by. In the end, Santa does not disappoint. *Characters:* Mary, Martin, Jimmy, Maggie, and Joey Carlson, and many cows and cats

NONFICTION

A Farm Country Haying

A history of haying and the development of haying machinery, with more than six hundred photographs and one hundred stories of haying memories submitted by farmers and former farm kids. It also includes a short, illustrated story of the Carlson family putting up loose hay with a hay loader on Father's Day in 1950. *Characters:* the five Carlson family members and a kind neighbor named Mr. Haber

A Farm Country Harvest

A history of harvesting grain with more than 150 photographs of threshing and other grain activities. It also contains a short, illustrated story of the arrival of the threshing machine at the Carlson family farm in 1950. All the neighbors arrive to help load bundles on rigs drawn by either a tractor or a team of horses, and Jack Drude and Billy Joe O'Keran plan some tricks that get them in big trouble.

Characters: the five Carlson family members, the neighbor families Droeser, Drude, Shaurel, and O'Keran, and the owner of the threshing rig and his crew

A Farm Country Silo Filling

A history of corn harvesting and machinery with more than four hundred photographs, including the many kinds of corn harvesting and the history of the invention of the silo. It also contains a short, illustrated story of the Carlson family mounting the pipes on their silo and filling the silo by hauling bundles of corn to the ensilage cutter at the silo's base.

Characters: the five Carlson family members, plus Martin's father

OTHER BOOKS BY GORDON AND NANCY FREDRICKSON

Visit our website www.gordonfredrickson.com for details and excerpts.

BOOKS FOR CHILDREN
If I Were a Farmer: Nancy's Adventure
If I Were a Farmer: Tommy's Adventure
If I Were a Farmer: Field Work
If I Were a Farmer: Making Hay
What I Saw on the Farm
Raising Little Duck
What Colors Are Tractors?

POETRY
Farm Country Moments: Poems, Pictures, and Memories

MEMOIR
Out of Wedlock, 1948: A Two-Part Memoir,
by Nancy A. Fredrickson

NOVELS
Discovery
The Dance
The Search
A trilogy of novels scheduled to be completed by 2025.

FANTASY STORIES
Joey Meets the Ghost Elf and Other Stories
The title story has Joey in an exciting adventure with a ghost elf who has superpowers, and the short fantasy stories that follow were written for Mrs. Deem's English class by Jimmy Carlson, Maggie Carlson, Mary Schroedler, Jack Drude, Robert Plathe, and Billy Joe O'Keran. Also included is Joey Carlson's "The Dog and the Garden Ghost," which he wrote for Jimmy in the novel *Discovery*. Coming soon.

ACKNOWLEDGMENTS

I thank the entire workforce at Beaver's Pond Press, Saint Paul, Minnesota, who have supported us through the publishing of seventeen books. We especially thank my managing editor, Alicia Ester; my editor, Kellie Hultgren, who offered many valuable insights to make my novel a better story; Abbie Phelps, my proofreader; and my designer, Dan Pitts.

I thank all those who went through the trouble of mailing photographs to me; although I decided not to place most of them in the book, they provided great reference material and gave me encouragement.

I thank my friends who graciously read drafts of my novel, especially Joyce Tornio and Judy Malz, who are my two dear sisters. I also thank Judy for creating the artwork for the front cover of *Discovery* and Nancy for collecting the photographs for the back cover.

Beyond all other measures of gratitude, I thank my dear wife, Nancy A. Fredrickson, who tirelessly and enthusiastically read many drafts and revisions and provided me with the kind of loving encouragement every artist needs.

ABOUT THE AUTHOR

Gordon W. Fredrickson was raised on a small dairy farm in Minnesota, served three years in the United States Army after high school, graduated with a teaching degree from the University of Minnesota, taught English to grades nine through twelve, directed high school plays and musicals, and has written fifteen books about farming for children and adults with the aim to enlighten and entertain. His wife, Nancy, coauthored several of the books as photographer and photo editor.

Gordon and Nancy have downsized from their hobby farm and presently reside in a townhome less than twenty miles from where they grew up. Visit their website www.gordonfredrickson.com for details and sample pages of their books.

Discovery is the first of a trilogy of coming-of-age novels, set in the 1950s, that reveal the multitude of conflicts in the daily lives of teenagers, many of whom are inundated with adult responsibilities while facing events over which they have little or no control. Although each novel stands alone, taken together the trilogy provides a wide scope of conflict, events, and resolutions that aim to define the era and its challenges.

The first book, *Discovery*, reveals hidden conflicts in a deceptively well-regulated farm community; the second book, *The Dance*, further intensifies the conflicts and deals unexpected outcomes to its characters; and the third book, *The Search*, provides unsettling but growth-driven temporary resolutions for each of the ensemble of characters.

Immerse yourself in a past era and discover that life then was no less complicated, and the issues of love and discovery no less traumatic, than in any decades since.

WANT TO READ MORE ABOUT THE CHARACTERS IN DISCOVERY?

Join them in Fredrickson's next novel, *THE DANCE*, and experience the rambunctious Saturday night gathering where hardworking people dance and drink to celebrate life and release frustrations accumulated over love, work, and life.

Violence and lust lurk under a thin veneer of civility, and the dance becomes a symbol for all of life's energy, both creative and destructive.

Forthcoming in late 2024.